UNEXPECTED UNPLANNED AND INTO THE UNKNOWN

F. D. Brant

F. D. Brant

GRESHAM, OREGON

F. D. Brant
P O Box 522
Gresham, Or 97030
www.fdbrant.com

Book Layout © 2017 BookDesignTemplates.com

Unexpected Unplanned and into the Unknown/ F. D. Brant. -- 1st ed.
ISBN 978-1-946179-15-9

Books Written by F. D. Brant

Science Fiction Adventure

Survival Trilogy

Time of Isolation

Desperate to Survive

A Taste of history Past

The Harsh Lands (The Complete Trilogy)

Stand Alone

Of Gods Strangers and Messengers

Contemporary Christian Fiction

The Woman in the Snow

To be released at the end of 2017

Post-Apocalyptic

Discovery Trilogy

The Ones Before

Discovery

An Ancient Fire

CONTENTS

AND THE SUN WILL RISE

Jay had worked hard to get the two days off, and to get the permission necessary so that he could finally do what he had always wanted to do. At least as far back as he could remember, which, if he truly wanted to admit it, wasn't that far back since he was a youngling, not quite old enough to enter the world of 'dults, who were too young to be elders. Still, he admitted to himself, he really wasn't but a year or two away. And once this happened he would be required to leave all his imaginings behind. And while he knew that others had made the climb, that trek to the peaks that lay outside of his hidden town, hidden village, for him it would be a desire fulfilled.

He had always, again as far back as he remembered, stared at what appeared to be the dizzying heights those mountains presented. They always seemed to have a whiteness on top that never disappeared, reminding him of the few times that his family could afford to make frosting for those cakes, which only were there during the family yearly celebrations, for all surviving another year. Every year a different family member was required to provide the cake, and while it had always been a privilege, it was also a burden, since the necessary ingredients were not always available and were always expensive.

So his imagination always said that what was on top of those peaks were great amounts of that delicious frosting, although he knew for a fact that it was frozen water. He remembered that day when he learned that hard fact, and the disappointment was so great that he ran back to his shared room and cried. Of course he was only a few years old then – a child. A time when most of what was around him was a great mystery, of myth and magic, where his imagination soared to those magical realms back then, not that it had waned over time. But he had learned more, understood more now than he did back then. As time had passed him by, the veils that hid many of the mysteries disappeared and became real. He knew with these changes that he had lost something, but had also gained. But it also meant that he had learned a hard lesson for that gain. Life is full of compromises. And as you gained one thing, you would lose another – always trading one for another, always giving up something else to gain whatever one strives for. Was the loss worth it? It was a question he couldn't answer since he found that there was no way to go back and try the other direction.

While he hadn't fully understood this concept, he was beginning to see it work in his own life. Just like this adventure he was taking. He would be trading his time to climb those peaks, to be alone, to test his strength and resolve, and be away from his friends and his family – and, especially that girl. He didn't know what had changed but suddenly he found that he was attracted to girls where before it had been just the opposite.

He had been the runt of his family – small, scrawny, but quick. Then came that day when he realized that he was looking into his mother's eyes instead of looking up at her. This was followed by a similar day when he did the same with his father. And now he towered over both of them by at least a head. In fact for whatever the reason, he became one of the tallest in his village. And while he hadn't filled out yet, and had the awkwardness of learning how to handle his new body, he could feel the changes coming about that would give him strength and coordination. But that was for the future, as he found that he still did stupid things because of a lack of experience or not using his body right. Brown hair, blue eyes, rather nice looking, and one could easily tell which family he came from. Apart all of them had been mistaken for each other.

He thought that it had to be worse for girls, but very few talked to him, so he really had no way to know for sure. But it had to be that way. After all, for many years the only way one could tell the difference between them was the way they acted. But as they approached the time of 'dults, their bodies changed shape. And, he had to admit, it was then he began to become interested in them, and at this point they seemed to become even more of a mystery. When he would have a look of consternation on his face because of girls, and his mother was around, he could almost see a secret smile on her face. And while he really never put her in the same place as these mysterious creatures, he realized later that she was. It was both a shock, and a revelation. Mom was a girl!

With these changes, not only to them, but to him, he found things happening that he didn't understand, and could be embarrassed by them. Like that feeling in his loins if he let his mind drift in a particular direction. And he could feel something happening and it wasn't something he could consciously control — giving away his thoughts, and if anybody was around to witness it, he would blush, feeling the heat in his face, embarrassing him more. Why was this so? He guessed that it was all part of growing up. He just wished that confidence was part of it. He felt so awkward and out-of-place especially when he tried to talk to girls. Some of his friends had no problem with this at all, and seemed to draw girls to them. While he could only watch from a distance and daydream about how it would be – could be.

The town, or village, where he lived was isolated, and as far as he knew unknown. It was that way for protection. When people left to trade with other distant towns they always went the long way that allowed them to approach these trading centers from different directions so nobody would know from where they came. It was a very dangerous world out there with raids and destruction happening all the time. He had been told about the roving bands of raiders and other bad people who only destroyed. He didn't know what had brought all of this on, or whether it was something that had always been. He just knew that their safety was their isolation. With a desert on one side, and those mountains behind, their location seemed an unlikely place for a town to exist, and that had always been their safety.

Yet, such a location also meant that many of the items necessary for survival had to be purchased since it couldn't be grown locally – too little water and too little workable land for the crops. They did have a couple of small mines where they dug out stones that others wanted. And it was this more than anything else that kept them supplied with the necessities. Again it was a curse because others wanted what they had and it was another reason for the care of keeping their town and its location safe, hidden, and unknown.

While such thoughts were always with him, today they were deep inside, as he headed out the gates ahead of the rising sun. From others he had learned that most who had conquered the peaks had taken 3 days to do so. He didn't have that luxury of an additional day, so thought he could do it in the two days allotted him. If not, then he would go as far as time allowed before turning around and coming back. At the gates he ran into a sleepy guard who smiled and waved him on once he had been recognized, stating, "Be careful and watch out for those wild beasts. And I know you've been told and from the size of that pack I'd say you're prepared, but I'm required to remind any who leave . . . You do have your emergency supplies, right?"

He nodded his head, returned the smile and was out of sight pretty quickly. With the darkness he knew that dawn and the grayness of that time was just about upon him. For him his night vision was great and besides he was on familiar ground so he had no problem moving along. Shortly it would not be so and he might have to stop and await the dawn, but hoped that it wouldn't be necessary. His impatience was driving him on, and he thought that while he was still excited and fresh that he needed to push as much as he could. Later when the going became difficult he could slow down, be careful. Heck, he had to be because if he got hurt there would be no one to help him. So with anticipation he pushed onward and upward.

* * *

Hours later, taking a break, he wiped the sweat off his brow, and looked out over the panorama that lay before him. *What a view!* It was as if he could see forever. He was partially surprised that there seemed to be a light haze hanging over the desert. Not only there, but from here the town lay within that haze making it virtually invisible – not that it would have been visible anyway. There were hills and such between him and his home now. Thinking about it he thought that it had to be mid-morning, and while he felt that he made good progress – he had stayed on the trails as he had been admonished, after all – looking up it seemed that those peaks were still far away. Although, in truth, he knew that it was an illusion. *Well, I guess I'd better continue. Otherwise I'll never make it to the top and really look out over this place.* He honestly had never seen what the other side of these mountains looked like.

He found that the silence of this place was overwhelming. Even though he had considered the town a quiet place, there was always something going on, some noise, or some conversation. So, to be here where, only the rustling of the brush, the sound of the wind through the trees, and nothing else, was a new experience. Heck, he could almost hear himself thinking. This brought out a laugh since he had been accused, much too often, of not thinking something through. And, if he really wanted to be honest, there was truth to that statement. But like so many of his age he would vehemently deny it, but know within himself that it was the truth.

* * *

The shadows were lengthening as the sun began to disappear behind those peaks he was trying to conquer. He really wasn't too far from his goal, but the chill in the air, and those shadows were warning him that he had better find some shelter for the night. It really would be stupid to try to find a campsite in the dark. With reluctance he looked up at the distance he still had to go feeling the urge to just push through. But that was the foolishness of youth telling him to do so. And here there could be none of that foolishness, so with a sigh he began to search for a good campsite. After what seemed too long a time he found a rock face that provided a wall that he could use as a reflector for his small fire. The area was surrounded by numerous boulders partially hiding his camp from the rest of the world. And he had been told too many times that this was not only critical, but could mean the difference of him surviving the night.

The night crept in slowly and suddenly he realized that for the first time in his life he was alone. There was no one, just him and his small fire. With this realization he felt a brief chill, as the sensation ran up and down his spine, causing him to shrug his shoulders to shake it off. He could feel the goose bumps run up his neck and down his arms before disappearing. He hoped that he had enough wood for the night, but with his inexperience he had no way of knowing – truthfully this was the first time for any of this. Still the fire was comforting as well as warming. Picking a place between the fire and the rock wall he put down his sleep sack trying to remember to clear the area of all the rocks and small pebbles. Again he had been warned that without the standard bedding that each and every rock would be poking him throughout the night, and even with the padding that he had brought for that purpose, it wouldn't matter.

Again with it being so quiet he began to hear things creeping through the bushes, and when the winds came up, chilling him, and hiding those sounds, he felt his imagination running away with him. With his mind doing this he began imagining all sorts of creatures and such that had to be watching him and his fire, waiting patiently for a time that they could come in and attack him. Even though he knew that all of this was just that, no matter how hard he tried, he couldn't keep his mind from doing it. So he grabbed his long knife and small axe and kept them next to him as he ate his night meal he had cooked over his fire. *Why did it seem,* he thought, *that the food cooked over an open fire appeared to taste so much better?* Well, he personally had no answers.

While eating he stared out beyond the trees and saw a sky full of bright stars. So bright that he felt that he could almost reach out and touch them. In awe he stared at the raw beauty that surrounded him. Until this very moment he hadn't realized that the lights of the town, dim as they were, didn't allow one to see the stars as he did now. He wondered what other things he had missed because he lived in that village. Then one streaked across the sky disappearing somewhere in the distance. *Wow, a falling star!* He had forgotten about them. So he watched the skies more carefully trying to see more of them. But each time one would show he would catch it from his side vision, he always seemed to be looking away at the time it would arrive. Suddenly he awakened. He somehow had fallen asleep and looking around he could see his fire had burned down to coals. Carefully he stood up, stretched, and added wood to his fire, placing a large log on it in such a way that it should last most of the night. He watched as the smaller sticks caught fire, with the large log beginning to burn felt his fire should be okay. With that he climbed into his sleep sack feeling the comfort of the heat on his back from his fire and drifted off to sleep.

* * *

Jay awoke in the gray of dawn after a less than a restful night. He realized as he came out of a deep sleep that he smelled smoke. Through the fog of his mind he first panicked, which brought him fully awake. Then he smiled rather sheepishly, as he remembered that he had a campfire right next to where he was sleeping. So, of course he should be smelling smoke. It was then he realized that the odor wasn't of wood burning from a campfire. He only remembered smelling this once before and he had been so much younger then. It was when the fire alarm had been rung in the square of their town. When this happened everyone was required to report and help suppress the fire. Being a child he hadn't been let close, but remembered the house burning with flames coming out of the windows and huge clouds of black smoke rolling high into the sky.

As he wiped the sleep from his eyes, in his mind he re-lived that moment from his past. First, even with the distance that he was from that fire, he could feel the heat and it was unbelievably hot. Then the wind shifted blowing some of that evil smoke his way and as he breathed it in he began coughing immediately as it took his breath away. It smelled awful. It was nothing like the sweet smell of the smoke off the cooking fire, or those fires in the winter that heated the house. He realized that it burned his lungs leaving his throat raw, and he speaking with a raspy voice. It had forced him to back away even further.

Now worried he stood up and looked down towards his town, the village, but knew that he really couldn't see it. It was the only place that the smell could be coming from. In his hike to this point he had passed nothing that had been built. All that surrounded him was the natural world, so his conclusion was that something in the village was burning. Still, how did the smell get up here, he wondered. He was a long way away, and usually during the night the winds were going downhill not up. It would have had to been something pretty large to overcome the natural way of things. This pushed impatience upon him, and left him in a quandary. Should he head back and lose his only chance in the foreseeable future to climb this peak, or should he head back now?

Suddenly a heavy black cloud of smoke rolled in on him definitely smelling the same as that day from the deep past. With that his mind was made up. The peak could wait. Something bad was happening and he needed to be there, it was time to head back. Quickly he packed, took out some of his travel rations and chewed on it as he carefully started his return trek. With the uncertain light he had to be sure of his footing, and because of this it was slow going causing impatience, worry, and dread to drive him.

Eventually he reached a point, as the skies lightened enough to see easily, and he, from his position, could overlook the valley where the town was hidden. It didn't bring relief as it appeared that the whole town was burning, pouring out great clouds of that black smoke, which was climbing high into the sky in a dark column that was easily visible against the blue sky and the desert sands. Something horrible had happened and he wasn't there to help. *Why now?*

Looking at the distance he still had to go he knew that there was no way that he could do much to help with what he was seeing. But maybe he could get back soon enough to do something – anything. And because that smoke was so heavy and visible he found that he was having difficulty concentrating on the trail. And as he continued to watch, he was feeling helpless at not being there, but stuck up here on the mountains. And it had taken him all day yesterday to reach the point where he had camped. At least going back down it should be faster. Still how much faster, was the question for which he had no answer. It would be too easy to become careless, and if he injured himself, he would be useless to the village in its apparent time of greatest need. So he pushed as fast as he dared and watched as the rising of the sun continued to climb higher in the sky, the never-ending column of black smoke, and the trail, cursing the distance that still lay before him.

Eventually, as the sun started to dip behind those peaks, he was back on familiar ground and picked up his pace even though his muscles ached and his lungs burned from the exertion. As he came around that final corner to where he could see the guarded gate he stopped in his tracks with his mouth open. Before him was the gated entrance, only the gate was broken and barely hanging on its hinges. As he stared, he saw something lying on the ground, and as he cautiously approached saw it was the same guard that had passed him through this same gate the day before. When he looked closely he could see that his eyes were open staring sightless into the sky. At that moment he realized that this man was dead. It caused him to jump back for a moment. He had never seen a dead person before.

At this point with the shock of seeing this dead person he began to hear the roaring of the fire – the sounds of crackling and popping, and the overwhelming smells of burning buildings. He was almost afraid to go through the broken gate, beyond that wall, to witness what was on the other side. Yet, he couldn't remain here either. The sun had set behind the mountain peaks and in the fading light the raging fire within those walls was becoming the dominant light.

Mentally preparing himself he tried to be ready for the worst that his mind said had to be there. And because he was young, his imagination was no match for what he found when he finally entered. Immediately he could see that most of the town was burning. A good portion no longer had the intensity of some of the other fires, speaking of having burned up what fuels was available. There were weird dancing shadows everywhere created by the raging conflagration that he saw before him. And everywhere he looked he saw bodies. Panicked now he ran towards his home, but found his way blocked by the intensity of the fires. Taking his time he worked his way around trying hard not to look at the dead.

Every once in a while, as he tried to find an alternate way to his home, the smoke would overwhelm him forcing him to his knees leaving him barely able to breathe. He found that he was choking and coughing heavily, with his eyes closed against the burning ash and smoke, causing his eyes to tear heavily as they tried to clear out the grit, and acrid smoke. And finally coming in from the opposite direction he found his home – what was left of it anyway. It, as well as most of the homes that were close, were down to hot smoking coals and ashes. And where the front door would have been he saw his uncle lying dead face down. He sat down heavily not knowing what to do. Even though he didn't want to admit it to himself, he knew that everyone he ever knew, all of his family, all of his friends, all of the townsfolk, and all of his plans, hopes, and dreams, were dead.

Tears were running down his face, and it wasn't because of the wicked smoke. Normally he would have been ashamed of crying, but now he didn't care. His body was wracked by the deep and heavy sobs that escaped his lips and he didn't know how long he had remained in that position feeling the deep misery, the self-defeating blame, he put upon himself. Again, if he wanted to be honest, he knew that there would have been nothing he could have done to prevent this, or to survive this if he had been here. But his mind, his thoughts continued to accuse him.

Where the night had gone he didn't honestly know. But it was the heat of the day that brought him back to reality and when he looked up he could see that the sun was well on its way to the high point. He could remember Jon, the uncle that lie in death right here in front of him, always saying, "Bad things happen, and many times there is nothing anyone can do to prevent them or change the outcome. But the one thing one can always count on is, *the sun will rise*. And if that is so then one will find a way to go on." He had to admit that the sun had risen on this day and his discovery of death and tragedy hadn't changed this fact and presently this new day was almost half over. Although, if he wanted to admit it personally, he really hadn't noticed any of the passing time being so lost in his personal misery and what lay around him.

So much death . . . so much destruction – everything that he ever knew . . . gone, with no way to ever get it back – ever. Then panic set in when he suddenly realized that the ones who did this could return at any moment. And that brought other thoughts of why were they not still here? He stood up quickly and looked around in every direction. But with the heat waves created by the still burning fires, and the heavy black smoke it was impossible to see very far in any direction. He knew that he wouldn't be able to do anything for the dead, and as far as he knew he was the only one who lived, but what to do? One thing for sure, he couldn't remain here. So retracing his steps he returned to the broken gate that he had gone through two days before to begin his adventure.

Once there he hesitated. He had no plan, no idea where to go, had never been on one of the merchant runs, as they were called, had no idea how far away, or whether it was safe to make that trek, so he stopped frozen with indecision. One thing for sure his meager supplies that he had for his adventure wouldn't last. He would need to prepare, and do it quickly, since the raiders could show up at any moment. And in his mind, he felt that it had to have been raiders. Still, the way he felt right now, maybe it would be for the better if he could join his family, his village, in death and be done with it. But if he did that there would be nobody to remember, nobody to seek revenge, nobody to speak for the dead, and he felt that somebody had to. And at this moment, as far as he knew, it could only be he himself. But what could one person do? Where did one go to find help, let alone seek revenge against the size of force that must have attacked this place? He had no answers, but if he remained here, then, in the end, it probably wouldn't matter.

He remembered the storage place where a large number of emergency packs were stored, and he wasn't far from where they were stashed. So, if his luck held, and the cache hadn't been discovered and looted, he could resupply from there. He felt that he would need to take as much as he could pack, since he hadn't a clue how long it would be before he would have a chance to resupply, or hunt, or whatever. So he went down the wall from the entrance – just a few steps really – since these emergency kits had to be reached quickly, if they were needed, and felt relief when the supplies, or at least the hidden entrance to the supplies, seemed untouched.

He pushed back the vegetation that covered the entrance, pulled open the large door, and climbed down the ladder into the cellar that lay beneath the wall that surrounded the village. It wasn't a large space, and he knew that there was a similar one on the other side of the town. But as far as the location of that one he was unfamiliar. He had assisted in supplying this one and inspecting the kits to be sure that they were in good condition. In fact it had only been in the recent past that he finished one of those inspections so he knew what was here.

It was dark inside, yet with his intimate knowledge of the layout of this place, and where everything was located, he felt he didn't need a light. Besides, the space wasn't very large, and it would be easy to grab and go. With some speed he stuffed his pack as full as he could and began to leave when he remembered that there were a few weapons stored here also. He turned to the opposite corner and felt around until he located a bow, a quiver of arrows, replacement strings, and a few more of the knives. He really didn't know what he needed since he had never been a warrior. Still everybody had at least had some basic training in the uses since they needed to hunt to supplement their food supplies.

Once he emerged from the hidden cellar, he carefully closed it back up and re-covered it with the vegetation, hoping that it would be overlooked – if the raiders returned to continue to strip the remains of the village. If it remained hidden then sometime in the future he possibly could return and grab some additional kits. The next thing he noticed was the sun was beginning to set. Where had the time gone? It couldn't have taken that long to do what he had done? Yet the sun didn't lie. It moved across the sky in its leisurely fashion each and every day, setting at the end of the day, and rising at the beginning of the next. *Yeah,* he thought, *and the sun will rise.* Well, if he didn't get moving it might not rise for him.

He immediately headed out of the broken gate and retraced part of his route that he had taken the day before. *Had it only been a couple of days ago,* he thought, *when I headed out this same gate to begin my big adventure?* For him, with all that had transpired, it felt more like a lifetime. In that short time he went from a member of a family to being an orphan and none of it was his doing. He knew of a hidden area that wasn't too far away – a place where he had played as a child. Yeah, as one, this place seemed magical and hidden, but now as a youngling and about to become a 'dult, he knew better. Still it provided some protection, was out of the way, and was a place where one wouldn't generally search for someone.

And before he knew it he was there. Slipping through the vegetation that blocked the small trail he worked his way among the boulders, and then inside. Sometime in the past the water had undermined these large rocks creating voids that as a child he and others had considered caves. It was here, when time was allowed for play, that they would have great adventures. Thinking of this brought a smile to him, although it was a sad one. He knew that none of the other children, no other younglings from his village would ever have adventures here again. Most likely he would be the last to spend time here in these hidden places. If one didn't know they were here, and because of where they were located, no one would even be curious enough to see what could be here. So for now it was his refuge.

He could feel the emotions begin to overwhelm him again, and at first he fought it, but eventually, in misery, gave into them, and once again cried deep body wrenching sobs that further exhausted him. Despair rode high and he had no plans, no ideas as to what to do, where to go, or how to really survive. He had only faced the normal everyday problems someone his age always faced. Nothing had prepared him for what he was now facing. So once his crying subsided he sat there in one of those hollows not moving, feeling drained – spiritually, emotionally, and physically.

Even though he didn't feel that it was possible, somewhere during this time he fell into a deep troubled sleep, having nightmares and bad dreams from which he could not wake. He was chased, in those dreams, all night long, by unseen demons, and armies of horrible creatures. And however it happened, he somehow had been able to stay just out of their reach. Finally it was the chill of the dawn that brought him out of these dreams and back into the waking world. He found that he was still sitting upright, propped between a couple of those boulders. He found his clothes soaked in sweat, and he felt that he hadn't slept at all. It was then, as he remained in the twilight between waking and sleeping that he thought he heard voices.

Oh if only everything I've experienced could be a bad dream. If it was, then he had to be in his camp near the top of the mountains. But if he was hearing voices, he couldn't be there, and everything he saw, everything he remembered truly had happened. In the semi-darkness he reached for his pack and found it stuffed with the emergency kits and knew that it all had transpired, and everybody he had ever known was probably dead. *So where were those voices coming from?* And if there were voices that meant someone was in the area. And from the sound it sounded like many which could only mean the raiders were back. Had he stayed in the village another night instead of retreating to where he was, then he would have been discovered, and he suspected after that nothing else would have mattered. *Now what?*

He had to get away from here. Yes he probably could stay where he was for a while, but it wasn't safe, and it wasn't a place where one would want to stay. It was to be temporary while he figured out what he wanted to do. Well, with the return of the raiders, if that's who they were, he'd have to leave and get as far away as he could. But he knew that he couldn't leave in the daylight. He wasn't the best at moving quietly, or flowing through the wilderness, and remain unseen. He would have to wait out this new day, and again those words from his uncle came unbidden into his mind, "and the sun will rise", and it meant he had a full day to wait them out.

He knew that it would be an uncomfortable one, since where he was, wasn't meant for someone his size. When small one could scamper through the small voids with ease, but now it had been a tight squeeze just to get inside. He hoped that whoever he heard wouldn't go out of their way looking for survivors. He hadn't fully thought about it when he made his way here, and because of his mindset he hadn't considered the tracks that he would leave, and didn't know if he had left any. In a way, the direction he came went along a well-traveled route, which had both gravel and hard packed soil. So there was a good chance that he left no sign of his passing, but could he be sure? The simple answer was no, but he couldn't leave now and correct this error. All he could do was hope that he hadn't left a trail.

He waited out an uncomfortable day hearing, many times, voices getting stronger as the raiders moved up and down the trail outside the wall. Fortunately none of them seemed interested in looking in his direction, and at no point could he discern how many, but it seemed to him to be a large group. He could hear the cursing when someone burned themselves on something that was still hot, and the laughter from others as they would rub it in. Eventually, and he didn't know how or why, he dozed and awoke with a start a several times. During the times when he wasn't frozen with fear, when the voices were near, or when he dozed, he wondered where they had come from. It was his guess, since they hadn't come by him from the mountain side that they must have come out of the desert. But that seemed impossible. There was nothing out there to support anything. Well, that was the belief anyway.

With those thoughts he guessed that most likely, they only swung into the desert to locate hidden villages that would be using the desert as protection. And from the desert it would be easy for the raiders to locate these villages, which would stand out against the backdrop of the mountains. And once located determine the best time to attack and do what they wanted. With them running around the area of his village he felt that once it became dark he would have to retreat into that desert himself – that very dangerous desert where the rumors said that no one survived. It truly was his only chance for escape. And by doing this by night he felt that he would have a greater chance to survive. But, if he wanted to be honest, he really knew nothing about living in the desert at all.

After a long day, and with the night approaching, he made his decision. Soon he would work his way away around the village and head out into the desert and to his destiny . . .

* * *

Jay was on his third day in the desert and wasn't sure at this point whether the decision to escape into the desert had been such a good idea. He'd been warned of the dangers, and the importance of remaining on the trails. But he felt that it was something that he couldn't do with the raiders still in the area. Once daylight had arrived, on that first day, he could see the raiders working the desert's edge and sending patrols deep into the surrounding areas. And he found that it was close to impossible to hide. There wasn't anything here to block one's view for vast distances. The only thing in his favor had been the fact that he had traveled all night to get as far away from the destroyed village as possible, and he felt it was the only reason he had escaped.

Now he wasn't so sure. Yes, remaining off the trails had prevented him from being discovered by the raiders, and if captured, whatever they would have done to him. But now he was lost and the heat of the day was beginning to build. He thought he had brought plenty of water with him, but found with the heat being generated that he had gone through it twice as fast as he expected. There was just a bit sloshing in the bottom of his last portable water container and nothing visible giving him any idea of where he could replenish his depleted supply.

The heat waves were beginning to dance, distorting the surrounding landscape, causing mirages to form, tempting him to chase lakes of water that retreated as he approached – something he had been warned about. He had headed east towards the rising sun when he had left, of course it had been night, and with what water he had remaining he knew that there was no way to backtrack if he had wanted anyway. Besides, not that it wasn't obvious, death awaited him back there also. So why not let the desert take him instead? He needed to find shade, but where? Everywhere he looked there was open barren land with those wicked plants that had those barbed thorns and needles that seemed to reach out and attack. He had learned early on and the hard way to keep his distance.

As the heat continued to build, he felt the sweat begin to drip down and into his eyes, burning them from the salt; he looked to his right and saw an old wash that might hold some promise of shade – even if it was simply a high bank that was high enough to cast a shadow. He had been heading generally east so this change of direction moved him in a southerly direction. The sun wasn't to the zenith yet and was a couple of hours off, but it was almost too hot now. He headed down the wash, which deepened and became more of a ravine, narrowing and deepening significantly so that the sides were above his head. Here he found some deep shadows that for the moment were cooler than the surrounding land.

Taking a deep breath he sat down in the sand that covered the ground feeling the coolness that it provided. He knew that this was only temporary. Soon the sun would be overhead and this respite would disappear. At that point in time he didn't know what he'd do. He'd been searching desperately to find some place to wait out the day, but had found nothing – once again, now what? As he leaned against the wall of the ravine, his breathing eased and he drifted off into a troubled sleep, reliving what he had found when he returned to the village that fateful day so many days ago. It haunted not only his sleep, but many times, when awake, his tired mind would drift off, reliving what he had discovered. Could he ever get away from those horrible images and memories?

* * *

At least two more days . . . two days or more without water . . . trouble, deep trouble. He couldn't think, his vision was blurring . . . His mind wouldn't work . . . his mouth was so dry that it hurt. His steps were uncertain, and he truly had no idea where he was. He found himself lost inside a number of broken canyons that held the heat but no vegetation. He had, at one point, thought he could work his way back to one of the major trails . . . He'd been warned that it meant death if one left them in the desert. But somehow he had become turned around, and somehow had missed any and all that might have existed. He never realized that there were mountains and canyons existing in the desert. Shaking his head, as he tried to clear his clouded mind, he thought. *Well stupid, what did you think? Did you think that it would just be a flat sand covered area where nothing grew?* This drew a weary smile. *Of course you did.*

He didn't know when it happened but somewhere along this time he awakened and it was night. He must have passed out. The cool night air was a relief from the heat of the day. But he had learned that it was also a curse, because once the sun was gone from this tortured land it became unbearably cold. And because he assumed, yeah assumed, that the desert was hot he hadn't added any real items to keep him warm at night – not that it would have been easy to do so. Soon it wouldn't matter anyway. He was close to death and knew it. He wondered how it felt to die and knew honestly that he didn't want to. Did he have a choice? And once again those words from his now dead uncle entered unbidden into his mind, "And the sun will rise", probably true, but would it rise for him, or would the previous day be his last sunrise?

As these thoughts were going through his mind it was then that he realized that he smelled water. It was subtle and seemed to appear and disappear with the soft down canyon breezes. At this point he realized that he was sprawled in an awkward position and his arm was aching from being under him. He rolled over on his back, barely conscious, and stared into the clear night sky. Again those stars were so bright and the night so clear, it was like he could reach up and touch them. It seemed that he couldn't focus for very long on anything and thought that it was probably from the lack of water. But that smell said it was close. Still, with the coolness of the sands under his body, he felt that it was impossible to move. *Just let the sands and the desert take me,* he thought.

He must have drifted off once again because the next time he became conscious the moon was full and overhead adding its light, creating an eerie landscape bathed in shadow and soft light. Again, that subtle smell of water – tempting, out of reach, *where is it coming from*? He slowly pushed himself up off the sand, stood up and immediately fell back down. He began to laugh hysterically, and found that once again he was lying on his back staring up at the moon and stars. *Have to be more careful – didn't think about being dizzy.*

More careful this time, he stood back up and leaned against an embankment that was close by, waiting for his head to clear and to get his balance back. Once this was accomplished he began a slow methodical search for the source of the smell. But it eluded him as it continued to drift on the night breezes. A few times he thought he had to be close only to lose the scent once again. He could feel anger rising in him and the unfairness of the water to remain out of his reach, and then realized that the anger wasn't helping. With his clouded mind he was having difficulty remaining on task, but knew if he didn't it would be over, done, and like his village, he would be no more.

After what seemed to be half the night he had finally narrowed his search area down but had yet to locate the water. The smell was tantalizingly strong but still remained out of reach. Eventually he could hear what he thought was running water, but immediately doubted it. *After all, this is a desert; there shouldn't be running water here, right?* Honestly he knew next to nothing about deserts so he really had no idea if water ran in the desert. In the uncertain light of the full moon he tripped over a large rock that was hidden in the shadows, fell hard, hit his head, and was unconscious once again.

When he climbed back into consciousness dawn was breaking, and before him at eye level was a raised portion of a rock layer. It sat above the sands and was probably only a couple of inches wide. It was here that he could both hear the running water, and smell it. Turning his head and trying to peer into the space he found it too dark to do so. Looking at the layer of rock he could see that it was slowly rising in height as it turned around a corner and went out of sight. He also noticed that the ravine that he was presently in began to run downhill and continued, like that rock layer, out of sight.

Crawling and following the ever-widening crack around the corner – it remained much too narrow to be able to climb into – he felt his frustration grow. Then the ravine suddenly dropped off. He slid up to the edge, looked over and down and saw that it was a little further straight down than his own height. Carefully he lowered himself over the edge, hanging by his fingertips, finally letting go, had a rock roll under his foot, and as he slid further down the ravine he began losing some skin off his arms and hands in the process, which burned. This was followed by his sitting down hard with a feeling that he had just bruised his tailbone. With the rattling of falling sand and stone he ducked and protected his head but none of the debris hit him. Well, if it had, not hard anyway.

Looking to his right, with the sun just about to rise, providing plenty of light to see, he noticed a large crack running parallel to the drop off that he had just descended, and it appeared to be wide enough that he could squeeze through. Although he had no idea if it ran very far into the hillside, was a dead-end, or whether it was just another false direction. He found the floor of the wash or ravine at this point was solid rock with loose debris making it a slippery dangerous surface. He had to be extra careful. Leaning against the rock wall he turned sideways and pushed into the crack, found himself wedged for a moment, let out his breath, making himself thinner, and pushed into the darkness and stopped.

He crouched down and pulled in the pack that he had removed before attempting to slip into the crack. When he crouched down it let in more light, and as his eyes adjusted, he opened the pack, grabbed a candle out of one of the emergency packs, lit it, and looked around. One of the first things that made itself known was the fact that right in front of him appeared to be a large drop off. How far it went down, or how dangerous it was he didn't know. Had he continued he would have found out the hard way. Taking a deep breath he noticed that it was cold. So much so that he involuntarily shivered. He saw that there was what appeared to be a slight trail that went back in the direction where he first smelled the water.

He was finding that his strength and reserves were gone and felt if he sat down now he would never get back up. Carefully and using his will alone he worked his way back, now inside the mountain, or hill, or whatever. The sound of the running water was becoming stronger as was the smell. It pushed him onward. Then rounding another corner, and in the shadows, there before him was a large pool of water. He couldn't believe his eyes. After all the mirages and illusions he wasn't sure it this was real or not. So with care he approached the small tank, felt the air cooling further, leaned down and touched the surface of the liquid and was rewarded with the feeling of wetness and seeing ripples run across the surface – it's real!

He had never had anything that tasted as good as this water. He almost jumped in and let his parched body soak in as much as he could absorb, but thought better of it. Carefully he lay down and sucked up as much water as he could hold and immediately regretted it. He felt sick, and wondered if there was something wrong with the water and he had made a mistake. It was then he realized that it was him being greedy and drinking too much. So he carefully slid back and leaned against one of the walls, closed his eyes, and concentrated on his queasy stomach, and willed himself to keep it down. After what seemed too long he felt better and realized that he was still thirsty but refrained from drinking any more until some time had passed. Then he returned to the pool of cool water and drank sparingly.

He didn't know how long he had remained there, but suddenly realized that it was becoming darker in this, well he wasn't sure what he'd call it, maybe cave? But there were a number of cracks and openings that allowed light in, and he always thought a cave would be dark. Still, until he came up with a better word, cave would have to do. It meant that night must be approaching and he had been in here much longer than he thought. It also meant that at some point he had probably fallen asleep and was unaware of that fact. The candle he had lit had burned almost all the way down. At first he thought that he should head back outside, but changed his mind. There was enough room here to lay out his sleep sack, and as he looked around he found an old abandoned nest made by some desert rodent. And with all the small openings to the outside he could build a small fire, keep warm, and know that the smoke wouldn't build up inside forcing him out. "Better get to it," he said.

* * *

Waking up the next morning, cold and shivering, he grabbed some of the old nest material and quickly built a small fire. The wood was so dry and old that it hardly put out any smoke, but at the same time burned and turned to ash quickly. The supply was limited, so he decided to use it to get warm, and eat a travel ration instead of trying to cook something over the fire. He found that he was still thirsty and between bites of the travel ration, which seemed overly dry, he drank vast volumes of water. In fact his thirst was greater than his hunger, and he found that he had at least half of the travel ration left when he felt full.

Going back in the direction that he had originally came he took care of nature, although his bladder didn't seem to hold much. No surprise there, with the lack of water he was sure that there wasn't much to get rid of. He couldn't tell the time of day only that it was daylight and some of the light was streaming in through the cracks. He remembered hearing running water, but this tank seemed to be filled by water dripping from above – at least that's how it appeared. So where was the running water? He went back to this small tank and remembered to refill all of his containers. For now he was reluctant to return outside. Honestly he had no idea where he was, and through those days without water he was sure that he probably had been turned around a number of times.

Besides, if he wanted to be honest, there was enough mystery here to keep him busy. And again, if he wanted to admit it, there wasn't any place he needed to be. His home was gone, his family was gone, and as far as he knew, everybody he had ever known was gone. So why not spend a few days and discover what was here? At least he still had plenty of food, and while the tank had dropped a bit in water level, it appeared to have already refilled. But, it didn't appear to overfill and run off somewhere. How was this possible? And from what he could determine, while water was dripping into the tank, it wasn't enough to refill it this quickly – another mystery. Standing there and trying to determine how it refilled he found he needed another drink of water. Was he ever going to quit being thirsty? Taking another drink from the tank, once again he found that he couldn't get enough and felt his insides stretched just about as far as they could go. Shaking his head he thought, *really?*

Getting up he wondered if this cave ended here. It was something to think about. Initially it was all about the water, but now curious, he wondered how the water got here. Yet, in front of him was what appeared to be a solid wall, but he had to admit he hadn't done any real exploring. So with care he skirted the pool of water and was rewarded when a portion of the wall curved out of sight. From where he had been the whole area was in deep shadow and revealed nothing. The curve became more of an "S" curve and when he completed the last portion of this curve he stopped and stared in awe. The walls glowed in a faint luminescent light making it easy to see. But what added to the surprise was the fact that there were stair steps carved into the floor leading one downward. And it appeared the walls had been worked and were not natural. *"What is this place?"* He asked himself.

There seemed to be a natural downward direction and after a while the tunnel twisted again. He suspected that it had been slightly curved anyway, but the curve was so subtle that it was almost unnoticeable. Yet this twist to the left was major and like the first turn into this tunnel there was a second turn in the opposite direction. Suddenly the tunnel ended. There appeared, of all things, to be a door. *A door? Really?* This seemed so out-of-place here. He ran his hands over it and it felt cold. It was then he realized that the door was metal and not wood as he expected it to be. Still why would a door be here at all, let alone a metal one? He reached out for the door knob and hesitated. He wasn't sure if he was ready to face whatever was on the other side. Things, since finding his way into this cave, had been strange enough, and he wasn't sure if he was ready to face whatever danger there might be. Standing there undecided, he felt his curiosity rising. So, once again he reached out and this time turned the knob.

To his surprise it turned easily, *how can that be?* As far as he knew he was the only one around here. He had seen no sign or tracks, no footprints, no fire pits, nothing to indicate that there was anybody around at all, so why did the doorknob turn so easily? With no answers he pushed the door only to find that it didn't budge. This brought a nervous smile and a bit of frustration to him. *Why isn't the door opening?* He leaned harder into it and once again nothing happened. With his hand still on the knob he leaned back ready to put all of his weight into the door only to find that it swung outward easily. And because he wasn't expecting it he lost his balance and fell hard, feeling it in his bruised tailbone. *Really?* He thought.

Rolling over, rotating around, and propping himself up on his elbows he looked into the space beyond the now open door. *Why did it open outwards? All of our doors open to the inside.* It made no sense to him at all – and, of all things, there was light streaming through the doorway. Pushing himself up, he dusted himself off, took a deep breath, and with a growing nervousness carefully peered inside. He had to close his eyes from the bright light that seemed to be shining from inside of this room. The soft glow on the cave walls didn't come close to this. In fact he couldn't remember anything inside a home that was this bright. Only being outside in the bright sunlight came close.

In what he figured took much too long, his eyes finally adjusted to the light. He rubbed his eyes and wiped away the tears that had formed, blinked a couple of times and then looked around carefully. It appeared to be just a small rectangular room with nothing in it. No windows to let in light, although if he wanted to admit it, where would the light come from? After all, this room was inside a cave, so windows wouldn't be something that would be necessary. As he continued to study the room, other than the bright light it seemed ordinary. Yet, he couldn't find the source of that light other than it seemed to be coming from the ceiling.

Looking down at the floor he found that it was covered with something that was hard, almost like sheets of stone that some of the better homes had back in his village. At this point when he thought about the village it choked him up, as once again, he realized that it had been destroyed along with everyone that lived there. It was then he saw another door with a sign above it, and while entrance was a word he was unfamiliar with, it was close enough to the one they used to understand what it meant – employee, no idea. The lighted sign simply stated, EMPLOYEE ENTRANCE. Thinking about it he wondered where this could lead, and if he wanted to continue. Still, being young, and being curious it drove him onward.

He reached for the other doorknob, and this time when he turned it he pulled the door towards him and like the other one it didn't budge. *What's going on here?* With a firm grasp he decided to push like he did on the first door, and this time it moved easily away from him. It dawned on him, at that very moment; the doors were designed to swing away from a room. To his mind this was stupid. It meant if someone was on the other side they would get hit with it, so why? With only he here there was no one to ask, so he quietly moved into the next room. He looked back and on the wall next to the door was a sign that stated, STAFF ONLY.

Looking back into this newly discovered space he found a room that was unbelievable in its size. It was like one could put at least one if not two of the biggest houses from the village in here . . . and possibly more. He had to admit that he had never seen a single room this size. He saw what he assumed were chairs sitting in rows, and what looked like one long counter where one could stand, but for what purpose he didn't know. And there appeared to be many places along this counter where there were small access points for people to do something. He noticed that most had small signs that stated, CLOSED NEXT WINDOW PLEASE. *Closed? Next window please? What's this all about? And why are these openings called windows?* Behind, on the wall, there appeared to be a large sign that stated in bold letters, <u>Welcome to Helm's Deep. A valley in middle earth from the fantasy series by J. R. R. Tolkien, The Lord of the Rings. In this valley lay a fortress, a place of last refuge, built into the mountain and an appropriate name for this place where you are presently standing.</u> Even though there was a brief description of this "Helm's Deep", he hadn't a clue to what the sign was referring to, or who J. R. R. Tolkien, or what The Lord of the Rings was all about.

Looking down he noticed that the floor, which was similar to the one in the room that he had just left, seemed to be covered in a thick layer of dust. And there were no tracks, no marks, nothing, showing that there hadn't been anybody here in a long time. Looking back he could plainly see his tracks in that same dust. "What is this place?" He whispered. "And why am I whispering?" He didn't know why, only that it felt right. Quietly, so not to disturb anything, he moved across the area to one of those "windows", as the signs said, and looked behind. He noticed that against the back wall there were places for people to sit and work. He hadn't ever seen anything like them, but the ones who had made the trading runs had described what he was seeing. If he remembered right, he had been told these things were called desks. In his mind, in the past, he thought desks were more like tables but now knew he had been wrong.

Going further down the counter, which sat in a small alcove, and away from the STAFF ENTRANCE was a solid wall, which extended behind him as he faced the counter. On the wall opposite of the STAFF ENTRANCE and away from the counter he found a couple more doors – three actually. The three doors were between the counter and another open entrance on the far wall opposite of the counter. Two had strange symbols, one looked kind of like a male, and the other he assumed had to be a female, but it was a guess. Even though there was no one around, he decided that he would only be allowed through the door with the male symbol. But the door had no handle, only a rectangular piece of shiny metal. Shrugging, he pushed on it and found, with some effort that the door swung open, and as soon as he released the pressure the door closed. This was novel. What made it do this? None of the doors he had ever gone through would close themselves like this, unless closed by the wind. He pushed it a number of times, released the pressure, and watched it close. *Who are the people who had created such a thing?*

Before entering, he wondered if there was a way out, since this side didn't have any knobs or handles. It was a good question because he didn't want to get stranded behind a door he couldn't open. So carefully he pushed it open far enough that he could see the other side, which lay in deep shadows, and to his surprise it did have a handle. He reached around and awkwardly grabbed it and found that it felt solid. So with some confidence he entered what seemed to be a darkened room, only to jump when the light suddenly came on. It startled him enough that he let the door close with him on the inside. This wasn't quite his plan, but there was nothing he could do about it now. He stood very still for a short time, and the lights went out and he found himself in absolute darkness.

This was almost worse than the surprise light. He turned around to grope for the door only to have the lights come on again. *What the heck is going on?*

Carefully he worked his way further into this area; past a wall that seemed to keep anyone from the outside seeing what was happening in this place. One of the first things he noticed was the walls were partially covered in some type of small, well stones came to mind, but wasn't sure if that was accurate, and they were cold to the touch. Going around the wall he looked into a large room that looked similar to a privy, more or less. Although, he had to admit, he had never seen anything like what was here. On one wall there appeared to be basins with reflecting glass above them and the opposite a place where males could stand and relieve themselves, plus closed areas with many swinging doors that were partially open. Going to one of them he pushed the door all the way open and found, in gleaming white, something that could easily pass as a privy. He assumed that the other side or door was for girls, females, alone, as this one was for males. And from the size he figured it could handle his whole village, if such had been necessary – not all at the same time of course, but it wouldn't have taken long for everyone to use what was here.

He wondered how it was that the area where he was would light up, and then when nothing moved, turn off. He was still in awe of the lights anyway. He couldn't discern what was making the light. He was used to candles and lanterns and the smells associated with them. But there was no smell, there was no flame that he could see, there wasn't anything he was familiar with at all. In fact it was more like bringing the sunlight inside. He exited this; well again since he wasn't familiar with what it was called, he would call it a privy. He stood looking back across the room to where he had entered and saw that he had left that particular door open. He thought maybe it would be a great idea to close it, but shrugged instead. As far as he knew he was it. There was nobody else around, and besides, it would be an easy way to know that he had already been there.

So with a decision made he decided to explore this large room some more. As he looked around from his vantage point he could see other doors and at this point he remembered the third one, walked over to it and directly on the door was an attached sign stating, SUPERVISOR. *So, what is a supervisor?* He really didn't know. He tried the doorknob and found that it didn't budge. Trying harder it refused to give in to his attempts. Finally giving up he then saw another door on the other side of the room to his left. This one, like some of the others, had a lighted sign above the doorway stating, SECURITY. Again the word was unfamiliar but curiosity drove him on and he went to the door and was able to enter here. Once inside he found a smaller version of the counter here and on the other side of this counter was what appeared to be a partial glass wall. At least he thought it was glass, although it seemed to be frosted. Between the wall and the counter were a number of desks like he saw behind the counter in the larger room.

Again, it appeared that he was the only one here. He noticed that the counter ran the full length of the room and since there was no way around it he decided to jump over it instead. It wasn't something that would be difficult. Heck, he'd scrambled up rocks there were more of a challenge than this. So vaulting over the counter he worked his way back towards the partial frosted glass wall. Off to his right was an open doorway that held no door. Going through it he found he immediately entered a hallway that moved him to the left and then another open doorway that led him behind the frosted glass. Only on this side it wasn't frosted and he could see clearly everything that was happening on the other side. *How is this done?* He asked himself. Of course there was no one here who could answer.

It was at this moment that something else caught his attention. Behind him was a wall of, little windows? He didn't know what else to call them. Curious again, he moved closer to them and froze in his tracks. In each of those windows there appeared different scenes, which at first he assumed were paintings. But the images changed, and moved, and did impossible things. There were chairs here and he grabbed one only to find that it moved easily and rolled back on what he had to assume were wheels. *Wheels on a chair, who'd have thought it?* Not sure, he gingerly lowered himself into it and stared mesmerized by what he was seeing. It was then he realized that he was pivoting back and forth in this chair. *Wow,* he thought, *I've never sat in anything like this!* He didn't know how much time had passed as he stared at the ever-changing scenes. Only that suddenly he heard his stomach growl and he felt hungry.

He had set his backpack on the floor next to the chair, grabbed and opened it, taking out another travel ration, and with his supply of water, ate and drank, not really paying much attention to his eating. He realized that one of the windows was showing the area outside in the desert where he had been earlier, with another showing where he had entered the cave. And the window next to this one was showing the very cave where he had spent the previous night. *How is this done,* he wondered. The rest of the windows showed different things including the large room he had exited to get here. Much of what the others showed was well beyond him, and where or what they might represent he didn't know.

Suddenly movement caught his eye and he looked back at the window that showed the desert. In the distance it looked like someone might be approaching. Still he or she was too far away to do any more than say that it was an individual, yet there seemed to be a familiarity to whoever this was. Fascinated he stared, wondering how this was possible. He had to admit he hadn't a clue. As the image got closer he realized that the individual was female, and she was without clothes. He immediately was shocked that it should be this way, and found his body reacting to this revelation. Even though he was alone it still embarrassed him, but there was nothing he could do about it other than stare. Even though this female, this girl was still in the distance, something continued to tug on his mind. It was like he knew her. It was something in the way she moved, in the way she walked.

It suddenly dawned on him that the person he was seeing, the girl who was approaching was his younger sister, which made him feel a little ashamed with the way his body was responding. But, once again, he couldn't help it. Then he saw, as she became more visible, dirt and filth covering her body, as well as what appeared to be wounds, including a large bruise that stood out on her face. She seemed to be caked in blood, and he could see it covering her in a number of places. She was also barefooted. *How has she made it this far, and in her condition?* He watched, fascinated by what he was seeing – still not sure if what he was seeing was real or not. He saw her stumble and could tell from her ragged steps that she was barely standing, let alone walking, and at the end of her strength. Not waiting any longer he retraced his steps back out through the doors, back into that cave, avoided the hidden hole, and headed back out into the desert.

Once back outside, he had to wait for his eyes to adjust to the daylight, and he to adjust to the heat. It was cool inside of the cave and building. Now he had to figure out how to work his way around the drop-off he had dropped down to find the entrance to the cave. First he headed further down the ravine and found a way around, headed back towards where he had last seen her in that window, and found nothing. Had he imagined the whole thing? Taking a slow breath he looked around desperately and could see where the sand had been disturbed, and began to search. Shortly he came upon her prone figure. Somewhere between the time where he had last seen her in that window to now, she had passed out. And if he wanted to be honest, probably close to death.

She looked like hell. It was obvious that she had been severely abused, and how she had escaped this abuse or her captors was an unknown. He had to add to this going this far into the desert in her condition and those visible ugly wounds without anything or anyone to help and to have survived long enough to reach this point. Now he worried that she may have been followed. He quickly, but carefully, picked her up. He could feel her flinch, and moan in pain. All the exposed skin was reddened from sunburn, and there was a deep cut on her scalp. He needed to move quickly and get her inside of whatever it was that he had discovered. At least he had an extra set of clothes that she could wear until they could find something else. That's, of course, if she survived, and there were no guarantees there.

With the extra burden it took him much longer to get back inside that large room. He propped her up in one of the chairs so that he could go get his backpack. And once back to where she was, laid out his sleep sack and placed her on it. She hadn't moved and it was only the rising and fall of her breasts that let him know that she was still alive. He needed to clean her up and tend to her wounds, but didn't know where he could get water unless he retreated back to the tank. Then he remembered the privy and immediately went inside. There were those basins there. Standing in front of one he could see that they were made to hold water but didn't have a clue where the water was stored. There were no pitchers here, as they used back in the town, so how did the water get here?

Frustrated, he leaned on the basin, and ran his hands everywhere he could think. In one of his passes he ran his hand under the silver thing that extended out over the basin, jumped, when water came pouring out. After a brief time it quit. He did it again, and water was produced again. He'd never seen anything like it. Quickly soaking down a large rag he had brought with him he returned and began washing her down, carefully cleaning the wounds, and cleaning her up. It took a few trips back inside the privy to rinse, clean, and return to her to get the job done. It was an uncomfortable job, but it had to be done. Other than a brief attempt to keep him from touching her, and some moaning from pain, she never awoke. Eventually she almost looked like Elsa who was only a year and a half younger than he.

He carefully checked her over once again to be sure that none of the wounds were infected, opened up his sleep sack , placed her inside, and let her continue to sleep. Of course she had been unconscious, otherwise what he had to do would have awakened her. Now all he could do was wait. Knowing personally his condition when he found this place, he knew that shortly her need for water would be overwhelming. But until she awoke, he felt it better if she remained unconscious, or asleep.

* * *

It was five days later, and Elsa was better. She still seemed to be haunted by what had happened to her, and she remained abnormally quiet. He could see the fear in her eyes, and her pleading that he remain in her sight. Because of this, he hadn't been able to do any more exploring, but right now her needs outweighed his curiosity. He returned to the security room a number of times to watch those windows, but no one showed. So, as far as he knew only the two of them had escaped. Although, his sister hadn't escaped unscathed as he, and he knew that it would take time for her to overcome all that had happened to her. He knew the physical wounds would heal in time, but she was a long way away from her fun-loving self. She was withdrawn, and seemed to jump at any shadow. Time might be the only thing that could heal this. Well, at least one could hope.

So he would put off his exploring, his discoveries for now. To bring back the sister he knew and loved was more important anyway. And once she was back, then they, together could learn more about this place, this mystery that he had discovered here in the middle of the desert. And maybe it was a place where they could start over, but that was an unknown, for the future. And for now, until she returned to whom he knew, this would be their private oasis from the rest of the world, and the horror that both of them faced and left behind.

THE DEEPS

He looked around with depression lying heavily upon him. As far as he knew he was the last person, the last human, the last of his kind on earth. Ed had just finished the ceremony, and the placing of his father's body into the crematorium. His father had died of old age, which meant that he wasn't young either. He was now returning to his room so that he could grieve, and come to terms with the conclusions that lay heavily upon him. "Well Ed, it's been a good run. We've ruled this planet for a long time." He laughed a bitter laugh before continuing. "Yeah, but the dinosaurs lasted longer."

This place he was living was simply known as "The Deeps" to all who lived here. It was known by that name because it was deep underground. Supposedly it was a last refuge for mankind. Instead it would become the final resting place, the final ending, and unlike the imagined glory at the end, they would die in a whimper. With his passing – there hadn't been a female, a girl, a woman, to carry on their species – the candle's flame would extinguish, marking the end. *Would the world outside care?* "Did it care when we replaced the dinosaurs?" He asked. He snorted by answering his own question, "Of course not."

He wondered what if anything would replace them as the next in what would have been a long line of "top dogs". Again it was all idle curiosity since he wouldn't be around to find out. He walked the long empty hallways, past open doors that led to empty dormitories, past the family units, and on into the section where the elected leaders lived. It was a trek that took time. This facility, when built, had been meant to hold thousands of people, both single and married. It was to be the place from which mankind would start over. Again this brought a bitter smile to his face. *Such thoughts, such plans, such hopes, such gall, and here I am the only one left, and from what I or we know or knew, nothing survived when the worst happened.*

Yes, he hadn't been around then, but it was written in the records, shown in the vids. All that took place, the passing of the act, the blueprints created, the location chosen, and the place constructed. It all happened in record time. It had to because all the earth, all of mankind knew what was coming, and the odds of being missed was too small to contemplate. He knew, again from the history, the records all that lived here were required to learn, they were just finishing up the storage of supplies, and beginning the preparation to bring in the first who had been selected to begin the overall functioning of the facility.

He, as a descendant, as well as the ones before him, had been part of the original crew, the team that was placing all the supplies into the storage areas, testing all the electronics, making sure the radios, computers, the communication systems functioned. They were supplying the libraries, the electronic sides of this. Almost all the books, entertainment – movies, and such – were in digital form. If hard copies were needed then the massive banks of printers would produce what was required. And then once used be recycled so that the materials could be used again.

Because no one had any idea to the severity of the damage to the planet this place had to be completely enclosed, completely self-sufficient – self-contained. The facility had great greenhouses, hydroponic gardens, and actual artificial parks that had much greenery to help with the recycling of the air. Again, because no one knew how much damage would be sustained, they had to plan for the worst, including the loss of atmosphere for an unknown time period. So, if necessary, this facility could be, would be sealed, with equipment located and protected on the surface so the conditions could be monitored.

And once the event happened, then periodically, people in environmental suits would go through airlocks to sample the outside air, and see how this old world fared. Yes, things had come to fruition quickly, but in the end, yes in the end, it hadn't mattered. *It wasn't soon enough.*

Something had happened out in one of the belts where the asteroids lie. What the event was would probably have been eventually discovered, but whatever it was caused a chain reaction, caused chaos in one of those asteroid belts, and like a shotgun blast sent hundreds, maybe thousands in towards the sun. In that chaos it had been nearly impossible for even the supercomputers to track. As the debris came towards the sun, and thusly the earth, there were collisions, changes of direction, influences from other planets and moons, and too many other things to be able to make even rough predictions. If luck held earth might be spared, but the data spoke of a more likely outcome. And it wasn't pretty. The worst case scenario destroyed the earth, making it a barren rock circling the sun. Other predictions were from complete misses to everything in-between. Yes, it was obvious the gas giants of the solar system would absorb much of what was flying inward, but not near enough.

Unfortunately, with the delay that light added to the equations even an accurate timeline couldn't be developed. The only fact that was truly known was the event would happen . . .

While the crews and teams were running the supplies into the storage areas, there were technicians on site testing all that was installed, and construction still happening. With the pressures of limited time chaos reigned supreme inside. With tempers flaring, and people in each other's way all the time, adding to the friction, somehow they pressed on. But there was little that could be done about it. There was no time to run separate shifts, to allow separate areas to be free of workers. And as these many workers pushed to get what they were trying to complete, flaws were found, and work-a-rounds had to be created. It made sense, since nothing of this scale had ever been attempted, let alone built. So what appeared to work on paper, didn't necessarily work in the real world.

Yet, even with all the pressure, the time limits, it really did appear that they were going to make it, to succeed, and soon the now empty facility would be teeming with life and the hope of humanity for a real future . . . *A real future, right.* Ed thought. *I'm it, and that's no future at all.*

Yet, as the history continued to flow through his mind Ed was unable to stop it. He didn't know why this was happening. Maybe it was because he had just placed his deceased father in that final place, but knew there would be no one to do the same for him.

How many generations had lived here, ending with me? He had to admit that he really didn't know. The only thing he did know was in the end, as it had been stated too many times back at the beginning, as well as in the lessons, the gene pool was too small, and somewhere along the line they would be doomed because of this. Nobody knew when it would happen, only that it would. Well, he was the end of the line, period. There would be no one to grieve for one Edward Carson.

Before he realized it he was back to his space. As a kid, and unfortunately there were no others, he had free reign of this place – this facility. But in the end, he felt that he had been everywhere, had discovered all the hidden areas, and was left with no mystery, and no adventures. He had read much of the stories that were available, and laughed inwardly are the sheer audacity of what was called Science Fiction, writers talking about what the human race would be doing in the future. Well, he was the future and it wasn't anything like those stories.

Of course he fell into the world of movies for a while. It was a place to escape from what was the real world. And, he suspected, like all kids, he really liked the world of Star Wars. Still, according to what his age was at the time, he found others more to his liking. He knew that at the time of the building of this place there had been advances in 3D, but unlike the Holodeck in the Star Trek series, there had been no true immersion. It still required those ridiculous glasses to make it work, although he had to admit it was fun dealing with the illusions these early attempts created. And those rides that combined the two effects with motion made it feel even more real. Still by spending his life here in "the deeps", he could only guess if that was how it truly felt. Then, of course, there were those recreation times where he was allowed to play video games. Still, even with the depth and amount that were available, he eventually ran out of the type he enjoyed playing – but all of this was part of the past. What the future held, other than death, he had to admit he didn't know.

He sat staring out at nothing, and probably, if he wanted to admit it, thought about nothing. It was hunger that finally brought his mind and musings back to reality. Sighing he got up and headed for the kitchens, the places to get a meal. There were a number of them located throughout the facility so that anybody from any section wouldn't have far to go to get fed. And the decision had been made, when the facility had been built, to keep the eating areas communal. To keep everyone in contact with each other hoping that it would prevent any member from becoming self-important to the point of believing they were better than the rest. Whether it would have worked he had no idea. There never were enough survivors or residents to find out.

He knew that through the time they had been here originally, and for a short period, their small population grew, giving hope that maybe they could beat the odds and the gene pool wasn't too small. But that was short-lived, and he was the final proof. With that brief population explosion it marked the end of expansion, and from that point on until now, it slowly became less and less until the whole facility had a total population of *one*.

After finishing his meal he headed over to the library – one of the many. He was in the mood to watch the vids of the final days of any who were on the surface of the planet as suddenly the skies lit up with streaks of fiery light as the first of too many entered the earth's atmosphere. Much of that early bombardment burned up, but there was too much, and before any could arrive, other than the crews and teams already at "The Deeps", the earth shook with the violence of too many strikes. It had happened during a shift change, and with only a skeleton crew, due to a brief holiday break, with this further reducing the ones left inside the facility. Fear reigned supreme as the strikes, which could be felt as earthquakes, even here in The Deeps, sent worry and shock through those few. And before the communications ended, and the vids being sent were cut off forever, much of the earth could be seen in flames as the atmosphere heated, the forests and cities burned, and the carbon dioxide rose. It truly appeared to be the end. Who or what could survive such an onslaught?

The fear within the deeps was overwhelming because any who witnessed the event felt there was no way for the earth to survive, and thusly any attempt to save at least a few would come to failure. And as the days moved into months, with the strikes continuing, all felt that it would only be a matter of time before even they, deep in the bowels of the earth, would be destroyed. Yet, as time continued to move, the strikes became fewer and fewer until one day they realized there hadn't been either a sighting or an earthquake generated by a strike in a while.

With the limited views they had back then nothing they saw gave them much encouragement. There lay a heavy layer of smoke blocking out the sun's light (much of the sensors and cameras close to their refuge survived), putting the earth into something that was called a nuclear winter. And it was obvious to them whatever or whoever might have survived the devastation would lose to this created winter. Killing whatever or whoever still lived out in the real world.

There were a number of security offices throughout the facility. There had to be because this much humanity in such a confined – here he laughed as he thought, *yeah confined* – space there would be conflicts. And if the place was ever discovered by the ones who were on the outside, then they who lived here would have to protect what they had. Most security stations monitored the interior, and only a few watched the outside. In the early days the security offices that monitored the outside were manned fully. The fear was that eventually they would be found (again if any had survived), and there could be an overwhelming force which would lay siege to "The Deeps" if they could find it.

Some of the other security offices were used to ensure the ones who were lucky enough to be here remained honest and part of the group. And eventually, as the years moved on and no one ever showed up, even these outward viewing security offices were rarely visited. And now for Ed they were just another set of doors and smoked glass – doors which reminded him of his isolation and the fact that he was the last man on the earth. *King and servant – yeah right!* He thought sarcastically. *So now what? Would it be better if I returned to the surface? Allowed the desert to take me? Or should I live out what few years I have left here where I know everything?* Good questions all of them, but today wouldn't be a day to answer them.

The death of his father was too fresh on his mind, and he knew that it would be easy to allow these emotions to cloud his judgment. Besides, whether he remained here or returned to the surface the results would be the same, only *when* would be different. So he continued his walk down the empty corridors, of both time and of distance to finally reach his destination. Once at the library door (again, one of many) he paused, took a deep breath, let it out slowly, entered, but stopped just beyond the threshold. Now that he was here, he wasn't sure if he really wanted to be. After all, what he had wanted to do would have only reinforced his loss, and the emptiness he felt.

He stood there for what seemed like forever before turning around and heading back out. Now with no specific destination in mind he began wandering the halls, again depressed, and letting his mind and his feet take him wherever they might want to go.

He passed by the rooms where the ones who were selected could put on the environmental suits and check out the conditions above. Early on there was some who had volunteered to do this, many never returned, and it was assumed they were killed, and any who did return found nothing promising. And later expeditions seemed to confirm this as some of the ones who had been on earlier teams and had not returned were found. Again, after much time, and no successes, even these forays outside were abandoned as too costly in lives. After that the security cameras were only used to observe the outside. And the images they presented gave no hope.

Eventually the skies cleared, and the sun's light once again penetrated all the way to the surface of the planet. And it appeared that somehow the atmosphere had also survived the onslaught. Then, after much discussion and arguments, a final team exited the facility using what was now ancient environmental suits – the population had been dropping drastically at this point – and returned days later. What they reported wasn't promising. The desert around the facility was huge, and had grown. Mountains could be seen in the distance, but if there was any vegetation at all, it couldn't be discerned. It gave the appearance it would take thousands of years for the recovery to happen, if it ever did.

When the volunteers had gone to the surface, they were expecting the solar vehicles to be usable but instead found they had deteriorated from lack of maintenance and were worthless. This meant the only real exploring they could do was on foot, limiting what they could actually see and confirm. And with limited distances and time everything discovered pointed to death and destruction and a very little recovery. There also was no sign of any having survived. As far as the evidence found and presented, they were it. They would have to remain where they were.

With this discovery and discouragement no one ever asked again to go topside and see. It brought a depression upon the ones remaining and soon after there were a number of suicides as many felt there were wasn't any reason to go on with a world that could no longer support life of any kind. It had been a dark time in the history of this facility, and there had been some actual fighting as the ones who were left took up sides, became factions, and began to attack one another, furthering the shrinking of the population. Again something they couldn't afford to do. But it truly had been too late all the way back at the beginning, and slowly, very slowly they could see the proof happening right before them.

And again the predicted day had finally arrived – there was only he. Ed found he was down in one of the maintenance areas and didn't even know how he got here. Then he shrugged, the area needed to be inspected anyway. Fortunately most of the equipment had been mothballed since there was no need. It meant if something broke there would be plenty of spare parts available. And if necessary a different plant or steam works could be initiated and the old one shut down for repairs.

Hours later, and quite dirty from having to crawl around and look into tight corners, he showered, and headed down the hallways to catch his evening meal. Once finished he'd head back and catch something on the tube, not that he hadn't seen everything that interested him a number of times, but it was a way to finish out this day when the human population of the earth had shrunk to only him.

* * *

What had it been? Three weeks since he became the last one? He knew they still tracked time the same way as it had been before the event, and if he looked at the calendar it would probably read somewhere in the month of June. The year, he hadn't paid attention in forever. He knew from the archives there had been an argument as to how to track the years. Some thought it should begin from the point when they sealed this place from the outside world, others wanted to continue as it always had been. In the end it was tracked both ways since no one could decide.

And if he wanted to admit it, again since he was the last, why would it be important or matter anyway? Once he was gone there would be no one who would care, and there was a great chance there wouldn't be another intelligent species arising that would track time the same way anyway. Still three weeks had passed and in a sense, even with all this space, the walls were closing in on him. He swore he could hear voices, see shadows, and it felt as if the ghosts of the ones who had lived out their lives here were watching him, judging him, and shaking their heads, seeing the end close at hand.

He had decided, in the near past, to go back over the vids of his parents. Not that it mattered. He knew, again from the history of the original occupants, from the vids and records, the idea of monogamy had been thrown out. To have the greatest chance of survival everybody had to spread their genes as widely as possible. It wasn't the best of solutions, and had created its own problems, since most were of the belief that monogamy was the best way to go.

Some of the issues were obvious, especially for the women because they knew that this fell mostly on them. They would become nothing more than baby factories, sperm depositories, with no love or support for what lay ahead for them. Many rebelled, but when desperation reigns such rebellion didn't last long. And whether they wanted to be a part of this or not, they were forced against their will to participate. It was the reason for the brief population explosion, but the widely mixing of the genes from this – experiment, for lack of a better word – didn't save them in the end, and again, he was the proof of that.

It was probably six months after the sealing of the facility they knew there would be no others. This led to many arguments, discussions, anger, fear, and chaos. Eventually, even though with some reluctance, they put into action their plan to give the human race a chance of survival. The exam rooms were turned into production rooms – more of reproduction rooms really. They determined for the best success that each woman would have three males leave their seed inside of her, and this would be done one after another with only 5 minutes between encounters. To help the females they would lie on the exam tables and use the stirrups to support their legs and make it easy and quick. Then a few days would pass and the procedure would be repeated with a different set of males.

Each male would be given a random room number, a time, and once there would be assigned a number ranging from 1 to 3. The guard at the door would admit each one, announce the number to the waiting female who wouldn't be seen by the males, and the timer would start. The process was a simple one, the male would touch the female on her leg to let her know he was there and ready, at which point he would perform the act and leave. No talking was allowed to further the anonymity of the participants. The second reason for this was simply the chance to reduce jealousy, and the possibility of violence among the members of "The Deeps". By no one knowing who either the father of the child, or which female each male may have mated with, other than when the child resembled a particular male, or possibly a female or male of a different race, it could have been any of them.

It had been conjectured, somewhere in the past, that in the wilds a female (before civilization and written history) would mate with more than one male, and like in the ideas of the fittest surviving, it was thought that even on the level of sperm, the fittest would be the one to fertilize the egg. And within a short period of time, where in the past the attempt to prevent pregnancy was paramount, now it was the opposite, and all of the fertile females were carrying. And once they came to full term, then 3 months would be allowed before they would try again. All would be responsible for the care and the raising of the new generation coming out of this, with the hope of success.

Part of the problem from this desperate attempt lay in the fact that this process was a slow one – nature made it that way. Once a child was conceived then the mother would carry the child to term and hope for a successful birth, this followed by 16 to 18 years of life before the children would be at a time in their life where they could add their genes to the mix and enter into the program. And with the few women who were at the facility at the time of sealing, they could generally only add one life a year to the population, and only for so long before their bodies would give out.

Then there was the age factor. A woman could only safely produce offspring for so long before genetic errors, personal survival, and the ability to become pregnant arrived. And many of the women who were here at the facility were close to the end of their child-bearing years, adding to the odds of failure. This didn't mean that there weren't problems on the other side. Males or men had issues also. No they didn't carry the burden as the women, or pay the price, still there were no guarantees they were fertile either. And add to the mix there were no doctors or nurses – they wouldn't have arrived until the first of the ones who were to occupy this facility were to arrive, which, of course, never happened – only added to the complications.

Without nurses and doctors, midwives and such, there was a greater chance of losing both the birthing mother and her infant, furthering the chances of failure. And each time it happened it weighed heavily on the population, because there were no others to replace the losses, replace the females who died in childbirth. And as time and desperation drove the residents of "The Deeps" on, the inevitable happened and the population had dwindled down to his mother and father.

Of course, with his parents there was no choice. They were the last of each sex to be alive, and if anything, the vids of their relationship showed they were not compatible at all. But desperation creates strange bedfellows, and it was obvious as he watched the vids this was the case here. They had nothing in common, and it was painfully obvious for them to come together physically was a difficult proposition. Yet, eventually he was conceived, and it was while he was still young – 6 or 7, if he remembered right – his mother died.

He could tell from the desperation in his father's attempt to save her, it was important – critical really. But at that age one didn't understand other than the hurt from not having her around. Her skills had been computing and as a dietician, while his father was an engineer. Ed, more because of the need, had no specialty, but kind of a cross-section of everything. This allowed him to repair anything that might break down, and break downs did happen. Things just naturally wore out just like their bodies. Time, it seemed, tore everything down.

He remembered, after her death, things seemed to fall apart – especially between him and his father. He didn't understand it at all. After all, he really was too young to understand. Yet, after what seemed to be too great of a time both of them fell into an uneasy routine, an uneasy understanding, and a shaky relationship. What else could they do? There was no one else, only the two of them. And as time moved past both of them he realized, in most ways, he had taken after his mother's side, and since he knew how poorly the two of them got along, he could see it would be the same with him and his father.

Yeah, it had been tough. They had compromised a lot. Even still there had been fights, arguments, and disagreements, followed by anger and silence between the two of them. Still, they had no choice; they depended on each other just to survive. This eventually led to an understanding of what could and couldn't be discussed. And the years moved rapidly until here he was – alone. *Alone*, such a scary word. He had learned, through his studies, they were a gregarious species, ones who needed others. Yet, when there were no others what did one do?

The obvious answer was – die. *Well that option would be coming soon enough.* Heck, if he was younger, by about 40 years, maybe it would be worthwhile to head back to the surface if for no other reason than to be able to say he had been there. But he was now in his 60's. All he could do is shake his head and ask, *where did the time go? Wasn't it just yesterday when mother had passed away and I tried to hold back the tears? Wasn't it just yesterday when I was no longer a child? And yet only a short time ago father joined mother and all the others before them in death. Now what? Yes, now what indeed.* No answers, and in truth, no one to ask.

* * *

How much time had passed? How long had it been? He didn't know the answers for those questions, but somewhere along the line he suspected he had flipped out – had gone crazy. It was the only explanation he could come up with. When he finally came back to reality he looked at the clocks that measured the passing seconds as well as the passing days, weeks, months, and years. To his surprise he found two years had gone by since he became the last human, the final flickering candle burning down to nothing, the end of the line. He found the clothes he was wearing, which weren't much if he wanted to be honest, were filthy, caked in ground in dirt, torn and worn out. And he stank – speaking of missing too many showers. Looking in the mirror he could see a white beard half way down his chest, and his eyes still held a wild tint to them speaking to him – saying it would be easy to fall back into the insanity which had gripped him.

Better take this slow and easy. Don't know what I did, or what I might have destroyed, or hurt, but I really do not want to repeat it. Taking a deep cleansing breath he stripped off the rags he wore and entered the shower setting the water jets to as hot as he could stand, letting the streams of hot water wash away the layers of dirt, and the steam to help clear his mind. He leaned against one of the walls and let the hot water massage his back, and he had to admit it felt great. Once he decided to get out of the shower he'd shave off this beard, and get into some new clothing. It was time to take on those responsibilities he probably had ignored when he wasn't right.

Another two months had gone by, and he had been quite busy during this time. It had taken all of his energy and effort to fix everything, to inspect the equipment, and to bring everything up to date. Once finished he finally sat down and watched the vids, cringing as he watched himself during his period of insanity tearing through the facility, screaming obscenities, breaking things, running around naked at times, and at other times spending time in his room rolled up in a fetal position, rocking back and forth, and only humming. And if he had said anything at all at those times it was unintelligible. What had brought him back to reality and sanity he didn't really know.

And truthfully he didn't know what had sent him over the edge either. The only thing he could say was the fact he had reached the age of 67, and wondered how many years he had left, but honestly he didn't know. And maybe, if he was completely truthful with himself, it probably didn't matter.

During these times, after returning to sanity, he began a complete rediscovery of the huge facility. There were a number of areas, when there were more here, that were generally sealed off, or no longer visited. And these areas, because of no usage, had all the security cameras, and sound recordings turned off. The areas were powered down, and minimal light and support was maintained to conserve energy. Since the assigned had never reached the facility, and the population never reached a point where the space was needed, well over three quarters of the unused space became just that and was never used.

Sure, as a kid it was a neat place to explore, but in a very short period of time, after the first discovery of this vast area, and his sneaking into it, he found it to be boring. It simply was a darkened cold area similar to the one where they were living, with exactly the same rooms, same layout, only the area still had all the materials marking it an area never used. Things such as plastic sealed mattresses, and furniture, unopened kitchen ware, and closets with hangers that had nothing on them, followed by a light layer of dust, further identifying the lack of use. In other words, it was like a new – and since he had only seen them in the vids it was only a guess – house, or apartment complex.

Again, as a kid, every once in a while, during these unauthorized excursions into the closed areas, he found tracks of others before him. Most were the same size as his tracks, stating other kids had done the same thing. But every once in a while he would find what he had to assume were adult tracks. Why or for what reason adults had come here, he hadn't a clue, but suspected it could have been for breeding. It was the only thing that made any sense. Since here, no one could or would watch you, and it was one of the reasons he liked to come here. He could be truly alone, although at this point in his life, he had no idea what he would give *not* to be alone. Once again he laughed a bitter laugh, *Oh how the times have changed from back then to now.*

After his return to normalcy, and with his travels around the facility to do the required maintenance, he found one of the doors open into one of the closed off areas, and since he was it, he knew he had to be the one who had gone there. So with the completion of the work he decided to return there and see what he had been up to during those 2 years of insanity. So with a plan in place, he brought the lighting up to where one could see, but not to full power. It would still be a place of shadows and illusion, but he wouldn't need any additional light to walk those hollow empty hallways, rooms, family units, and storage areas – all which at one time held a promise of a future only to have it not fulfilled.

The first thing he noticed was a feel of time and of unfulfilled promises, a smell of an area long unopened and sealed against all. It spoke of age, and the emptiness almost caused him to turn around and leave. Yet, looking in the layer of dust on the floors he could see his tracks, speaking loudly he had been this way in the near past. So with his utility belt, and wearing a hard-hat which had a headlamp, he began his exploration of this wing of the facility, one, other than his time of insanity, he had only traveled when he was a child. And this was probably 60 years in the past, or there about.

From the stride of the tracks in the dust he figured he must have been running, but why? What could he be running from or to? Since he was out of his mind at the time he didn't know. Curious he pushed on until he entered one of the large storage areas which had never been used. His steps echoed and the area was in deep shadows with only a few of the emergency lights burning. He looked high up on one of the walls and there, written in his own hand in large letters, and he suspected it was from one of those paint aerosol cans, were the words, THE END IS NEAR. He almost laughed. *Isn't this something one saw in those old comic strips where someone would have signs over their shoulders shouting this to the world? And how did I ever get up there to spray those words?* He had to admit he didn't know.

Although, if he wanted to admit it, there was some irony in this statement written in paint, and obviously it was a fact. Yet, was it the truth? Good question. Since, when one looked out through those sensors that had survived the onslaught of the falling rocks from space, and the time since the incident, this old world was slowly returning. So it would only be the end of mankind, a slight bump in time when we existed. *And when the earth has healed herself from the damage, there will be nothing to mark our passing into history – nothing at all.*

He spent the next month following his path throughout this sealed wing, finding places where he had damaged things – superficial for sure, but he still had. Other places where there were additional writings on the walls which made no sense at all. *Definitely the sign of an insane mind making sense out of nothing, and living in chaos,* he thought. He really wondered what had triggered the insanity, and really had no clue as to what ended it. Or maybe, he really was insane, and what he was doing presently was only a dream. How would he know the difference? *There is nobody to ask, now is there.* This stopped him for a moment as he looked around and at himself seeing the dirt on his clothing from the cleanup he was doing. Slowly he had been repairing the damage, cleaning and removing the painted words on the walls, and preparing to reseal the wing.

He went to one of the rooms and sat down in one of the chairs and thought about it. No, if he was asking himself about his insanity there was a greater chance he wasn't. But could he be sure? Of course not. And as far as he knew he could be asleep and all of this might be a dream, and he'd wake up and find his father still alive and they could laugh about it when he told him about the dream. He took a deep breath, let it out slowly, and shook his head. He knew better. Sighing, he pushed himself out of the chair, did one more circuit through the wing, and left it for the last time, sealing the door behind him, cutting the power to the area, other than the minimal necessary to keep it operational, and headed back to his personal unit to shower, get into some clean clothing, eat something, and if time permitted, maybe a trip back to one of the libraries. He wanted to watch some more history from the beginning of their time, and maybe something from before, when the world was filled with people.

Another two weeks passed as he double-checked all of his work, but even with this needed work he could tell that the loneliness of this place was settling in heavily. It was then he got an idea and headed for one of the large meeting areas or assembly rooms and surveyed the area, taking measurements, not that he needed to, since all he really had to do was bring up the plans for this place, and headed out to one of the fabrication areas. There were a number of these fabrication areas throughout the facility, and great thought and energy went into them since it was felt these facilities would be the reason "The Deeps" survived.

It was a known fact they wouldn't be able to think of everything, so to have the ability to create whatever was necessary for that unseen or unplanned event was critical. Although, in the end, these "fab" areas were not responsible for the failure that lay upon the facility – it was time itself. *Time on both ends.* Not enough in the beginning, and because of this, enough time to show that the conclusions at the time of the sealing were correct. And again because of the limiting factors of time, the measurements from the plans to the final product were not necessarily the same and further reason to measure. Besides it gave him something to do, and he to admit, he did have the time.

Once he reached the fabrication space he drew up what he wanted, studied it a while, made a few minor changes, input the data into the system, and had the fabricator produce half a dozen large monitors. He felt he needed more than this, but would get these mounted on the walls and make a judgment call from there. Now all he had to do was monitor the process, and be in the right place at the right time when the monitors came down the automated assembly line – which he did. At this point he loaded the 6 monitors on a small fork lift and drove back to the assembly room he had chosen.

After moving the units inside the room he found he was sweating, and he looked up at the time and found the day was over. *Where'd the time go?* He realized at this moment his stomach had been warning him he hadn't eaten since breakfast. Shaking his head he headed back out the door, shut the forklift down, with plans on taking it back to storage tomorrow, headed to one of the kitchens, prepared a meal, and headed back to his room. The one thing he truly had was time – well time until it took him like all before him.

Yet, once he had finished eating and taking that hot refreshing shower, and was looking at some program from the past on the tube, he realized that he really hadn't been watching or listening at all. So he shut it down, grabbed some reading material, but again found he couldn't concentrate on it either, he sighed and stared at the ceiling for a while. He was antsy and realized he wanted to complete his planned project, but made himself wait. The monitors were only the first part of it and there really was no reason to rush, even with impatience pushing him.

Finally, after his restlessness pushed him on, he left and walked the empty halls until he settled down, and headed back to his room, climbed into bed, and after sometime of being awake finally drifted off into a dream filled sleep where "The Deeps" was filled to over capacity with others like him. It seemed so different from the reality he faced.

* * *

He wished he knew more about programming and computers. It was his mother's specialty, but he couldn't ask her now could he? He looked around this large assembly room to the rows of bleachers and the center area where whoever had called the assembly would speak. What he had planned for this area would give him the feel of what it was like to be surrounded by humanity. But, of course, it would be nothing more than an illusion. Still when one was alone as he, such an illusion would be all he had.

As he had mounted the monitors on the walls he found that he had to add additional ones so that most of the wall space would be covered. All of them were placed above the bleachers, yes those never used empty bleachers that had shown a promise never fulfilled, which had made the job of mounting them more difficult. This was followed by the speakers he set up in the corners pointing towards the center. All of this was the easy part. Then came the wiring of the whole mess, followed by failure after failure, when what he was trying to accomplish, refused to work.

He had yet to find a program on either the servers, or tower computers that would allow him to control this area as he wanted. It was then he remembered that some of those FPS games he used to play as a child had the capability he was looking for. Now which one was it, or was it more than one, he couldn't remember. After all, it had been years since he had even thought about those days of gaming on the computer. Maybe he should go down to one of the libraries and head into the areas designated for gaming and see if he could find the one he remembered.

* * *

It was a month later when he finally got back to his project. He had a large smile on his face as he headed back down the hallway to his room. *Nostalgia, what a ride,* he thought. Because of the time since he had played any of these games he had forgotten how intense and how much fun they were. *Rusty – that's an understatement.* Games he used to fly through with ease now were difficult, and he found his avatar in the game world was dying a lot even on the easy setting. Yet, almost like back in his youth, he found himself being drawn back time and time again. Finding himself immersed into those fictional worlds once again – with the hours and days passing him by, leaving him completely unaware of the passage of time. Finally, with the marathon sessions, he tired of the games once again, but vowed to come back now and again so he could immerse himself in these worlds.

Well, tomorrow he'd head back into the assembly room and try to continue where he left off. Now, if he could only remember why he'd quit in the first place. Still, he was sure once he got back into the room and picked up his notes he would be able to pick it up and continue. But it was the end of another day, and it could wait until tomorrow. Tomorrows would be with him until they were taken away, and he went the way of every other individual who had lived here, and any who had lived on this world. Yes, time for a shower, a meal, and maybe a book, and then to bed.

* * *

"Ah yes, that's right. I went to check out those devices we used, well I used, that allowed the screen and the game program to track movement." It meant with the properly mounted hardware when he turned his head, or looked up or down, the scene on the monitor would change to reflect his view. An example that came to mind was some of the games where you were a pilot of a plane. With the equipment you could turn your head and look out the sides to see if your team was still there, or if the enemy had gotten a drop on you. Now he wanted to adapt this to this room. Well, there was only one way to find out if it would work. At least the program to operate the hardware was separate. He just had to figure out how to make it work with what he had in mind.

Taking a deep breath after too many tries and failures, it still wouldn't operate like he wanted. To help create the illusion he desired required those 3D glasses. He wanted the area to feel as if it was filled with the images, and not just on the screens of the monitors. Taking a slow, deep breath he left the assembly area to clear his mind and maybe get something to drink. He'd been pushing it, and as in those immersive games the hours had flown. If fact when he had looked up at the time he found that not only had he been here all day without a break, but half the night. It was close to midnight. *Guess I'll call it then, and come back either tomorrow or the next. I've got to figure out what I'm doing wrong.*

He then spent the next two days in the library researching the subject to find out what he missed, and realized it simply was a command line, which was optional in the gaming world. Because so many of them were set up to interface with the VR system, he had forgotten that most other programs out there weren't, and the reason for the existence of the command line. So using the old DOS command "COPYCON", he wrote it, ending it with the "COM" extension finishing it with the "CTRL Z" command to tell the system he was finished with the file. He then inserted the command line into the proper folder and ran the program again. He held his breath briefly as it came on-line. He then hooked up the device to his hat, placed the 3D glasses over his eyes and watched the screens as they showed a nature scene, turning his head he watched as the views changed with his movement, giving the illusion of depth. This brought a huge smile to his face. *It works!* Not only that but the sounds shifted with his movement adding reality to the scenes. *Yeah!* He thought . . .

With a nervousness that was almost overwhelming he went back to the library. He would be choosing what he would view in that room he had created. He wasn't sure if he really was ready for it or not. When it came right down to it he had only been around three people, including himself, since he had been alive. Now, he planned on virtually – figuratively and in actuality – surrounding himself with thousands, and he truly had no idea how he would act and react to this. He remembered his father disappearing at times, and he would find him watching one of the monitors, with the sound turned way down. When he would look over his shoulder he would see some sporting event from the past. At the time it held no interest, so he would leave and go do something else. But now, since it was only he, he had to admit he was lonely. And maybe those sporting events would be the very thing he needed.

Still, could he handle the crowds, the ones who would show up at these events? It was a question for which he had no answer. He had been in the assembly room a number of times watching many scenes from the time before the impacts. Seeing much of the beauty of the world, but at the same time he avoided any that showed the cities and towns, and especially the humanity. He found the only thing missing was the smells, the scents, the feel of the moving air, the changes in the feel of the air, and the different temperatures as one hiked around. Of course, that was what it said in the books. He personally didn't know since he had lived here in this enclosed environment for his entire life. Yes the small parks, green houses and such gave one a little sense of how it could be, but not really.

So he sat here looking over the lists. He knew, from watching his father, that football (and there were two different versions of this sport) had been very popular. He knew, from the archives, that even here in this place they had played versions of both in the parks. Of course this was when there were enough people to form teams to play. It had been a long time since such had been a possibility. He finally chose American football, more because it had been a favorite of his father. But before he could decide on what to pipe to the computers and screens in the assembly room he needed to understand it a bit more, learn something about the teams, and begin to see how it was actually played. So he spent the next couple of weeks watching, pausing the images when he didn't understand something, researching his questions, and coming back and watching the game again.

Eventually he began to see the complexities of the game – the continual battle between the ones who had the ball – the offense, and the ones who tried to take it away from them – the defense. He found, as he continued to watch, that at times he could actually predict what play or counter play would happen. And he began to learn the tendencies of certain coaches, as the ones were called, who seemed to be in charge of the teams. He found he was becoming emotionally involved at times, with flights of joy as a big play would happen, and anger when there seemed to be a bad call or something unexpected had taken place. And he found, like most, he began to develop favorite teams. Yet, this wasn't necessarily what he had set out to accomplish. Still it passed the time, and he didn't feel so lonely.

Eventually he chose the game he would move to the assembly room, set it to begin at a certain time, headed for the kitchen to grab some food and drink, and mentally prepared to enter a room, which would become what was called a stadium, join the crowds that would be filling that stadium, and watch the players on the field – all virtually of course. He remained standing, still not certain if he was ready for this. He had tried to watch the crowds during the games he viewed on the regular screen, since the cameras always panned the crowds during the games, but it wasn't the same. Taking a deep breath and looking down, he could hear the game start, the cheering of the crowd as their team was introduced, and he found he couldn't move. The sounds alone were overwhelming, how could he enter that virtual stadium and sit among that many people? He honestly didn't know.

He found himself standing outside of that room. (There next to the doorway he had mounted a shelving unit and had placed the needed equipment necessary to make the images inside that room become 3D.) Here was the hat with the wireless VR unit, and many of the glasses necessary to create the illusion of depth. Still from all the noise emitting from the room he couldn't eliminate the fear that had frozen him at the door. Shaking his head he thought. *Now this is stupid. They are not really there. It's only a projection, an illusion. So why can't you go inside and join these fans who aren't really here?*

Truthfully he knew the answer. It simply was because he had never been among so many, even if they weren't real. Well, that wasn't the complete truth. At one time these people were living, breathing individuals living out their lives before death and destruction from the skies ended all of that. Still he stood there and listened but remained firmly in the hallway. Eventually he took another deep cleansing breath, shook his head, turned around and headed back to the library where he shut it down. He now knew it would take a few days, a few attempts before he could be brave enough to enter that room once one of those simulations were running. Maybe he could work up to it?

It was then he decided to slowly work into it using some of the other videos that combined the natural world with cities and towns. Once he got used to these cities, maybe then he could handle the crowds. So for the next couple of months he ran an old series that explored the world from the air, only zooming in on people now and then. These he ran one after another until there were no more to see. He had to admit when seeing the world this way it had been a beautiful place. And even some of the cities seemed to hold their own particular beauty. And another part of all of this came to light, there didn't seem to be a place where people hadn't been. Even the vast oceans seemed to have traffic on them all the time. Well, soon he would try again. Besides his 68th birthday would be arriving soon. Maybe he would attend a game to celebrate.

* * *

He spent a number of days researching the teams, and for whatever reason, he thought he would try to watch a Green Bay Packers game, maybe followed by one of the teams on the opposite coast. It would be a tough decision – well not really since this was only entertainment, a way to pass time – because there seemed to be a lot of teams. Finally he decided on one that was the furthest in the southwest – a team that never seemed to quite make it all the way to the championships but would cause problems for the ones who did. Besides it would mean he had a team from both sides, both, as they were called, divisions. And this meant a team from the northeast, and one from the southwest, although this latter was considered to be residing in the west – right along the coast. Sometime before it all ended they had moved to a larger city to the north. Besides, when they wore their old uniforms, identified as the powder blues, they really looked sharp.

He had learned through his research that there were pregame shows and decided he would watch one of these in the library before going to the actual game in the assembly room. He felt it would set the atmosphere, and even with all the preparation including some smaller events where a lot of people were present, he still wasn't sure if the size of the crowds at these games would still overwhelm him or not. Well, there was only one way to find out. Tomorrow he would be another year older, and another year closer to his end. Might as well enjoy the time he had left.

The pregame show was interesting. This must have been a popular sport. The show lasted three hours. Three hours, can you imagine such a thing? He had sat through the whole thing and then set the game to begin after a delay. He needed to hit the facilities, go to the kitchen and grab some snacks, and he wanted to be inside and sitting when the game started. This way he'd already be there when it began. In preparation he had brought in a small table and a comfortable chair. One thing about those bleachers, very quickly, they became uncomfortable, and if he was to be here three hours – the length of an average game – he wanted to be comfortable. The one thing he still didn't understand was the stated length of a game being sixty minutes, yet it would stretch out to three times that long.

Finally he was back in the room and set up with drink and food. Looking up at the clock he had a couple of minutes so he took a deep breath, closed his eyes, and waited. With his eyes remaining closed he heard the sounds of the crowds and the movement of the people, followed by the loud speakers announcing the start of the game. With effort he fought down his nervousness, and brought his breathing back under control. Slowly he opened his eyes, and almost panicked when he found himself surrounded by literally thousands of fans. This sea of humanity seemed to press in on him, and what made it worse was how close they sat next to each other.

It took all his willpower to remain here, but he did, although for the first few times he could only remain there in that room for maybe five to ten minutes before he had to *pause* the program. He had to keep reminding himself that they really weren't here, and it was all an illusion. He even had to take off the glasses to convince himself. Eventually as time moved on he could feel himself relaxing a bit, and then he put the glasses back on, and carefully looked towards the area where the field was and began to concentrate on the players trying to ignore the crowds. It took all of his will power, concentration and effort but eventually he found he could. And if he could become more comfortable with it maybe he would take in a couple of games a week, heck maybe more. After all he had years of the sport, and of course, other sports locked away in the libraries.

* * *

It was the time of the week to take in another game. Searching out the archives he learned these football games were generally played on Sundays, a single game on Mondays, and sometimes on Thursdays. So in keeping with the traditions of his ancestors he decided to do the same thing. Even though he had decided to originally follow those two teams, over time, he found that according to the season, as such a thing was called, he would follow different teams.

Of course, there were other sports. Soccer, or the other version of football as most of the world called it, basketball, rugby, baseball, and so many others. So if he tired of one he had others to watch. It was during these searches for others he came across the winter sports, and found the Olympics. It was a gathering of world athletes who competed for their individual nations – nations that no longer existed, and to win honor for themselves and their nations. Still it was much too easy to become, as he found the phrase in the libraries, "a couch potato".

He could see, from the articles in the various papers and magazines (digitally of course), the passion many had for sports. He found many examples of merchandise that supported all levels of the sports world – from the most amateur to the pros. The amount of time and effort expended on the competitions were unbelievable. And as he delved into this world of competition, he found this seemed to exist on all levels of humanity. Be it sports, jobs, education, or whatever, it seemed the human species thrived on it. *I guess in a way my father and I did also. Maybe it's just a part of being human. Well, one thing for sure, I can't prove or disprove it. I have no one to compete against.* This got him to thinking about other parts of what made them, well, them. Here he laughed. He remembered during the time of growing up and his studies that there were many who had spent their lifetimes pursuing these subjects and had barely moved the discipline forward.

Besides, if he wanted to be honest, there was no reason to do this, the studying and researching of psychology and sociology, because he was it. It was at this point he heard one of the warning buzzers, stopped his walk down the corridor, headed to the maintenance office where the panels would show him where the problem was, and realized at the same time he had been ignoring his duties. Nothing built by man could last forever, and when he looked at the calendar he realized he was months overdue on some of the needed maintenance, repair, and work. He had allowed this obsession to surround himself with the sea of humanity to take precedence over all his other duties. Now he hoped it hadn't ignored this work for too long.

Once at the panels he found there were two problems. Well, in a sense only one, but the first had created the second so he had to shut down the second to prevent additional damage, and once shut down go solve the first. The problem he faced, was while most of the facility had redundant systems, in one area they were not so lucky. There were a number of water storage tanks, but they were all together and linked to one another, with a single main line coming into the facility. There had been no time to set the water system up as the rest had been. So it had remained a single weak point, but there had never been any real problems.

If any of the tanks started leaking it could at least be closed and locked out of the system until repairs could be made. But there was really only that one main line into the facility and if it began to leak it would mean the facility could be without water until it was repaired. Apparently this line began to leak. It must not have been too bad to begin with since the system hadn't shut down, but now the flow of water into the facility had been reduced, while the flow out of the tanks was greater. Even with an identified leak, water still needed to flow otherwise areas critical would be without. Apparently the leak or leaks had reached a critical point. So he now needed to locate and repair it, or eventually he would be without water. Because he was alone there would be a great possibility it truly wouldn't affect him, still it would impact other things such as food production.

While it was something he could do, in truth he wanted no part of it. Yet, what choice did he have? None really. Disgusted with the prospect, all he could do is shake his head. Looking up at the clock he found it was late afternoon, almost too late to begin the project. Maybe he should put together a tool kit, at least the basic tools, and maybe for the first time in his life actually head to the surface. Yeah he'd been close, to the doorway exit fifty years in the past, but that was as far as he had ever gotten. In fact it was as far as any of the three of them had gone.

Once they had reached that second door, the one on the far side of the airlock, opened it and stared out into the enclosed garage area where those old vehicles were stored they had stopped. They could feel the real air, the uncontrolled environment, the different smells, the feel of the heat radiating into the enclosed area, and in truth it had been too much. So they stood there as long as they could and in silence and in agreement closed the outer door and headed back into the facility. Yes, as a young person he had been curious, but after actually seeing and feeling it, his curiosity died. And he never asked again, and never wanted to wander the garage slash storage area or the wastes beyond that door.

Unfortunately someone had to – if only to inspect the water supply lines, to make sure the tanks remained sealed. Once the water entered into the facility it was processed, used, and then reclaimed and sent to the gardens and hydroponic tanks to keep "food on the table", to keep the greenery green, and to provide a few ponds to give the illusion of the outside. Of course with only three of them there wasn't much to process and recycle. So much of the water use went to keep the gardens alive, and the hydroponic areas producing. Again at a minimal rate since there had been only their single family, and now only him.

This meant the water in those tanks changed rarely, and the circulation pumps kept the water flowing between the tanks keeping it fresh. Now, somewhere a leak had formed. And while it had been in the original plans to set up monitoring points, it had never happened. In the end the only monitoring that had been set up was acoustic in nature. Something which would pick up the sound of flowing water, which meant something such as a pinhole leak wouldn't be picked up. It would only be after the leak had grown large enough to be heard, the system would send out its warning. This meant that a leak could go for years before it became large enough to be heard – at which point it would have become serious, and a threat.

At least the environmental suits still functioned. He couldn't see himself heading out in just his overalls, the clothing he wore when he did maintenance within the facility. Although he really hadn't tried working in those suits so he really had no idea if was even feasible. He knew, from the archives, that the suits allowed one mobility, and to move freely in the world, but none of the vids ever showed anybody doing detailed work. It was more to operate the vehicles, and to move around. Well, maybe he should at least put one on as he put his tools together and see how flexible it would be.

After about an hour in the suit he gave up. There was no way he could make it work. This brought anger to him. The last thing he wanted to do was to expose his body to the outside air, but he had little choice. At least he could go out into that large garage, and off to one side was the entrance into the area where the water tanks were located. He could at least start there and begin his search. Again he looked up at the clock and with the time of day decided he would do the searching tomorrow. He felt it too late to begin now. Besides he needed to search out the blueprints and trace to water pipe locations so he wasn't searching and remaining outside for too long. Well, not really outside since he would still be in the enclosure. Just outside of the controlled environment. Still, there had to be a way to use those suits.

* * *

He wasn't sure if it was his imagination or whether he was truly feeling the difference. Especially since he was in one of the environmental suits and completely separated from the outside air. He found he wasn't brave enough to go outside without it. He was going to try to use it anyway. If it failed he could still remove it and go the way it had appeared he had to back when he tried to use the suit earlier. He hadn't seen anything living from the few times he had watched the feeds coming from the outside. As far as he knew the air wasn't breathable (although in his heart he knew it was just an excuse). And even if it was, he wasn't going to take that kind of risk. He knew, with his isolation inside "The Deeps", if there were germs out here, he could be vulnerable to them. Yes, he had been inoculated for everything one could catch, but that was from what they knew. No one had sampled the air to know how much had changed or mutated, so as far as he knew and even with all those preventative measures, in the end, it could mean nothing.

So here he stood inside the vast structure that housed the useless broken vehicles, the repair shops, supply storage areas for most of what was here, including replacement pipes, valves and such, welding equipment, fabrication shops for repairs to the structure, and whatever the original builders and planners thought such a place might need. He knew north of this area was the original gathering point, the Welcome and Processing building where the chosen were supposed to enter, but it had never been used, and if the truth be known, pretty much forgotten. In fact the building never received the supplies marked for it. Items such as food and drink dispensers, and while there had been plans for a kitchen area, it was never completed. And while he wouldn't need to go inside of the reception and processing area the pipes ran by and then over the sides with a trunk line that ran into the reception area so it would have water to supply the bathrooms, small dining areas, and drinking fountains. It also fed a small natural tank so that any worker out in the real world could refill their containers and not have to return inside.

He went to the north end of this vast area and climbed the ladder up to the entrance to the tunnel where the water pipes ran. He brought a flashlight to compliment his headlamp since he wasn't sure if the solar lighting would still work. It hadn't been tested in forever, even though it was one of those things that were supposed to be done on a regular basis.

Somehow once people quit coming to the surface, the inspections were never made, and even the large garage and supply area, while somewhat sealed from the outside, was never visited. And the vast amount of dust from the ages that seemed to lay on everything reinforced this point very well.

He grabbed and with some effort forced the handle that locked the door, to turn and open, listening to it complain and screech with each movement. It was a simple quarter turn handle since the door was a simple inspection access and repair door leading one into the inspection tunnel. Dust also fell off the door and when he finally got it to open, again with the hinges protesting, the lighting came on. Unfortunately not all of it and because of this there were dark areas, and shadows everywhere, creating pools of light and shadow. At least there was some light.

Taking a deep breath he headed into the manmade tunnel and with each step raising small clouds of fine dust which hung in the air further shadowing the tunnel. And even though he couldn't be sure it seemed to be warmer. Still this was more enclosed than that large working area and he felt more comfortable here. So carefully he worked his way down the long tunnel, past a turn and slowly over his breathing he began to hear the running water. It continued to get louder. Checking his position from the map he carried, he thought he had to be over the natural tank. There should be a window here so he could inspect it. Since things hadn't been checked in forever he figured there was a good chance that the tank was dry.

He began searching for the inspection window and almost gave up when his headlight reflected off the glass. It was heavily coated in dust and he had to brush it off to be able to look through it. When he did, and to his surprise it appeared to still contain water. That was good news especially if he ever decided to go exploring. This brought a smile to his lips, *exploring right. Something I might have done, oh forty plus years ago. Now . . . not.* The sounds of that running water was pretty loud now and he headed down to where the water pipe split and at that connection he could see that the "Y" piece had cracked and leaked. And it had been long enough that the leak had enlarged and was putting out a pretty good spray. And it had been this leak which finally had become large enough that the sound sensing equipment had finally heard it and made a report.

At least there was a valve just a short distance back and he could temporarily shut down the water. Now he had to head back, get the necessary replacement part, and if there wasn't one in storage or stock, to fabricate it on the equipment, come back, and because of the time that had passed since it had been originally installed, fight removing and replacing the part, turn the water back on, test and flush the system, and head back inside. Yet, before he went back inside he felt he should at least go back to where the tanks were and make sure all was okay with them. If this pipe had developed a crack, maybe there could be issues with the tanks themselves.

* * *

He had forgotten, well not exactly forgotten, how large those tanks were. Since that one aborted attempt years in the past of entering this area he had only used the cameras, the video system to monitor the tanks. Well, one thing for sure the vids made the tanks appear smaller, much smaller than their true size. All six of them were set on large concrete slabs that were set with a lip, and then filled with a combination of gravel and sand to give some flexibility to the supporting surface. After all both the weight of the water, and the expansion and contraction of the metal due to heat and cold would lead to small changes in the size of the tanks.

Taking a deep breath he realized that this would have to be another project at another time. So he did a quick cursory inspection looking for signs of leaks, and obvious cracks or split joints. He knew the tanks were lined to give them as long as life as possible. He could hear water entering one of them as the pumps attempted to keep it full. Since water use was generally small he suspected under normal circumstances the pumps would barely get a workout. But the leak required more usage which at some future date could lead to a failure of the pumps. Yes, like everything in "The Deeps" there were replacement parts, and replacement units. In this case it would take more than him to do it, so if the pumps failed it would come down to the water in those tanks.

Once finished with his inspection, he headed back into the storage area and began the search for a replacement part. It took him a few hours to do this because of the size of the supply and storage area. While the planners had tried to keep it as simple as possible there still was a myriad of different sizes and too many different plumbing supplies to just be able to walk in and grab one. He knew that most were inventoried on the supply computers, but they hadn't been used in forever, and when he tried to boot one up nothing happened. It meant he was stuck having to use the inventory books, and even locating them took a while.

Once located, he realized that there had only been an overview placed inside, with notes stating to refer back to the computer, which didn't work. He suspected he could go back inside the facility and with some effort find a system that dealt with the supply storage system, but he wanted to get this job done and not have to return to the surface any time soon. Even though he was getting used to the differences, it wasn't enough that he had a desire to remain out here more than once. Eventually he found what he was looking for, put it on a cart, grabbed the necessary sealant and gaskets, and with his portable battery operated tools, headed back to the ladder and stopped.

He realized there wasn't a way to climb and carry the replacement part at the same time. (The tools and sundry other items were in a backpack.) So he had to go find a rope which cost him more time. And when he had climbed the ladder and followed this by pulling up that part he wished he was about twenty years younger. He had to lean back against one of the walls, once he had it up with him, to catch his breath, and let his shaking muscles settle down. This wasn't going to be as easy as he thought. Then came the difficulty of moving everything to the work site, setting up, doing and completing the job. And with skinned knuckles, a broken nail or two, even through the suit, and a bump on his head that left him with a headache, he finally finished the job.

He was exhausted. In fact so much so he didn't have the energy to move. He sat there staring at the finished job and knew he needed to turn the water back on and head back, but that took energy – energy he didn't seem to have. He must have fallen asleep for a brief time because his snoring awoke him. Taking a deep breath and shaking out the cobwebs in his mind he pushed himself up, went back to the valve and carefully turned it back on, easing it open so the water wouldn't hammer the pipes and possibly lead to another leak or break. He left the damaged part there in the tunnel, after inspecting his handiwork, and slowly made his way back to the facility. Once inside he removed the suit, and headed back to his room where he went to his bed and fell instantly asleep.

It was hours later when he finally awoke, realized he was still in the work overalls, got up long enough to change out of them before climbing back into bed and falling into a deep dreamless sleep. He didn't know how long he slept since he didn't look at the clock when he fell asleep, only now after all this time he felt better and somewhat refreshed. Although he had to admit he was sore. He needed a shower, and found he was really hungry, besides needing to head to the bathroom to take care of nature. Sitting on the edge of the bed he looked at his clock and the date, and realized two days had passed, *Must have been really tired,* he thought. Sighing, he pushed up and went to the bathroom, took care of the nature call, showered, and once out felt better.

Once dressed in clean clothing he headed out to go to one of the kitchens and get something to eat, passing one of the many security offices along the way. For some reason he glanced into the darkened room through the smoked glass windows and saw a red light flashing. He didn't think anything about it as he continued on. His stomach was growling, and he needed food. And once there he grabbed something he could throw into the microwave, made some coffee, and ate a quick meal.

That red flashing light kept bothering him. This particular office monitored the unused above ground areas and the Welcome and Processing center, not "The Deeps" itself. What could it mean? *Well, when I finish here I'll go see – probably just letting me know that something has failed. No surprise there. Nothing new down here, let alone outside, heck even I'm old!* This brought a chuckle to him because it was all true. So he cleaned the kitchen and headed back to that particular security office, looked through the windows to see if he had actually seen what he thought he had, confirmed the light was still flashing and entered the office, headed over to the desk, which had the bank of monitors, sat down and turned the monitors on.

He figured that one of the monitors would show nothing other than snow, identifying a failed camera. But to his surprise all of them came on clear and sharp. The ones on top row were showing the desert, and the second and third rows showing the Processing and Welcome center, and the security office that was part of the building. These second and third rows duplicated the monitors in that other security office. Being that he expected the cameras to show nothing, he really wasn't paying too much attention, and was about to get up and go back out, chalking it up to a faulty light. Then movement caught his eye. *There shouldn't be any movement. Wonder if some small creature found its way inside?* He rotated back around in the chair and stared. *No, it can't be!* He was immobile for a long time as he watched in shocked silence.

For in the view of the cameras were two young people, a male and a female, dressed in what had to be homemade clothing . . .

THE PAST IN THE PRESENT SEEING THE FUTURE

Ed remained frozen as he sat in the chair staring at the screen. "No! No, no, no, this can't be right." Yet the screen didn't lie. It couldn't since it only could show what the security cameras saw. Looking down at the desk that ran the full length of the bank of monitors he thought for a moment, and almost panicked as his mind raced to solve what he was seeing. *So how long has this light been flashing?* He had to admit, he didn't know. He rarely even looked towards this particular security office, let alone took the time to look through the smoked glass to see what could be transpiring. For all he knew this light could have been flashing, well, forever.

With those thoughts he found the pressure easing somewhat. *Forever, yes, as far as I know this light could have been flashing long before I was born. Nobody really pays much attention to these security offices. Why should they? After all, nothing has ever been found on the surface. And as the population fell here it was easy to keep track of the ones who remained. And when it finally reached the point of only me I had no reason to consider any of these security offices other than empty rooms. So these images could go back centuries if I want to be honest.*

Still, he was fascinated by what he saw. Was this how he looked to his parents? He had never seen anybody young like this. The images were silent, although he could tell they were talking, and rather animated in their conversation. *Isn't there sound attached to the cameras?* He was sure there had to be, which meant he should be able to hear what they were arguing about. It had to be an argument from the body language. The male appeared to be somewhere close to probably his twenties, and the female couldn't be much younger. So were they ones who would be a mating couple, or something else? He honestly didn't know.

Again, from the history in the archives, he knew before the shutting of the doors to this facility that it was common for a male and female to commit to only each other for life. So were these two such, or were they something else? If only he could get the sound working then maybe he would know. As he watched they walked around with the male apparently trying to make some point, and the female, well he could see fear in her movements. Was he threatening her, or again was it something else? "Damn, without sound I cannot determine anything." Frustrated he began to look around for a switch, or a dial, or something that would allow him to turn on the sound. He had to admit he never paid much attention to these places and their operation since there was no need. *Well, there is a need now.*

If this female, young girl was in trouble he felt he should help her, but at the same time that male looked formidable, much more than what he could handle especially at his age. Still these images could be from the deep past and he was watching a recording that was playing back in a loop waiting for someone to find it. And if this was the case he was getting himself worked up over something that had happened a very long time ago, and whatever transpired was ancient history. So how could he determine whether the feed was in the present, or from the past? Looking around the small room, which was still bathed in shadow, he could see nothing that would help. Getting up he headed back to the doorway and flipped on the lights for this room leaving him temporarily blinded.

Blinking hard a couple of times he finally was able to see once again and began looking around the room. Initially he saw the work stations, the storage lockers that contained the equipment a security team could use. Such things as flak vests, riot gear and weapons, flashlights, the gases in the form of grenades, flash bangs, and other sundry items, all locked and inaccessible. Well, if it came down to it he was sure he could find the keys somewhere. Yet, if he remembered right, the keys were locked inside a safe. Well, he was sure that if he searched he probably could come up with the combinations to the safes, but right now it wasn't important. Turning around towards the opposite wall he saw a breaker panel, and next to this another panel that appeared to have switches, toggles, and dials.

Going over to this panel he found a number of dials marked with numbers underneath. Turning towards the monitors, which were now on his right, he saw corresponding numbers under them. Looking at the one that presently had the images showing he turned back to the panel and turned up the dial with the same number. At first he had it too high, and it hurt his ears as the sounds came bellowing into this small space. He quickly turned it down, sat back down, and began to listen, figuring he could come to a conclusion as to what was transpiring. Only to be disappointed when he couldn't understand a word they were saying. *What's this gibberish? Is this some foreign language or something?* At least from the tone he could tell there was frustration coming from the young male, with the female almost pleading about something. Just what the discussion – argument was about he knew no more now than when he had no sound.

Finally there was silence between the two with the young male heading through the door to the security office in that building. He watched as his image shifted to a different monitor. Here he watched as the male easily vaulted the counter and headed through the hallway back to the bank of monitors, sat down heavily in one of the chairs, crossed his arms, shook his head and said nothing. It was obvious from his posture he was unhappy about something.

Looking back at the first monitor where he had seen them originally he saw the young female head for the rows of chairs sit down and begin to weep. It was obvious that whatever this was about had come off badly. He only wished he knew what it was all about. Still, this could have been the past and really meant nothing to him at all, other than something new to watch, a change from his daily routine. Somehow he needed to find out whether this was a recording, or whether what he was witnessing was in real-time.

He could feel his heart going out to what he was witnessing on the screen. Even if this, in the end, turned out to be from deep in the past, it gave him a chance to witness others, and the apparent troubles these two were facing. In a sense it gave him a personal view of the tragedies that had to span the whole globe to include the period of time when the disaster struck. Families being torn apart and destroyed – with the resulting terror, and the pain of loss – communities becoming ruins, leaving desolate vacant lands, leaving all with no place to escape, and the dashing of the ones, like he was witnessing here, hopes, longings, and future, forever. Maybe it was a good thing they were becoming extinct. Still seeing these two gave him hope that there could be others alive and surviving in the aftermath of the worldwide destruction. But, once again, if these images were from the past it truly meant nothing.

He remained there for the longest time deep in thought. This definitely created a dilemma. Somehow there had to be some type of closure to the tragedy he had to be watching. If this was indeed from the deep past maybe they had come to seek refuge here at "The Deeps", only to never get a response from the residents. Maybe what he was witnessing was the frustration of finding the Welcome and Processing center and getting nowhere. These two pinning their hopes on being able to join the only ones who had any true safety from the fire in the skies, and when getting no response of any kind lost any hope leading to this argument.

He suspected if he stayed with the video he would eventually see them leave and disappear out of the range of the cameras never to be heard from again. But he knew, in truth, he was only building this scenario from too little information, and most likely it would prove to be wrong in the end. Still, as he remembered telling himself, even if this was from the deep past, at least it is a change from the daily routine, the daily rut he found himself in. Maybe he should be trying to solve the questions he had in front of him instead of creating fantasy.

* * *

Jay was really worried. He and Elsa had been here for a while now and when he had been able to grab those emergency kits, filling his pack to almost overflowing, the supplies would have lasted him a long time. But now with his sister adding to the mix he knew they would be out of food soon. Since they had been here, at whatever this was, he had searched for anything to add to the dwindling supplies, but he had found nothing. With no need to search for water, which was a relief, he felt that an important – critical really – element was taken care of. He knew they could survive longer without food than water. Yet, without food they would still perish in the end.

So he approached her, with some trepidation, since he could feel the fear, the doubt in her. Things that spoke of what had happened to her at the hands of the raiders – unspeakable things she had no desire to talk about. And knowing her condition when he found her he had a pretty good idea of what had transpired. And it was something he wished on no female, let alone his sister. Still this problem wouldn't solve itself and he had been wracking his brain trying to come up with some solution. The problem lay in the fact that they were in the middle of a desert. Well, it might not be the middle, but somewhere in this vast desert meaning that food just didn't magically appear. He had come to the conclusion that he would have to go back to their destroyed hometown and hope those hidden supplies; those hidden emergency kits hadn't been discovered. At this moment it was the only solution he could come up with.

The problem lay in the fact he knew he would need to do this alone. With the condition his sister was in he couldn't, wouldn't take a chance of her, first revealing them to the enemy, and secondly giving them a chance to get her back and finish what they had started with her. And since she had, and again he had no idea how, somehow escaped and stumbled upon and found this place, although that wasn't accurate. She had been wondering the desert, in bad shape, naked, and with nothing to help her, with obvious injuries that had been inflicted by the raiders. If he hadn't been here she would have died.

He had been fortunate to have something for her to wear, even though the clothing was a bit large for her. Still without it he didn't know what the two of them would have done to cover their bodies. So he gave thanks for the small things. He figured that the edge of the desert and their destroyed village couldn't be too far away. He knew that he had become delirious at some point in his journey and hadn't a clue where he was and how he got here himself. Still with her arriving on the scene it seemed to indicate that their home wasn't that far away.

He had hope that he could convince her to stay, to be strong, and to wait. There was no other way. Although that brief time when the water stopped had him worried – it almost panicked him. He – they had gotten to a point where they were taking the water for granted – wasn't prepared, and to have it stop like that was shocking. They tried through most of what he considered a day to get water to come out of those . . . spigots? He had thought briefly to head back out and see if that natural tank still held water, but thought better of it when he looked at Elsa. But eventually he heard, again they heard water flowing into something and when they tried those spigots the water had returned, although initially it was dirty, but as they let it flow it became clear once again. And since then, even though it was only a short time ago, the water remained. So whatever it was that had caused the temporary loss had somehow been fixed.

Taking a deep breath he approached his sister and said, "Elsa, I need to talk with you." He could still see defeat and fear in every fiber of her body. He just didn't know how he could fix this. It was so far beyond anything he had tried to do, or experienced. When she came over she looked up into his eyes with that fear riding there, but at the same time he saw trust. She remained silent and waited for him to speak. *So how do I say this so I don't destroy what little is left of her confidence?* He had to admit he didn't know. "Elsa", he said gently, "we are running out of food, and it won't be long until there's nothing left. I've been trying to come up with some way of getting us more . . ." At this point he could see alarm flash on her face as she interrupted him.

"Jay, no! I know what you want to do, but I don't think it's safe at all. You can't go back there. And if you go ahead and try I *will* come with you. And neither you nor I have any idea if the ones who attacked, killed, and burned our town are still around. If I lose you what's to become of me?"

Taking another deep breath and slowly letting it out he wasn't sure what to do or to say. "Look sis, if I go it will be by myself. I will not put you in such a situation where you are in danger again. I'd never forgive myself if something happened to you. At this point there is only you and me who survived this. You are my only family. But, both of us know we have to get food from somewhere, and it has to be soon. Otherwise we escaping what happened will mean nothing. We'll die right here. And you know I'm right on this. When I grabbed these supplies the raiders never found the cache. And if one of the hidden caches has been discovered since then, there's the second one on the other side of the village. At this moment it's the only place I know of where I can get us something.

"You must stay, you must not worry. I don't know why we found this place, but there has to be a reason other than chance. So please trust me on this one. I'll be careful, and if they are still stripping the ruins then I'll have to wait them out. I promise I'll come back to you." He could see the fear rising up in her, and see her breathing becoming heavier and more rapid.

"Promise? How can you make such a thing", she screamed. "We both know that such things mean nothing, nothing at all. I don't know why we are alive or why both of us escaped, but at this time you are all I have brother! I don't want to hear any more." At this moment tears were welling up in her eyes and she turned and left him standing. At which point he, with frustration riding high, headed back to the room with those windows that saw things beyond, he didn't know what else to call them.

Elsa watched her brother leave. She could see the frustration in every step he took. She turned around went over to those chairs and sat down with the tears flowing down her face. *Don't you understand brother? You don't know what they did to me, how they hurt me, how they laughed and joked over the pain and misery they caused me. But not only me but there were others, and I had to watch as others like me were . . . were raped and tortured. I watched as others like me died from the abuses, and then it was my turn once again at their hands.*

Can you not see that they tore me up inside? And when they were through with me they threw me away like some trash. I must have passed out at some point and I think they thought I was dead like all the others. It was then; it was night when I became aware. I hurt, oh how I hurt, and I found myself piled among the bodies of our friends, of our people. Somehow I got away; somehow I escaped, only to wake up here with you. You are all I have, and right now I don't have the strength to go on by myself. Don't you see brother, I can't lose you. I really can't stand on my own right now. I just can't . . .

* * *

Was what he was seeing in the present or was it a recording, Ed didn't know. And it was frustrating to him also. If this was simply a recording of a past event then it was unimportant other than something to add to the archives, but if this was happening now, well, if this was in the present he needed to come up with some solution to what he was seeing. And with all he had known, up to this very moment in time when he saw this transpiring on the monitors, he felt his and mankind's end coming. But if this is real and in the present, then he wasn't the last human, the last man on the earth. Had some survived, after the devastating damage caused by the bombardment, and the following nuclear winter? It surely appeared that might be what had happened.

Still, until he could determine when these images were recorded he wouldn't know. Looking closely at the monitors he saw in the bottom left corner in small black print sitting inside a small box two letters "RT". "RT"? *What the heck does that mean?* He got up and went over to one of the many filing cabinets that were here and began to see if he could find anything, a manual, something that would help him translate this cryptic script. As he searched he continued to glance back at the monitors to see if anything had changed, but the two young people remained separated and in the different rooms.

Finally under the "M" folders he found something on the monitors. Unfortunately it was a general guide, which could either be something about the equipment, or something about how they worked. And in the end it wasn't what he needed. Finally giving up he went back to the monitors and stared. *Who are these people, and why are they here? Are they part of or maybe descendants of some of the ones who would have been part of the original ones who were to live here? Or does it matter because it's not now?* Well, it was all speculation, and he wasn't getting any answers here. At least the systems automatically recorded anything that showed up on the security cameras. So if push came to shove, he could always replay this anytime he liked.

It was then he realized that when he had been in one of the libraries and watching a vid on something that happened in "The Deeps" from the past that there was letters on the monitor or screens there, inside a box, sitting on the bottom left of those same monitors or screens. Now if he could only remember what the two letters were? One thing for sure what was happening above in the Welcome Center, so to speak, wasn't going to change. So he got up and headed for the closest library so he could find a past event to run. He didn't care which one he only needed to see what those mysterious letters were. And maybe he could find something there that would help him identify what he was witnessing.

* * *

Jay found he was swinging back and forth in one of those chairs. Somehow he had to convince Elsa. And he needed to think it through. He knew she had been through hell, something no young female should have to face, let alone any. But they needed supplies desperately. And he had only the one sleep sack which they shared. Not at the same time of course, that would be wrong. Plus she had the only change of clothes he had brought. When he had escaped it wasn't with the idea he'd find any others alive and he would only need to provide for himself.

Maybe that was the way to approach this. They needed more clothing, another sleep sack, and definitely much more food. Somehow he needed to stuff a couple of packs full to give them a chance. He wanted to spend as much time as they could here to give the raiders a chance to leave the area. He knew the two of them couldn't stay here forever since other than the water, there was nothing. He knew they could probably go back to the village for a while which would keep them supplied in food, but that would eventually run out – for he and his sister of course. So sometime in the future both of them would have to find another place to live. *Maybe a new village that would take us in,* he thought. *Yet, for now, getting enough to be able to continue here in the desert is critical.*

Again, somehow he had to convince Elsa. He'd never forgive himself if he gave in to her, brought her along, only to have her captured once again by those same raiders. And he was sure if that happened she wouldn't get a second chance. *There is no way around it, she has to stay here where it's safe – it's just that simple.* Holding his breath for a moment, before letting it out slowly, he headed back out into that main room to see how she was doing. Once back through the door he could see that she was still sitting in those line of chairs with her head down, and it appeared she was still crying – not a good sign at all. *What to do, what to do?*

* * *

Why does it seem when you want to run something, find something, especially since you've recently seen it, that you cannot find it? Shaking his head Ed, sitting at one of the stations in the library, took a deep cleansing breath, made himself relax, and concentrate. *This should be easy.* Of course it should. But he had to admit to himself it had been awhile since he had pulled up any of the recorded history on the vids. The last time had been years in the past when his father had died. Since that time the libraries were a place to research, and if he watched anything at all it was the piped programing that came into his room.

Then he remembered his experiment he had set up inside one of the assembly rooms. Even though these sporting events had happened long before the creation of the facility he wondered if there were any lettering in the left bottom corner of those screens. He decided, since the space was set up to begin at any time, he would make a quick trip there and start one of the games and see. If nothing was seen he could always return and see if he could find what he was looking for. With the decision made he headed out of the library down the hall to that room.

Since he had no plans on taking in a game he didn't worry about the 3D glasses, and as he entered he stopped a moment and looked at the sitting area he had set up for himself. *What a mess. Didn't I clean up after myself the last time I was in here?* The obvious answer was no. There was trash and empty containers, scraps of food and snacks still sitting on the small table he had next to the chair he sat in while he watched. Taking another deep breath he thought, *Okay, I guess this will be my next project getting this place cleaned up.* But it wouldn't be now; he had other things on his mind.

He sat down grabbed a remote that was buried under some of the trash on that table and started a game. He looked and in the left bottom corned in a small box sat the letters "PB", with a second set below those stating "RP". Now he had three sets of letters and he had to admit he still didn't know what they meant, but if what he was seeing here was a recording, and these were the letters being used to identify the video as such, then the one he was witnessing in the security office had to be real-time. Then it struck him – real time, RT – that's what it had to mean, which meant the letters he saw here had to mean "RePlay, and Play Back".

He needed to get back to the security office and see what was happening. He could feel his emotions beginning to run away with him. He wasn't the last person on earth! This was going to take time to understand. *All this time "The Deeps" has been sealed because we believed it wasn't safe to leave and there's been people living on the surface since the disaster.* This stopped him as he realized this fact. *Did the ones on the surface remember this place and that's why the two of them are here? And if these two are here are there others waiting outside?* This brought fear to him since he was an old man all by himself and there wasn't any way for him to defend this place from these two let alone a large group.

Yet, as he had watched them they seemed to be simple young folk who didn't know where they were. One thing for sure he needed to monitor the situation and keep listening to their speech, including the use of the playback function so he could begin to understand what they were saying. Right now with sound on or off he could only read their body language. And while such things could keep one informed, it lacked real information as to the why.

He could feel the energy flowing back into his system. He realized at that very moment that he had only been going through the motions of living. He was more letting things drift until he passed on leaving this great facility empty except for the ghosts. Now, yes now, he had a reason to carry on. But he had to be careful. Again who are these people, and why are they here, and what had led the young female to cry? Any and all of these questions he couldn't answer at this time. So with these thoughts he entered the security office once again to see if anything had changed.

Sitting down he saw that the male had come back out and was now sitting next to the female trying to console her, or something. Again without understanding what was being said he was only guessing. Yet, from the body language, again the only thing he could ascertain, Ed could tell this young male cared. It appeared that these two would be remaining there for some time so there was a good chance he would have time to familiarize himself with their language and begin to understand what they were saying and what was truly going on. So with a new project he began his study.

First off he knew that one of the side monitors could be used to run what had been previously recorded – all of this was part of his lessons. Now if he could only remember how to do it. *That's right. I need to set a date range, followed by which monitor number I want to watch.* He started by going back a few of weeks finding that the male was there and he was alone. *So when did the female show up?* It was a good question, so he fast forwarded and watched as the male seemed to be mesmerized by the monitors. It was like he had never seen monitors before. *Can that be right?*

Suddenly on the playback he saw a reaction from the young male, who immediately got up and rapidly left out through the employee entrance. Ed had to bring up a second monitor and set it up so he could follow the young male back out into the desert. The first continued to run showing nothing. Shortly he disappeared from the cameras leaving Ed impatient as to what was going on – he was now running the monitors with the playback function on normal so he could catch the details of what was happening. Time continued to drag with the male not coming back in view. He had almost given up when he saw him again and this time he was carrying the female and she was naked, dirty, and looked to be injured. *Had this male done this, or had someone else?*

Too many missing pieces, Ed thought. It was obvious to Ed that this male cared for this female from the care he had given her, but was it the other way around? He didn't know, and maybe the tears, and obvious fear this female was projecting, lay in the fact she didn't want to be here. But, again this was only a guess. Then another question came to him. *Where did she come from, and for that matter where did he come from?* It was another mystery. Even though it had been a long time since anybody had explored the surface there had been no sign of animals, let alone other humans. So now what?

He needed time to figure this entire mess out, and as far as he knew this was something he did have some of – time that is. Being old he didn't have any guarantees on the time he had left. Still if this female was being held here against her will, he would need to do something about it. *Yeah right. As if someone my age can overcome someone that young male's age. Still I didn't see any weapons other than a knife, and both of them have one. Hmmm, if she has one also is it for defense against this male, and if so why hasn't he taken it from her? Damn, there's too much here and by not understanding what they are saying I'm completely at a loss.*

He'd been drinking coffee and it was his bladder that reminded him he'd been observing the monitors for a long time. He got up and headed down the hallways to a public restroom which was only a couple of doors down. Shaking his head he wished he could understand them. Body language only went so far. It gave him an overall feel for the situation, the tension that seemed to exist between the two of them, but not the why. Well, if nothing else, this puzzle, this situation gave him something to break his routine. Something about emptying the bladder gave one a chance to refresh. It seemed that when it got to that point one's concentration flagged. *Yes, time to go back and see if anything has changed.*

* * *

Standing there and looking at his sister it tore his heart out. She had her back to him and probably hadn't heard him reenter the room. He could see that dejected look, and could hear her still weeping. Looking down at the floor briefly he tried to come up with something, anything he could say to convince her. And, he had to admit, even if he couldn't he didn't have much of a choice in this. They had to have more food, it was just that simple. And the clothing issue wasn't going away. Neither of them had anything else, and eventually – if they didn't starve first – what they were wearing would become rags.

In a way the arrangements for sleeping worked because of the need for one of them to be awake all the time. Even though they were hidden here in the desert, there were no guarantees – none at all. They could still be found. Although, at this moment he doubted it, still if he found this place that didn't mean someone else wouldn't. Then there was the other problem. There appeared to be only one way in and out, which meant if they were discovered it would be a trap, thusly why they both carried their knives all the time. And when they had their time to sleep, to keep the weapons close at hand, just in case.

He approached his sister and put his hand gently on her shoulder. He could feel her tense up before relaxing a little. She turned around and faced him, and he could see her eyes reddened from the crying, and the streaks left by the tears on her face. Jay went around her and sat on another chair, taking her hands in his and looked in her eyes, "Elsa, you all right?" He quietly asked. He could tell she wasn't but he really didn't know what to ask or say.

She shook her head, and in a meek voice said, "You know the answer. Of course I'm not okay. I don't know if I'll ever be okay again. What happened to our home, our town, to you, to me, to our family, how can one get over such things? Not me for sure. How can I tell you, how can I explain to make you understand? Right now you are the only thing here that keeps me going, keeps me from screaming, from being so scared that all I want to do is run.

"Yes, I know we're running out of supplies. You think I like wearing your clothes? To not have what I need, as a female, as a woman? We have only been here a short time and I have no way of knowing if I will end up carrying one of the raider's child from the many times they raped me. And if I do, what will I do then? Will I hate myself? Will I hate my body for being a traitor? Will I hate the child that would be growing inside of me? I don't know, and I'm scared. I wanted none of this. Yet, until my cycle is complete I won't know, and that scares me to death. And if I'm lucky enough to have that happen and I bleed, I still am facing the demons of reliving, in my dreams and nightmares, what happened to me. I can't run away from me.

"And I know logically that you must go, and why you don't want me to go with you. But emotionally I'm afraid I'll lose you as we've lost everybody we've ever known. And while I know you never wanted any of this to happen, neither of us wanted it, you are still the only one I can count on, the only one who can help me right now. And you are the one who is keeping me from bolting and running away screaming into the desert. I really have no idea if I can keep it together if you leave. And the problem with you leaving is when you would return – if ever. By not knowing what's happening, by not knowing if those raiders are still there, there is no way you can let me know how long you will be gone. Then there's the fact neither of us knows where we are, other than the desert. And both of us know this desert is huge.

"It's all of these things and so much more, so much more . . ." She trailed off to silence, and looked back into his eyes pleading for him to understand.

It continued to tear him up inside to hear what Elsa was saying. Some of it he knew, but other parts, like her possibly carrying a child from the raiders he hadn't considered. But now he understood, at least as much as any male possibly could. He stood up and pulled her up with him and hugged her. She returned the hug with a strength that spoke of the desperation in her soul. They remained that way for the longest time and he was sure both of them had their eyes closed. If there was some way, and at this time he knew it was impossible, he would love to seek some revenge on what those murderers had done.

For now Jay dropped the subject, but it was something that wouldn't go away. He'd have to wait until she came around. He knew she understood, but it was one thing to understand, and another to get past the emotion, fear, and hurt. He looked down with the love only a brother could give as she slept. It was his watch, although to be honest nobody, or nothing had disturbed them since he found this place. He wished there was some way to at least make the lights dim somewhat to make it easier, but he didn't understand anything about them. In truth he was thankful for the light because both of them would be in the pitch black darkness of a starless night if these lights went out. So he, and was sure she, accepted the unending brightness.

Taking a deep slow breath he headed for those windows to see if he could see anything moving – anything at all. So far, other than when he saw Elsa, there had been nothing. Every once in a while he could tell the winds were blowing when he would see dust blow past whatever was giving him these images. He really wished he knew where they were, other than the desert. But both of them had been quite out of it at the time of discovery. He found he was swinging back and forth in the strange chair he was sitting in. Something so simple, yet well beyond anything he had ever seen or experienced. And, in truth this place they were in could be described similarly.

He decided to head back out through the "employee entrance", whatever an employee was, and check on that natural tank. It had been a while since the water had quit flowing, only to return again. It kept worrying him that the water had stopped. If it happened again, there was always a chance it wouldn't return. So he wanted to be sure the tank still held water, and they could use it as a backup if necessary. So he headed out through the two doors, through that twisting tunnel and back out to where the water tank was located. He remembered, with the cracks and small holes in the wall, that there was a dim shadowed light allowing one to see.

Once he arrived the tank was full, but something was different he just couldn't put his finger on it at this moment. Taking his time and thinking a moment he leaned against one of the cave walls. Looking around he could see the pile of ashes where he had his fire, the partially dismantled nest he had used for fire material – all just as he remembered. So what was missing, what was different? It was silent, and he could hear the winds blowing, moving across some of the holes in the rock walls causing a whistling sound. It was such a lonely distant sound, as if the winds were crying out. *Maybe they were.* For him the winds could be telling of the loss the two of them faced.

After remaining for a while and coming up with no answer he headed back down the tunnel only to stop. It seemed the answer to his question was just out of reach. He concentrated hard on trying to bring it to the surface, but his mind refused, leaving him with a tantalizing hint, but still no answer. He shrugged, shook his head, and headed back to the building, thinking again about the silence. He finally entered back inside and watched his sister once again. It appeared she hadn't moved at all. This brought a smile to him, even though it was a sad one. So much had happened, so much had changed, and very little of it for the good. So what were the two of them going to do? He had to admit honestly he didn't know.

* * *

Ed had taken a break and headed out for one of the many parks within the facility. He needed to think, he needed to walk. *This is crazy.* From everything he had ever learned, had ever studied, the recordings of those final days, those final years showed no possibility of any surviving. Yet right there before him on those monitors were a couple of young ones. And the only possible way for that to be simply meant people had survived on the surface. This meant everything he ever knew, everything everyone in "The Deeps" believed was false. It meant all those years with only the three of them remaining, with the suffering and such, it was all for naught. If they had returned to the surface, explored, maybe they would have found others like them. This was a lot to take in all at once. To believe one thing all of one's life only to have the proverbial rug pulled out from under one shaking his foundation to the core.

After arriving at the park he walked through the grasses, by the flowering plants and finally leaned against one of the trees. Here in these parks, which were to be similar to other such places that had existed at one time on the surface, this was to represent what it could be like once the facility was closed down and the remnants of the human race returned to the surface to begin again. It was a place to know a little more about the surface, even if these were artificial, manicured, protected plots. It was more than the vids from the surface could provide, but less than reality. Still it was better than nothing.

Taking a deep cleansing breath, he slowly let it out, and stared out over the greenery that surrounded him – this area still made him uncomfortable. Slowly he moved from the tree he had been leaning against and headed down one of the many walkways that existed finally stopping and sitting on one of the benches. He needed to think, to understand, and somewhere along the line he needed to be able to talk to these strangers. This meant he'd have to figure out their speech. *What went wrong? Why didn't any of us ever see any sign of the ones who obviously survived? And why has it taken until now, right now for someone to show up and prove to us here in "The Deeps" that many had survived?* All good questions, and at this moment he had no answers.

He didn't know how long he had remained on that bench, but suddenly it seemed hard and uncomfortable. He also found he was getting hungry so he got up and headed to the closest kitchen to get some food. He had to admit that the last few days were full of life changing surprises. And as such all of this new information would take time before he could fully appreciate the consequences as well as implications.

Once he finished eating, and he found that the day was getting late, he needed to decide whether to return to one of the security offices to continue watching, or simply return to his room, call it a day, then return tomorrow where he could watch the archived footage, and be brought up to date on what was transpiring above, followed by watching the live feeds. *Well, I guess since it appears they aren't going anywhere, and I'm definitely not, I'll wait until tomorrow. I still need to get over the shock, and maybe a good night's rest will help.* He shook his head and smiled, saying out loud, "At least one can hope."

* * *

The problem both of them had lay in the fact that the lights never dimmed, never went out, so the only way they could judge anything was by being hungry, followed by being tired. Still, if they went into that room where the windows were they could tell the time of day by what they saw. But neither of them wanted to sit in that room all day watching. Elsa had been just as mesmerized by those windows as Jay had. But, after a while and seeing them show the same things over and over again, it became boring. Still there wasn't a lot either of them could do. Neither had figured how to get past any of the many locked doors they had found, and there was only so much area within this space, and both had been through all of the available spaces too many times.

This led to a number of times where they would sit and talk, about anything and everything, but in the end it would always come back to the reality that everything both of them knew was gone forever. At this point both would get quiet, drift apart, be with their own thoughts, and become introspective. With literally nothing to do the time seemed to drag, and their needs weren't getting any better. Both knew they needed more food, clothing, and at least another sleep sack. And the longer they waited the more difficult it would be to solve these issues.

Finally Jay, after another week had passed, said, "We don't have a choice. I've got to go and see if I can get us more. If I wait too much longer then it will become almost impossible. At least we still have enough so that I will feel comfortable with leaving you. And before you argue about coming with me I still say no. I would never forgive myself if something happened to you. Besides, with it being only me I know I don't have to worry about whom or where the enemy is, or worry about if you're safe. This way I can completely concentrate on what I have to accomplish. It means I know the only ones I'm going to see will be the bad guys.

"I know I can't give you a timeline for this, how long I'll be gone. The only thing I can tell you is I will be careful, oh so very careful. After all, I have someone to come back to, someone who is very important to me."

Elsa knew this day was coming and had been trying to prepare herself for it. But even with all the work she had been doing she found that when the day finally arrived it hadn't been enough. With some effort she was trying unsuccessfully to hold back the tears, and found she was shaking uncontrollably. She looked up into her brother's eyes and gave him a weak smile, reached out and grabbed him, hugging him hard once again. She wanted to say something – anything, but she was too choked up for words. All she could do was nod and watch as he grabbed his pack and headed out that door. She could tell that if there was a way he would stay, but there truly wasn't.

As he disappeared out the door she hesitated for a moment standing frozen. Then she remembered those windows in the other room and quickly headed there. Once at the counter she had to turn and put her back to it, jump and pull herself to a sitting position, swing over and jump down. She couldn't do it as easy as her brother since she was a head shorter than he. Once across she went down the hallway and sat in one of the swinging-rolling chairs. She watched the windows and saw Jay as he worked his way through the cave, head outside, and she watched his back as he disappeared into the distance. For the longest time she sat there staring at those windows knowing now she was alone.

She took in a ragged breath, and could feel the doubt and fear begin to build. She wrapped her arms around herself as if she was cold, and in a sense she was. It was a coldness of the soul that gripped her. Now it would be a waiting game to see if her brother would come back. She knew there were no guarantees in that. And after an unknown amount of time had passed and there was nothing new showing in those windows she headed back to the main room. Could she maintain control, or would she lose it? *Jay, please, please, please come back.* She pleaded. Without him here the time would really drag. And with no sunrises and sunsets she'd have no idea as to the passage of time.

After what seemed forever she got up and started pacing. In her mind she suspected that only a few minutes had passed, but there was no way to know. Maybe if she went back outside, stayed close to the entrance it would allow her at least some change of scenery, and to actually feel the heat and wind, and the roughness of the sand on her bare feet would be nice. At least it wouldn't be the same hard cold floor, and the light that never changed. She knew her brother had admonished her to remain inside, but she was now totally alone and didn't know if she could do this. Again, she wished there had been another way, or she could have gone with him, but he was right. If she was caught by the raiders a second time she wouldn't survive it.

In truth after waking up inside this place she had no desire to ever go back outside. It seemed safe, a haven from all the bad, and it had many wonders. Wonders that hadn't existed in their world. Even with her fears she had to admit this place left her curious as to who had built it, and why. Well, before venturing outside she'd at least spend this day here. It would be many days before Jay would return, and she had to be sure she could make what little food was left last.

* * *

Ed finally returned to the security office and began to look at the recorded portions he missed when he left. He found it easier this time to use the monitoring system so he could run an archives portion on one monitor while monitoring in real time on a different one. The first thing that surprised him, when watching the real-time monitor, was the fact this young female was now alone. Maybe the male was in the bathroom. For privacy there was never any monitoring of the bathrooms other than the entrances. From these locations it could be seen who was entering and leaving, but other than that this was it.

He really wasn't paying that close attention to the archives as the lack of the young male left he wondering what had happened. After what he considered a reasonable time to spend in the bathroom and with the male not making an appearance, he wondered if maybe he had left for some reason. But if he had left why was she still here? Again, too many questions, and no way to answer them. If only he could understand them then maybe it would make sense. But he couldn't.

Maybe she had killed him, and dragged the body outside. After all, there were weapons locked away inside the upper security office. Although from what he had seen so far, like here in "The Deeps" those weapons were well secured. With not much happening he started fast forwarding the archives and reached a point where there seemed to be a long conversation between the two of them ending in a hug. *Obviously they care for each other,* Ed thought. He glanced over to the other monitor and found the female sitting in one of the many chairs basically staring out at nothing. With that he went back to the archives and again fast forwarded the recording.

He had to stop it and back it up because suddenly it appeared the male was heading outside – *was this right?* He had rewound it too far and let it run from there. He watched it closely, and yes the young male did go out. He saw the female stand frozen for a few moments, and then head into the security office, having some difficulty with the counter, and head into the area where the monitors were located. Here he could see she was watching something. So with the zoom he peeked over her shoulder and could see the young male disappearing into the distance. *So he left. Why? Really, what's going on?*

He had to admit he didn't have a clue. His first thoughts he had back when he discovered them appeared to be wrong. No she wasn't here against her will, and obviously from the way they embraced they were close. So again what was this all about? He wished he knew. It would make it so much easier to put all of this in perspective – proper perspective instead of him only guessing.

* * *

Jay felt the heat as he exited the cave and found himself back in the desert. He hated leaving Elsa especially in the shape she was in. It had been a difficult decision not to take her with him, but knew it was the right one. Still he worried. She was in no shape to be left alone. That's why he wanted to get this done as quickly as possible, but what lay beyond here was something he had no control over. As far as he knew the raiders were still back there picking over the bones of the town. He remembered where he last saw his sister when she had first appeared in one of those windows, and he suspected that Elsa was watching him as he disappeared. He prayed this would be a fast trip.

Now, since both of them were *not* of the right mind when they found this place, what did that plaque call it, oh yes Helms Deep, he wasn't sure how far out they were. At least with the mountain range in the distance he'd have a landmark to go by. Still he'd have to be careful. With nothing to really hide behind he knew he could be seen a long way off. So he decided to head for an area to the south of where he suspected the village lay. Then he could use the trails in those foothills to come in from the south and have much to hide behind. Besides, once he was there he would rapidly find himself on familiar ground making it easier to move.

How does one survive what she, has gone through? To be violated that way, to be hurt that way, and find no mercy, and to be thrown away like a piece of trash when they were through with you. It has to take someone who is strong. Yet, she doesn't seem strong; she seems to be so vulnerable, so fragile, to be broken, to be fearful to the point of not wanting to be alone. How can it be both ways? He didn't have any of the answers. He knew that sex, for want of a better word, could be a great thing between loving mates, but a weapon that could destroy when it was used against one. And he could see that it had come close to doing just that. And now, through no choice of his own, he was leaving her, abandoning her, leaving her alone when she really needed him there. It tore him up, but again, what choice did he or they have?

Well, this trip had to be made as quickly as possible. Right now one of things he needed to remember was to leave a series of markers here in this area, so when he returned he could easily locate this place again. It was at this point he realized that where he was sat on the edge of an area they would have called the badlands. And there really wasn't anything in particular that stood out. This stopped him for a moment. He wasn't that far away, and looking back he could see that the wash he was coming out of appeared to be no different than a thousand other such washes that existed all over this desert. If he didn't mark the area somehow, then no matter how successful he might be back at the ruins, there was a great possibility he wouldn't be able to locate this place again.

He knew he needed to make time, to move as quickly as possible, but until he somehow marked his path he'd have to remain close enough so as to not lose the way back. He stood there for a while looking around trying to find something that would work as a trail marker and there really was nothing. *Now what? And maybe this is why whatever this place is has never been found, or has been written about in any of our travel writings.* Shaking his head as his thoughts continued. *This area is no different from other badland areas in this desert.* As he continued to look around he realized there were lots of rocks and remembered part of the training they learned back during the times of required learning.

It was a class called trailblazing. While where they were located really never required such a thing, it was felt that there was always a chance one could be away from civilization, and to help one from getting lost there was a way to use what was around them to mark a trail. And by doing this one could always return to their starting point, or retrace their movement so as to avoid repeating or going in circles. Turning around once again after looking to the mountains he decided he would build two cairns, followed by a third, which then would form a triangle with the one in the middle placed in the center of the wash back in the direction of the place he had discovered. That way all he would have to do is locate any of the two outer ones to be able to align himself to the proper orientation. From there it would be easy to find his way back.

Now he needed to build them in such a way that only he would recognize what they were, and what their purpose would be. Then as he headed out he needed to lay down marked stones for a certain distance followed by another cairn marking the starting point of his marked path. This was going to cut into time he felt he didn't have, but at the same time if he didn't do it, there was a great chance he'd never find this place again. One thing for sure, sand didn't hold footprints or tracks very well, so he couldn't count on simply backtracking. *Better get to it,* he thought.

* * *

Time was moving on. It always did. Ed found that no matter how he tried to slow it down time it just didn't. He had been watching this young female off and on for a week, and it was obvious she was becoming more agitated, more fearful. What was it that caused this? He knew when the young male brought her into the facility, through the upper entrance; she was naked, unconscious, and quite dirty. And he saw the love and care the male had given her. So he knew the cause of her anxiety wasn't him. It was also obvious she didn't want to be left alone and it was beginning to weigh heavily on her.

He could see her pacing up and down the main reception area, and then stop and sit awhile, then she'd be up again. At times her breathing became rapid, and he could almost see the fear on her face, and in her body language. At these times she'd head into the security office and look at the monitors, staying there for the longest time just staring. He suspected she was looking for the male who had brought her in, but as of yet he hadn't returned. He wished he could understand them, and then maybe he would understand why he left. He had to admit that his heart went out for this lost girl. Taking a few deep and slow breaths he headed back out the security office he was using to monitor the reception building and again began to walk the halls himself. He needed to think, and he really needed to understand their speech. It would make things so much easier.

* * *

Elsa was almost frantic. She really hadn't a clue to how many days had passed since Jay had left, but with only herself here she was going crazy. She needed Jay here and now, she needed someone to support her flagging confidence and strength. But there was only she, and as time continued to drag she found she was getting close to losing it. She felt she was losing control and if Jay didn't return soon, she'd head back out into the desert and run away screaming until she fell down somewhere far away from here, lost and exhausted where she would probably lie down and die. She was finding, more and more, she couldn't run away from herself, or her fears.

Oh Jay, I need you now, I need your support and your understanding, and even you're fumbling ways of trying to help. But you're not here, and that's not helping. Can I make it until you get back? To be honest I don't know, I just don't know. At least when the raiders were doing to me what they did I had no control over it, and because of this, everything seemed to blend into one long painful nightmare. But here and now every day is the same. There is no sunrise, no sunset, any night time, any mornings, dawns, and dusks. Just this unknown light that never wavers, never dims, never changes, and the number of rooms that are always the same, leaving me unsure of the passing time. How long have you been gone? She could feel the fear once again building. *What if you don't return, what will I do then?*

She shook herself trying to get these thoughts out of her head. *Jay you have to return, you just have to.* But she knew there were no guarantees in life. If she had believed so, then what happened to their happy lives when the raiders attacked and destroyed the town drove the point home. There wasn't one guarantee that Jay would be returning. Still she knew she couldn't dwell on that thought otherwise she would go crazy. Maybe if she at least took a trip outside for a brief time it would help. Taking a slow and cleansing breath she didn't know if she had to courage to face outside. She remembered escaping the raiders only to wake up here. Outside was where the danger lay, and she surely wasn't ready in any way, shape, or form, to face any danger real or imagined. Still . . .

Maybe if she only went out and up into that small cavern where the natural tank was. After all this wasn't really outside. She would still be inside of this, well in a sense neither of them had discussed where this was. So she didn't know if it was really a mountain, a desert hillside, or what, but whatever it was, this place, this building was inside of it. So by only traveling that little way it would be a change, but still provide her the peace of mind that she would be safe. She half smiled, even though it was a tentative one. And with her mind made up she, with her heart beating rapidly, headed for those same doors her brother had used when he left, and she suspected when he had rescued her.

She reached for the handle and twisted it, opening the door inward, which wasn't strange from this side, and entered into a small bare room. There she saw the second door. She thought maybe she'd leave the door open. Again Jay had said he had the first time he had entered here. This was more natural than the doors into the privies. When she tried to open the second door she wasn't sure which way it swung. Jay had told her the doors didn't necessarily open like they were used to. So she pushed and it opened. When she did she immediately felt a strong breeze flowing from the outside into the building. When she let go of the door the wind slammed the door shut bruising her knuckles. "Ouch!" She exclaimed.

Holding her breath briefly she shook her hand and looked at her knuckles. That stung! She turned around and with some reluctance closed the inner door, and then reopened the outer one, saw the stairs cut into the rock, and the slight glow that marked the beginning of the tunnel. While she remained in the doorway she was technically still in the building. Now she wasn't sure if she wanted to continue or not. Eventually her curiosity overcame her fear and she carefully stepped out, leaving this outer door open.

* * *

Jay had forgotten how hot the desert was. At least this time he had packed plenty of water anticipating the need. Building those cairns and laying out a path back to the area had taken more time than he'd allowed. So now it had to be nearing what was late morning. The zenith wasn't far away. Maybe he should have waited until dusk before setting out. But that would have meant another full day lost, and their supplies were getting thin, much too thin. So he really didn't have much of a choice. He'd waited longer than he should, but again there was little choice in that either. He had to be sure Elsa would remain behind where she was safe.

He knew she had agreed it was necessary back when he first approached her, but also knew with her mental and physical condition she shouldn't be left alone. And while she came to grips with these problems, and here he couldn't blame her one bit, they had dug dangerously deep into what was left as far as their supplies because of the delay. Now he needed to push on and move as quickly as possible through the desert where he wouldn't have to worry about being seen. This would be a worry once he approached the break between the desert and the hills beyond. Again he hoped by coming into those lands south of the ruins he could avoid being seen, if the raiders were still there. And he had no way of knowing until he was in the area.

In fact he had no idea how long both of them had been in the building underground. With no sunrises or sunsets, let alone night time they had no reference to the real time. He had gone outside a couple of times expecting it to be a certain way only to find that he was wrong. One time he had expected it to be around midday only to find it dark, and the other expecting a sunrise only to find it midmorning. As far as he knew, and again he hadn't really counted the number of emergency packs he had grabbed, they could have been there only a few days or maybe as much as a moon cycle. Anything was possible. Staring out at those distant mountains, those distant landmarks, he said quietly as he shook his head, "Better get to this. Standing here ain't making those mountains move and come closer."

He could feel the breezes coming up. It was a sign of the desert heating up. He needed to push while it was still somewhat cool, and then locate some shade and try and not move through the hottest part of the day. Even with all the water he had he knew he couldn't chance sweating it out and run out before getting into those hills and away from the desert. Looking around he saw nothing moving. He might as well be the only person on earth for all that he was seeing. So with determination he pushed off and set a fast pace.

* * *

Elsa had been asleep, and while it was a troubled sleep with nightmares and demons attacking her, at least she felt she might be getting some rest. Although how she felt once she awoke seem to contradict those thoughts. She felt tired, drug out, and always those dreams would stay through the twilight of waking up. Yet, as she slowly came back to reality something was different, something was wrong. With her sleep drugged mind she couldn't seem to figure it out. It was dark with a soft glow of light, just enough for one to be able to see. *Must still be night,* she thought. She rolled over and drifted off once again.

It must have been hours later when she awoke with a start. *Dark? But it's never dark in here.* She sat up with a start and looked around her. *What happened to the light?* There seemed to be light – soft light – coming from a couple of areas – just enough so that one could still move around the room and not trip over anything. She noticed that the room where those windows were located seemed to still have all its lights on, with the light shining brightly through the doorway.

She remained sitting up, still in the sleep sack and propped up by her arms. Carefully she slipped out, stood up and quickly looked around. She felt a foreboding rising inside of her. *Why had the lights gone out, and was there someone here?* That last thought scared her. She wasn't close to being over what had happened to her in the recent past, and without her brother here to help she almost panicked. Her breathing became heavy, rapid, and she felt lightheaded knowing she was hyperventilating, but couldn't control her breathing at the moment. With the lightheadedness she felt dizzy and leaned against one of the chairs, and quickly sat down. She didn't need to fall down and possibly hurt herself.

Slowly through some effort she finally got her breathing under control. So far, as she continued to search the area with her eyes, there seemed to be no other change. It was then she realized she needed to take a trip to the privy, but waited a little longer anyway. She wanted to be sure there was only she here. After a few additional minutes had passed and she had herself back in control she got up and headed into the privy only to be blinded by the bright light when it came on. Again, like her brother, this was like magic. Neither of them could figure why the lights came on and turned off when someone moved or stopped moving.

While there she thought about her brief trip out, well not out in the desert since she only went as far as the natural tank. It was just as Jay had described, and he had explained it was the reason he was still alive. Still he had mentioned hearing running water, but try as she may all she could hear were the winds blowing through the holes in the walls. So whatever it was he had heard either quit, or he had mistaken the sound. She could feel the heat from the desert when she headed towards one of the many cracks. She also remembered Jay warning her about a danger ahead so she decided to leave her explorations to just this tank, and headed back inside the building. She would let Jay show her the danger instead of blundering into it and it possibly leading to her death.

There were so many things about this place, this building under the ground that was beyond her understanding. And it wasn't just the way the lights here in the privy turned on and off by her moving. It was the magic way the water appeared in those basins, and a privy with water in it was a surprise. But what was even more shocking was the fact that when one was finished, and got up to pull one's pants up the thing automatically removed the waste and new water replaced the waste water. Again how it was accomplished was something she might never understand, but appreciated. Those privies back home could get quite ripe in the summer heat.

She went over to the basins and washed her hands, leaned on the basin and stared into the mirror. Even this was better than anything they had back home. The richest of the members of the community didn't have ones this good. And the room had a large number of them as if they were common. And since she had been allowed in the other side she knew they were there also. Who were the people who had built this place? While she, being female, really never involved herself with this kind of stuff, she did like looking at the way things were put together. And as such she paid attention to the little details and things that were pleasing to her eyes. And while this place had an impersonal feel to it, there were so many mysteries, and so much that spoke of the fact that whoever built this place hadn't any problems or issues. In other words it was a common everyday building, with nothing special or extraordinary about it. And everywhere she looked what she saw stated that this was so far beyond what they could do, making in her mind, her feel like some god or super being had come down and with little or no effort created this place.

* * *

It was almost dark on the second day, and Jay had been pushing and making good time. Every time he would stop and take a break he would build a marker. He had no idea if he would be able to locate them on his way back, but he hoped so. With his plan developing since he left Helms Deep he knew he was going to come out of the desert south of the town, and then work his way from the backside, kind of picking up the same trail he had used when he left to climb the peaks. For now that part of his life, that time seemed to be in the distant past and had no real meaning being trivial with what had transpired since. Had it been his life desire to do such a thing? Now it felt like it was shallow or something that had no meaning at all.

No full moon tonight. Yet, even without it the desert seems to almost have its own light. So if I'm careful I should be able to make a few more miles before I have to call it. I think by doing that then tomorrow I should be in the foothills. I really hope so because this means I'm going to be away at least 5 days if not more and I don't want to leave Elsa alone any longer than necessary. Still there was nothing he could do about it, nothing at all. He grabbed a piece of jerky and continued to push. Soon, very soon, he would have to be careful, but now he wasn't worried about being seen – tomorrow yes, tonight no.

It was now late on the third day and he was overlooking the village. From his vantage point he really couldn't tell if anybody was still there or not. The fires had died out a long time ago and if one didn't know better this could be just another ordinary day. He couldn't see the gate into the town from here so it wouldn't be obvious. If one saw what was left of the gate then immediately it would scream danger. He thought he could hear some rattling going on like someone had kicked a broken pot or pan. But this could as easily be some animal scrounging for some tidbit, or some scavenger picking over the corpses that lie inside of those walls.

He decided he would wait until dusk before moving closer. So he pulled back. The trail he used to get to where he was presently was one of the minor trails that took one to many of the towns and villages that hugged the desert. Most, like his, used the desert for protection, but sometimes it didn't matter. The bad ones found these hidden places and the results were usually the same – total destruction and loss of life. There was a place he had found where he could pull back and be unseen by any that might travel this pathway, and as he was just heading into his hiding spot he heard the jangling of small bells, and voices.

So he moved a bit faster and disappeared as a large caravan came into sight.

From what he could see, as they passed, it wasn't one that would stop at their village, but head further north where it was rumored larger villages, towns, and things called cities existed. He could hear pieces of conversations, and saw the number of guards and outriders that protected what was being carried. He heard one saying that they might stop at his village for the night, but heard another say that they had a different stopping place in mind further to the north, with the other agreeing. Soon they were out of sight, and eventually even the sounds of their passing faded and were gone. They were never even aware he was there, which was fine with him. His problems were his own and he figured he wouldn't get any help from them anyway.

It was getting close to dark, it was time to move closer and find out if the raiders were still here. So carefully he headed down the side trail off this main one and worked his way towards his hiding place in those caves he had adventures in when he was young. He figured that there was a good chance he would find a few diehards who wanted to strip anything of value that would be left, but didn't expect to find most of the raiders. He suspected they had already moved on. Still a few would be more than he could handle. And with these thoughts he slipped into those caves and listened, but all he heard was the returning of the natural night sounds.

Once it was full on dark he snuck out of his hiding place and carefully moved to the trail heading into the village. It was easy to discern as it presented a lighter track to the darker edges where no one traveled. He quietly approached the broken gate and looked inside seeing a single fire glowing somewhere in the ruins. It did appear someone was still here. So quietly he withdrew and returned to his hiding place and waited out the night. In the growing light of dawn he would come back.

* * *

Taking a deep breath and holding it she slowly opened the door from the privy and stared out into a darkened room. She was night blind for the moment since the privy's lights were bright. As she waited holding open the door the lights inside of the privy turned off making it even darker. It seemed like forever before her eyes adjusted to the gloom that now enveloped this place. If she was younger she knew her imagination would be running wild now. She'd be imagining all sorts of monsters and evil things hiding in the shadows. With those thoughts a chill ran through her body causing her to shrug, and shake it off. As she turned towards the light coming out of the doorway that led into the room that had the sign above the door stating, SECURITY, she began to breathe again.

She decided, since there was still light there that she would go ahead and go inside. If she went over the counter and back to those windows that allowed one to see other places maybe she could determine the time of day, and maybe figure out why there was no light here in the main space. So carefully, since she really couldn't see very well, she made her way through the doorway, over the counter, and headed back to that room. As it had been every time she watched, nothing moved. Although, from the light she was seeing it had to be either early morning just before the sun rose, or just after sunset. From what little information they received neither she or her brother had been able to figure it out.

Shaking her head she thought. *Now what? I can't necessarily move in here. There's no way out of here other than that one door. At least in the main area I can run back out into the desert if I have to, but here it's a trap.* She stood back up worked her way back down the hallway and leaned on the counter she and Jay were climbing over. *What to do . . . what to do?* It wasn't that the dark frightened her, well, maybe a little. With what had happened to her in the recent past this darkness did send a little fear, a bit of anxiety her way. If one or a group of those raiders found this place it would too easy to sneak in unseen and do to her what they already have.

She remained frozen and deep in thought. *Why has the light quit? After all it's been with us day and night since we've been here. Why now? Why now when I'm alone? I'd feel much better if Jay was here to help figure this out. But he isn't.* Making a decision, she boosted herself over the counter and went back out into the darkness and waited for her eyes to adjust once again. It was then she noticed a new subtle light coming from an area where there shouldn't be light. If she remembered right over there by that other counter, the one that had those signs that stated, NEXT WINDOW PLEASE, towards the end was nothing but a solid wall. So, were her eyes deceiving her, and the light was coming from behind that counter, or was it actually coming from the wall?

From where she was standing there was a wall between her and that location – more or less. From her present location the doors to the privies were on her left as well as that third door neither of them could open. Then there was the counter that paralleled the back or side wall. Between the two walls there was a slight additional depth added. A space if a door had been added to cover it would have made an excellent storage area. Both of them had been there a number of times and there was nothing on that wall at all. It was just a wall and nothing more.

She carefully worked her way past the privies and that locked door ending up at the counter and caught her breath. At this very moment her hands involuntarily came to her mouth as she stared. The wall was no longer there! *How is this possible?* She thought. There was a soft almost ethereal light coming through. So soft that it was almost invisible. Yet, at the same time bright enough to be able to see a pathway that went down. Not sure she stared. She was frozen and could feel her heart beating rapidly as well as her breathing becoming faster. *What is this place? Where does this lead, and what happened to the wall that was here?* All questions for which she had no answers.

For the longest time she stood there undecided. Yet the longer she was there with nothing presenting any danger she slowly felt herself relax. As she did she felt some curiosity building. *If this new space will stay open, maybe I can at least look a little way down that path and see if it is like the one into this place. Maybe I can learn something that will help us. After all neither of us knew this place existed, and now there appears to be more.* With her mind made up, being quite nervous, and with trepidation, she slowly approached this open doorway, stopped and leaned on the framework and tried hard to see what lay ahead. Unfortunately, like the tunnel into the building where she was this one seemed to twist out of sight. The only way to find out was to continue.

So with care and trying to be as quiet as she could she crept down the tunnel to that first bend, briefly went around it, and heard the wall close behind her. Now panicked, she ran back shaking with fear, and she screamed when the way back to where she had been was now blocked.

* * *

From the security office Ed watched her reaction once he had closed the portal to "The Deeps". It bothered him when he saw her reaction and fear. It wasn't that he was interested in her as a female. He was far too old for such thoughts. It was more to do with wanting to help. Although it was obvious she didn't know that. *What to do . . . what to do?*

CHANGES

Fearing the worst, Elsa sat on the floor with her back to the wall. A wall that only a short time in the past had been open and she had come through to this new place only to have it slide shut leaving her isolated. She was literally shaking from both fear and the sobs that were escaping her. *Why? Haven't what I've been through been enough? Oh Jay, if you come back I won't be there. But, I'm here even though there's no way you can know.* At this point she fell silent, too miserable to think anything at all. Somehow, and she didn't understand why, she fell asleep leaning against that wall. The only thing she could figure was in her misery she cried herself to sleep.

Other than the way out of here being taken away nothing had happened. She breathed slowly in and out and realized that she couldn't remain here. It was obvious whatever it was that had opened the pathway to where she was, had also closed it and she didn't have any idea how to change her situation. Standing up and taking a number of deep slow breaths she stood still for the longest time. She could feel the fear and panic trying to rise again. Using all the will power she still had she forced it away. So far it was quiet, no monsters or raiders had come to capture or recapture her, and do unspeakable things to her.

If she wanted to admit it, and she wasn't sure if she did and as far as she knew, only she and Jay were here. And at this moment, again as far as she knew, she was now the only one, unless Jay was responsible for this. It was a thought, but one she immediately put out of her mind. This wasn't something Jay would do. Besides she knew he was gone trying to get more food and clothing for the two of them. She had watched him as he disappeared into the desert, and she had checked back on those windows, as Jay stated she should – often. And there had been no one, nothing, just dust now and then, and little else. Besides she didn't expect Jay back for a few more days. He said that he expected to be gone at least 5 days at the minimum, and it could be up to 10 depending on what he found once he got back to the ruins. And as far as she could figure it had only been 3 to 4 days.

She found she was leaning again the wall, and it was cool, chilling her somewhat. She pushed off with her hands and tentatively walked towards that turn she had been at previously when the wall slammed shut. The whole area was bathed in shadows. Again such things allowed the imagination to run wild. Although there seemed to be enough light so she wasn't fumbling in the dark. The lights in this case were running along the walls right on the floor allowing one to see where one put their feet. While on the ceiling down the center ran another set of lights. None of them were bright and overpowering. Still they weren't very inviting to her either.

She really wasn't sure if she wanted to go down that twisting tunnel or not, but had to admit she really didn't have much of a choice. So with a large amount of trepidation she inched forward and with as much caution and courage as she could muster she worked her way down the tunnel. As she got fully inside the tunnel she felt a breeze. *Did this mean,* she thought, *there was another opening somewhere?* Yet, to her mind that made no sense. It felt like she was going deeper underground. There definitely was a gentle downslope to the tunnel. The first twist which was to the right had led her into a straight section, but now she could see somewhat in the distance another turn.

And even though it wasn't obvious, she felt it turned to the left leading back into the original direction.

She could feel her heart pounding in her chest and again her breathing was becoming rapid. She had to stop once again and get everything under control. Still there was no sign of danger. Just the gloom of the tunnel, the downslope, the movement of air, and that was it. Still, it didn't matter. All of this was unknown, and thusly had to be considered dangerous. She could feel a pressure pressing down on her and she almost turned around and ran back to that wall, but stopped. *And what are you going to do if you do Elsa? It's not like there's anything there. And you can hope and wish that wall will open, letting you back, but is that even realistic?* She could ask herself these questions all day, and know the answers, but intellectually knowing and being able to act were two different things.

Carefully she worked her way down to the turn, which turned out to be to the left as she thought, and stopped once again. She leaned against the left wall of the tunnel and tried to peer around the corner to see if there might be any danger, but was both relieved and disappointed at the same time. There was nothing but more tunnel. She pulled away from the wall and started to go down in this new direction when she froze, because, suddenly the sections ahead of her began to light up with a bright light. It scared her enough that she let out a small scream, the bright lights had begun furthest away from her that she could see and advanced towards her in rapid succession until the area above her head lit up. She was momentarily blinded, and had to wait for her vision to clear.

Looking ahead she saw what she believed was another counter, just like the one that existed in the other building. With no problem with her vision she slowly headed towards this counter.

* * *

Dawn was upon him and after an uncomfortable night Jay started to leave his hiding place. He stopped because he heard voices and the crunch of footsteps on the gravel pathway. The voices were too soft to be understood, but it sounded like either two or three individuals. Listening, it appeared to be a normal conversation anybody could be having, making him feel like everything was okay, and when he entered through the gate back into where he had grown up all would be as it was. *If only. Yes, if only all of this could be a dream, a nightmare, and everybody I've ever known is still alive, still going through their everyday lives unaware of the dangers.* But he knew better.

The sounds of the voices faded into the distance and he carefully came out and briefly followed behind at a safe distance. Before returning and heading back inside those broken walls he wanted to be sure those he was following wouldn't come back and catch him alone. He was hoping that whoever this was had been the ones who had been camping inside the walls. And if not, he didn't want to be caught between two different groups trapping him. So with care he followed until they joined the main trail through the area and headed south, the direction he had come from. He remained hidden as he watched them disappear down the trail, and waited longer to insure they weren't returning.

He waited until the sun rose plus a little longer, but they never returned. He didn't have a clue as to who these individuals were. They could have been part of the raiding party, or just some travelers passing through. With the passing time he figured he was safe from whoever they were and headed back to gate where he would be more than careful. He couldn't be sure if the ones he followed were the campers or not. As he approached the gate he first looked for any smoke that might be rising from a campfire, and saw nothing. Holding his breath a moment and letting it out slowly he could feel his nervousness grow. If there were still people inside, he could give himself away. And if they were the raiders he could forfeit his life, leaving his sister to die because of his carelessness.

Unsure, he peeked around the broken gate and saw nothing. Crouching down he worked his way inside, and again saw nothing moving – hearing only the winds that were beginning to blow off the desert.

With the amount of debris laying everywhere, and the remains of the buildings, visibility was poor. Plus it would be easy to step on something that would make noise giving away his position and alert anyone who was here. This also gave any who could be here plenty of places to hide making it doubly difficult to confirm the ruins were empty or if there were raiders here. Still, as with the ones he had followed, all seemed normal, well as normal as it could under the circumstances.

Taking another deep breath he stood up, taking a chance, and began to sneak around the ruins. Even though all had changed because of the destruction, he still knew the general layout of the town. Slowly and with care he searched out the site and with the sun reaching its zenith he was satisfied the place was empty. As far as he was concerned he had already spent too much time here, but felt he had no choice. Now it was time to find out if the caches had been found. So he headed for the one he knew finding that it had been ransacked. He had hoped it would still be safe, but he wasn't surprised as it was the more visible of the two. Now if he could only locate the other one. The one by the minor gate, the cache he had never been shown.

Jay worked his way down the wall on the north side towards the single small entrance that led out to the fields – small that they were, and the trails that led up to the hidden mines where they mined the semi-precious stones they sold in the markets and trading centers. Outside of this gate was a storage shed where the tools of the trade were stored, as well as the carts they used to haul the raw materials down from the mines to be worked. He knew the finished stones were stored inside the walls of their village, but were worked outside by the storage shed. Now if he could only remember what he had been told. Standing by this small gate he looked in both directions along the walls and couldn't see anything that would identify the hidden cache. Maybe this was a good sign. If he who knew it was here and couldn't immediately locate it, maybe the raiders hadn't either.

"Okay, so is it here inside the wall, or is it close to the storage shed and work area?" He had to admit he didn't know. So with care he worked his way up and down the walls on the inside and came away with nothing. This was followed by another search outside of the walls, in and around the storage area, followed by the work area. All, leaving him with nothing for all his effort, and still not a clue as to the location of the hidden cache located somewhere on this side of the village. Frustrated, he leaned against the wall, time was getting away from him and he wanted to be away and heading back into the desert by nightfall. If he didn't locate it soon he might be spending another night in the area and this was the last thing he wanted to do.

Could this one be up by the mines? He thought. *No, what's up there is emergency gear if something was to happen in the mines. Not the emergency cache for the town.* It had to be here and he had to be close. It was then he remembered that there was another building just inside the gate, a place where leather goods and such were stored – stuff used for the animals. And it was here in one of the corners lay the entrance to the hidden cellar. He came back inside of the wall and saw the building, and like all of the others, it was destroyed with most of what had been the building collapsed and filling the center. He'd have to dig it out to find out if the cache was untouched. But from what he could see it appeared that all the debris from the building was untouched. So the chances were good it was still there.

Now if what is there wasn't destroyed because of the heat from the fire when the building burned, then maybe I can get out of here soon, and have what we need for now. One can only hope.

* * *

Elsa stood staring not sure if she wanted to continue on or not. But what choice did she have? Her way back to what she knew was blocked and all she could do was continue forward. After her eyes had adjusted to the bright lights that now lit the tunnel she judged the downhill slope of the tunnel had increased. In fact she was only guessing at what she was seeing. It appeared to be a counter similar to the one above.

All she could see of it was the top and a little way down from her location. So far she had been it. No one had put in an appearance. She realized she could hear herself breathing and it was still a bit rapid – speaking to her that she was still quite nervous over the whole thing. *And why not?* She thought. *Anybody in this same situation would be.*

Where are you bro? Where are you when I need you here? In her heart she knew the answer, but that didn't ease the situation she found herself in. Finally after all this indecision she slowly went forward and down the tunnel towards what she suspected was a counter. It appeared to be crossway in the tunnel disappearing from sight to both sides speaking of the tunnel "T"ing at this point. "Why would it do that?" She asked herself quietly. As she approached the counter, which was farther away than she thought, she was able to finally see the base. And it was exactly like the other, except much longer. She noticed that where the counter ended on both ends, behind and on the wall that ran behind the counter, were double doors. At least that's what they appeared to be.

Leaning on the counter she saw that again like the one above there appeared to be desks behind and at eye level, if one was sitting, it appeared to have narrow slit like windows in the wall allowing the ones working at these desks to look beyond. Beyond to what she truly didn't know. And speaking of not knowing it appeared that the counter curved at both ends sealing off the workers from whoever was standing at the counter. At least she knew, from jumping over the one counter that was in the space that led to the windows that saw in the distance, that this wouldn't pose any problem for her either. Then she thought. *Why not?* She looked both ways and back up the tunnel from where she had just come from, turned around, and with the help of her arms boosted herself on top of the counter, swung around, and dropped to the floor on the other side of the counter.

She worked her way down in both directions and realized once she got to the end where it curved around that there was a portion that swung up with a release that allowed the ones who were on this side of the counter a way in and out. It was a simple arrangement, but one she would never have considered if she hadn't seen it herself. She swung up the countertop released the latch and opened the bottom portion. And as she did she felt a little resistance, and as she let go it began to swing back. *Wow, what have they done to it to allow it to return like this?* Thinking about it she thought it would be something nice to have. Still she knew that the doors into the privies had something similar. But there one could see what was responsible. Here there was nothing. Like her brother she kept asking, who were the ones responsible for this place? So many things existed here that in her wildest imagination she'd never thought about and yet so many seemed simple.

Simple maybe, but at the same time she had to admit she didn't have a clue to how or what made them work. She had gotten pretty much the same answer from Jay. Even though both of them had gotten used to what was around them, both of them admitted they knew absolutely nothing. She carefully let the swinging portion return and re-latch itself. She noticed with the top portion out of the way it would be easy if one was outside to reach in and release the latch and enter. Turning around she now studied the desks for which there were at least twelve of them. All of them seemed to have those swinging, rolling chairs that were in the room with the windows, making it easy for whoever was working to move from the desk to the counter.

As she turned back to the counter, when sitting in one of the chairs, she realized that the counter had a number of shelves which had nothing on them at this time. She wondered what might have been stored there, but like so much of what both of them had seen, she didn't even venture a guess. Then, as she turned around back to the desks (she was pushing herself around in one of those chairs) she noticed sitting between some of the desks what seemed to be sealed containers, but again unlike anything she had ever seen. Most of the containers she had ever been around had been constructed of wood. These looked far different. She reached out and touched one of them feeling the texture. It was cool to the touch and smooth – nothing like the ones made of wood. It felt, well she wasn't sure if it was accurate, but it felt sort of like heavy paper.

Paper, yeah right. Paper was expensive, and was a rare commodity in their town. Only the rich had it. So immediately she discounted her conclusion. But if it wasn't paper what was it? She looked closer and it appeared that these containers, where they closed, had some sort of shiny strips of something that kept them from opening. *What could those strips be?* Whatever they were, when she tried to open one to see what might be on the inside it wouldn't release. It was then she looked up and for the first time looked through the small window that was in front of her. It caused her to immediately stop and stare. *How can this be? No, this can't be real, there's no way,* she thought. But it seemed to be real. She slid down the open space between the desks and counter remaining on the chair and looking out the other small windows, and other than perspective what she saw remained. What she saw made her want to go through those doors and confirm it, but did she dare?

* * *

Ed watched through the monitors at the progress of the female as she tentatively worked her way through the tunnels. He could see in her body language that she had a lot of fear and seemed almost afraid of her own shadow. What had happened to her? From watching her explorations he knew there was a great chance that soon she would come through those double doors into the pre-area of "The Deeps". *Yeah, he thought, the shortened common name for what was originally named Helms Deep.* This park like area that was just beyond where she was presently was the final assembly area before one entered into "The Deeps" properly. This area provided a brief respite for those on their way to their permanent residence here, but, of course it never happened. Still the area had been designed to be relaxing and to ease the fears of those who were leaving everything behind.

He figured that she would probably remain in this area for a while since there were restrooms, and he had resupplied the food carts anticipating her arrival. With the drinking fountains, food, and restrooms it would provide most of what she needed since being locked out of the "Welcome and Processing center". Going back to the recording of the conversations between the male and female he was still working on trying to understand their language. He was close and it was like he could almost understand. Once he did he figured it would make the initial contact between him and this young one easier. Anyway he looked at it he found he was nervous. And if he was, how would it be for someone like her who had never seen anything like this place? From the reactions he had seen, it was the only conclusion he could make.

He found he had been making some progress in recognizing a word or two here and there. It appeared they spoke the same language he did, although it had changed somewhat, had been bastardized over time. It seemed to have words that probably had come from other languages. Here he laughed because in school it had been pointed out that English, the language he spoke was loaded with words from other languages. So it should be of no surprise that others had been added over time. For example he found both the word "casa", Spanish for house, and home being used. He didn't know if it referred to different aspects or whether the words were interchangeable.

It seemed they slurred their words a lot and spoke in a fast tempo that almost blended the words together. It could be that it was only the situation the two had found themselves in that had caused this, but he had no others to compare to. With this one close he had to put as much time in as he could to understand, and he hoped that once they saw each other there would be no confrontations that could lead to violence. He wanted nothing to happen. This person, and he suspected later, if the other one returned, between the two he should be able to find out what had been going on above with all these passing centuries, and possibly why none of the teams that had gone to the surface looking for survivors had ever found any, when it was obvious that somewhere there had been.

So he continued to study and become accustomed to their speech as he continued to monitor the girl's progress. *She sure seems curious.* Here he laughed as his thoughts continued. *Well stupid don't you think you'd be curious if this was the first time you had ever been in such a place? Of course you'd be.* She seemed to be staring through those small windows as she sat at one of the desks. Yet, at the moment it seemed she had no interest in going through those double doors that sat at both ends of the counter. Still her needs would eventually push her on. There was no way back, and there was only going forward into this new world. Eventually hunger, thirst, or a nature call would force her on through those doors.

Again how long she'd remain in this next area he wasn't sure, but the additional time one way or the other wouldn't matter. In a sense he needed it. Until the two of them met everything here inside would have to wait. This was critical, this up and coming meeting, possibly the most important thing, other than the passing of his parents that had happened to him in his life. *Why couldn't this have happened oh twenty to thirty years ago?* If he had learned any lessons about life it was the fact that life rarely accommodated one exactly when it would have been convenient, and here was a prime example.

Look, she's at the double doors! He watched fascinated, but it was obvious to him that all she was doing was looking. Again her body language said she wasn't ready. And as he continued to monitor the situation he saw her retreat back to the counter and lean on it obviously thinking. *Soon, little one, you'll come through those doors and sometime in the near future we will see each other in person for the first time. Yes, soon.*

* * *

Jay looked at the burned debris that had been the storage and supply building and wasn't sure he wanted to tackle the job that was before him. Maybe he could find a shovel or something similar to make the job easier. When he realized the job that was ahead of him he had made a quick trip back to the other location to be sure it had been completely stripped. He hoped it hadn't been and there would be enough left that he wouldn't need to dig out this other to find out if all the work he would be doing would be for naught. After all the raiders could have found it, emptied it, and then torched the building. There was no way to know. But when he had gone into the other hidden cellar, he confirmed it had been stripped bare.

Taking a deep slow breath he shook his head, the one thing he didn't want to do was spend a lot of time here. Every extra second meant a greater possibility of being discovered, to possibly have the raiders come back again, or just the scavengers that always seemed to know when something like this happened, and would show up to finish picking over the bones. And if they found anybody alive would make sure when they left that there would be no witnesses. Any and all of these could be here or back to finish what they had started. And one thing for sure he had no desire to become another victim of either.

As he made his way across the deserted and destroyed village it seemed to be much hotter than he remembered. But then again what he remembered was a living town, with all the homes and shops, the neighbors and friends, and the feel of life. Now it was all gone, leaving only the dust, burned and destroyed homes, shops, and a deep silence that spoke of the death that had been here. Eventually he reached the minor gate out through the wall and headed to the one building that seemed to be still standing. But even this was an illusion since it had been constructed of rock, the walls remained but the interior was gutted and roof collapsed in. Everything smelled of smoke.

He went by the building knowing he would find nothing of use there and headed up towards the mines hoping to locate a shovel there, but once again failed to find anything. One thing for sure he didn't want to use his hands. Too many things could easily be hidden in all that debris leading to injury. With his sister depending on him, he couldn't afford to weaken himself or return empty handed. It was then he remembered the dump area. There was a good chance he could at least find a broken but usable tool there. He quickly but carefully worked his way down to the dump area and found it was the one area the raiders hadn't stripped. Not that there was anything of real value here anyway. But as thorough as they had been it wouldn't have surprised him if they had.

It took a while but eventually he located an almost whole shovel. The handle had broken in such a way that for the work it was generally used for, it had become worthless, and thusly tossed. It would serve his needs, and maybe if the cache was undisturbed he could cover it and come back in the future if he needed. And at this moment, even though their present location was well hidden, there was nothing but water, so the likelihood of him returning for additional food was pretty good.

* * *

He was filthy, covered in ash and charcoal, but the cache had still been there. And somehow, and he was quite happy about this, the door into the cache hadn't burned. He didn't understand it since it was constructed of wood, but he praised whatever providence had kept it hidden and safe. He was now loaded down with as much as he could carry. He had two full packs, wearing one on his back and had the other mounted awkwardly on his front. It was uncomfortable as hell, and it made it difficult to move, but every one of these things he had was important, critical to their survival. He had found clothing for Elsa, and a couple of sleep sacks that he had rolled together as one. Now he needed to get back to her as quickly as he could, and do it without being seen. He felt good, now he only have that little section of desert to cross, avoid the dangers it presented, find his markers, and not be seen by any of the baddies out here. Simple – right?

Jay was almost back. He had almost missed his markers as he had swung further into the desert than he thought. But now he was on familiar ground and was heading over and around the ravine to head through that large crack. He had come close to running out of water, and had thought he had been followed a couple of times, but in the end it had been his imagination. He hoped that Elsa was watching those windows so she would know he was back. If she wasn't then his arrival would be a surprise, and he wasn't sure which he would prefer. Any way he looked at it the trip had been worth it. What he was bringing back should last them a long time giving them the necessary time to figure out what they would do.

With care he pushed through the crack – it was a bit more difficult with all he had this time – avoided the drop-off, and worked his way up to the pool of water. He continued to notice something different, but couldn't figure it out. But whatever it was wasn't important at this moment. It seemed the last time he had come to the tank he had sensed a change. Still, he was almost back and he couldn't wait to see his sister and show her what he found.

* * *

Elsa could hear her tummy rumble. She realized she hadn't eaten in a while and had no way to return to get anything really. She remained sitting in the one of those chairs that rolled and continued to look through that narrow window. What she saw seemed to be so inviting. She wondered how such a place could exist underground like this. At least she thought she was still underground. After all, when she had come through that open portal the pathway continued in a downward direction, and had only gotten steeper near the end where she was now. Still it could be a canyon or something. Unfortunately from here she couldn't see in the direction of the sky. This would require going through those doors.

Yeah, those doors . . . It was the first time she'd ever seen two doors mounted this way. Back in the town if a larger space was needed then a single large door that slid to the side was constructed and used. And to mount glass in the door was a real surprise. Again glass existed but not in the quantity she found here. And the quality seemed to be better also. She could feel the nervousness within herself and it kept her firmly planted right here in this chair. Even with the scene beyond those doors, beyond this narrow window appearing to be nice and inviting, she really had no way of knowing if it was or not. Still, she knew eventually she would have no choice. There was no going back, there was only forward. At least before coming through that opening she had used the privy so this part wasn't a problem yet – and yet was the key word.

* * *

Ed continued to monitor the girl. *Why is she just sitting there?* He didn't understand it at all. Yet all it appeared that all she was doing was swinging back and forth in that chair staring out through that narrow window . . . Nothing else, and no attempt to push through those doors. *How long is she going to sit there?* He was becoming impatient with this whole thing. Disgusted, he whispered, "There's nowhere she can go, other than into that park, so why isn't she moving?" He found he had pushed up out of the chair he had been sitting in, was out of the security office, and found he was heading in the direction of that park, realized what he was doing, stopped and went back inside, returning to the monitors.

He knew it would have been stupid, and could have wrecked any chance of a good encounter. He wasn't trying to capture her or make her his property, or do anything against her person, but from her perspective it could appear that was the way of it. *Let her make the first move, Ed. You've waited 68 years to find out you weren't alone. A little longer and some patience on your part might just make this go smoothly and work out. I really need to get her to trust me, and while I've got a rough handle on their language I've got to get her to speak slowly so I can understand. Then, and if this goes well, and once I understand what's really going on, I can probably add the male, with her help of course.*

He turned back to the monitors and continued to watch the girl, and every once in a while he would look at the one that gave him views of the Welcome center. He wanted to gain her trust before the male returned. He really had no idea where he had gone, or even why he had left, but Ed was sure he would be returning. And it would be so much easier if he could have the help of this female, and to have an understanding of why they were even here. Then there were the questions of where had all of the people been since no one from "The Deeps", or Helms Deep, had ever seen any sign of anything living, let alone others like him.

He saw her suddenly look up towards the ceiling grabbing his attention. *What?!* He quickly looked back to the Welcome and Processing center and saw the door from the employee entrance opening. He had the volume turned down but as he continued to watch he saw the male entering and saying something. From the body language it was obvious he was excited. Ed went over and turned up the volume and heard the male yell, "Elsa, Elsa, I'm back." And at the same time he watched the female and she was standing and looking up. "Damn", Ed exclaimed, "there's a speaker in there so the lower administration can keep in contact with the Welcome center." He watched both monitors as Elsa – that had to be her name – got up and headed rapidly back up the tunnel towards the point where she entered.

"Now what?" Ed asked. Not that there was anyone who could answer him. At least the entrance down to the lower level where she had come through was soundproof and she wouldn't be able to let the young male know where she was – although this complicated things a lot. He had hoped that there would be time before the young male returned to get things worked out, but *nooo*, Murphy wasn't going to allow that. He could see the hope in her eyes as she retreated back towards the wall, and looking at the male he, at this point, wasn't aware she was no longer there. Well, she was here, but not where he could find her. Frustrating – he was sure the young girl, Elsa if he had it right, was close to coming into the park, finding the foods, the water, and restrooms that were there. Now he didn't know what would happen, or how long it would be before she did give up and come into the park.

And he knew from what he had observed before that once the male realized she wasn't there he would panic and try and find her. Now, he wondered, should he let him in also? But not at this moment since the young female was almost back to the wall, which meant if he did open it she would rush out, and then neither of them would venture inside where he wanted them to go. Shaking his head he got up and headed out into the hallway and began to pace back and forth. It was getting really complicated.

* * *

When she heard Jay's voice she first thought he had to be with her. But the voice seemed to be coming from above her and there was no place for anybody to be above. Still she was sure it was Jay. If it was then maybe he could figure out how to open the wall and she could get back to him. Decision made she got out of the chair went around the counter and headed back up the tunnel towards the point where she had first entered these new tunnels. The light that had come on over her head when she reached this last section had remained active leaving the area bright. As she moved out of this section she had to stop and let her eyes adjust to the dimmer sections. It was frustrating. She wanted to be back with her brother, and it needed to be now.

Finally after what seemed too long she could see well enough to continue. She almost ran wanting to get there. But once back nothing had changed, the wall was still a wall. And once here she could no longer hear Jay. Back home with the walls between rooms it was easy to hear someone in another room and she expected it to be the same here. Unfortunately it wasn't so. She tried hard, even put her ear up against the wall – nothing! Then she began to pound on the wall hoping he could hear her pounding and banging the wall, but whatever it was made of absorbed the sounds she was making and she could barely hear the pounding herself. "Jay, I'm here!" She screamed. She could feel that she was beginning to panic, and she could feel her emotions beginning to overwhelm her once again. She slid down the wall to her knees and continued to beat on the wall and yell to no avail. It was at this point she realized he would never hear her or know where she was. Once again she began to cry – sobbing great body wrenching sobs that shook her. She turned once again and sat on the floor of the tunnel with her back to the wall whispering through the tears, "Jay, I'm here . . . Jay I'm . . ."

* * *

Once Jay had come through the door it seemed that nothing had changed. The light was still on, and he figured Elsa had to be in that other room watching those windows that saw into the distance. He went over to the chairs and placed everything he had brought back with him there and quickly entered the other room, vaulted the counter and went around to see his sister, only to find she wasn't there. This stopped him for a moment. *Where are you sis?* It was obvious this place was empty, and he knew there was no way to know the last time someone had been in here. Puzzled, he slowly headed back out to the main room.

Once there he noticed that the sleep sack was still on the floor and open. This increased his puzzlement.

We always pick this up so we don't trip over it. Why is it here? Looking around at the too empty room his eyes saw the doors into the privies and thought, *bet she's in there.* It seemed to be the only logical place she could be. So he sat down and waited what he figured was a reasonable amount of time. Yet, she never emerged from the privy. Reluctant, he went over to the door for the female side and pushed it open to call her name, but the place was dark telling him no one was in there. *She wouldn't have gone to the male side would she?* He didn't figure she would but opened the door anyway and was rewarded with the same darkness.

Fear was beginning to build inside of him. *Did she break and run outside and away? She said she had been close to it. Oh my, I hope not.* Now he was at a loss. If she went outside, and with most of the area covered in sand – it is a desert after all – there would be no way for him to track her. She could have run out in any direction and he wouldn't have a clue. Plus he had no idea how long she would have been gone, if she had started running. He headed back to those chairs and sat down once again. He really needed to think this through. *Oh Elsa, I hope you didn't panic and run away. Please let it not be.*

His anticipated happy return had turned to doubt and fear. Fear for his sister who was nowhere to be found. *Maybe she left a note or something – yes, a good thought!* Getting up he began searching all the areas and found nothing. Another thought entered his mind and he went to where they had stored the food once he had emptied the pack so he could take it with him. And from what he could determine she had been here until recently. It appeared from what was left that she was here up to at least 2 days ago. Still that was a long time to be gone and too much to be able to track her if she had left. *Now what?* Yes, now what indeed! After this time back together after the tragedy to have lost her now, and as far as he could tell that's what happened, would tear him apart.

Elsa, where are you? Did my leaving you alone finally allow those demons you are carrying inside of you win? By me not being here have I allowed you to lose it and run off screaming into the desert? Can I not get you back? Help me please, sister. I need you as much as you need me. Again, at loss as to what to do, he stood back up and looked around completely unsure.

* * *

There had to be a way to entice the girl back, but he had to admit he really didn't know how. And with her leaning against that wall he didn't know how long she would stay before she would give up and head in the only direction she could go. Ed thought once again. *Why now? Why when she was so close to coming into the park? If he had only waited another few hours before he showed up then she would be slowly overcoming her fears and finding what I placed out there for her.* He found his pacing wasn't helping other than keeping him from striking the wall in frustration, which would have hurt him more than the wall. So he went back inside the security office and watched both monitors to see how this was going to play out. To be truthful he didn't know.

Now the worry was that the male would go running off into the desert to try to find the young female not knowing she was only a short distance from him. Ed's goal was to simply get the girl to talk to him, and begin to build some kind of trust, followed by enticing the young male to join them. *I forgot all about that speaker and the connection between the Welcome center and the final counter into the facility.* Not a surprise really since nobody had considered any part of this area in generations. Now by not remembering it had come back to haunt him. He found he couldn't sit, so he stood and leaned on the table that ran the length of the monitoring station. He had to come up with a solution or this would get more out of hand, but what to do, what to do?

His heart went out for the young female who obviously was in distress, but if she would only come into the park then maybe some of it would go away. It was obvious she was going to remain against that wall for a while. How long he really didn't know, but a thought began to form in his mind. *Maybe . . .* He headed out and made a trip to the closest kitchen grabbed some wrapped food and drink, and quickly headed out towards the park. He hoped what he would be trying would work. And he wanted to get this part accomplished before she gave up and headed back down the tunnels. He didn't want to be seen yet. Maybe he still could get what he had planned accomplished.

* * *

She had cried herself out and felt exhausted, with no energy to move. Her brother was there only a short distance away. So close, yet so far, and there was nothing she could do to see him, to reach out to him, to talk to him. She had no idea how she had heard his voice but there was no doubt it was him. Still could it have been her imagination or had something happened to him? That scared her. Did something happen to him and he was in the beyond? In the beyond and somehow talking with her letting her know it was all right? *No,* she thought. *He said he was back. But did that mean he was back here, or did it mean he was back from the beyond?* No, she had to believe he was back from his journey to their destroyed home.

She suddenly woke up and realized she had fallen asleep. Well, no surprise there. She definitely had been on an emotional ride and she knew personally such rides usually exhausted one. Now she had another problem. It had been a while since her last trip to the privy, and if she didn't find another soon she'd have to figure out where she could take care of nature. She was sure it was the ache that had awakened her. She pushed herself up and slowly retraced her steps back down towards the lower counter looking to see if there was a place to deal with this, but it was simply walls and floor and nothing else. Again as she came around that last turn the light, which had gone out, came back on just like the first time, once again blinding her briefly.

Once her eyes adjusted she continued onward towards the counter. It was then she noticed a change. *If I remember right there was nothing on the counter.* Yet there appeared to be something there now. *How?* She stood there staring, but the distance was too great to be able to determine what this new thing was. Carefully she continued down and to her surprise it looked like a basket – although she had never seen one like this. Basket weaving was something all of them were taught, but this was rectangular, and all of the ones they made were round. How was it done? Plus, on closer inspection it had what looked like 2 lids facing opposite of each other allowing it to be sealed. With a handle in the middle it completed the basket. First off not knowing where it came from she cautiously cracked open one of the lids which simply pivoted. Inside there appeared to be sandwiches wrapped in some type of clear material.

Food was something she needed but now she was crossing her legs as the other need built. It was then she remembered that area beyond the double doors. If she couldn't find a privy or something similar then it would be better to relieve herself there under one of the trees. So grabbing the basket and with no choice pushed through those double doors on the right and immediately to her right she saw a sign with the symbol that was on the privy doors above pointing to the right. Setting down the basket she whispered, "Thank you", and literally ran, found, and entered the privy.

* * *

Jay was at a complete loss. While his journey had an unknown outcome, since neither of them knew if anything was left when he returned to the ruins, and there was some doubt of him returning safe and sound, the last thing he expected was to come back and find their refuge empty. He sat down once again in one of the chairs that ran in rows and tried to think it through. *Was there a struggle? No, no sign of that at all. And the two doors he needed to come through were closed.* Although, if he wanted to admit it, he suspected that the drafts would have closed at least one of them if they had been left open. But he doubted the draft could close both of them. So that meant she would have closed them.

He suspected if she had gone over the edge that this would be one of the last things she would have done. If one was eager to leave then closing doors would be the last thing on one's list, unless . . . Unless what? If someone had been chasing her, she could have slammed the door in their face to slow them down. But, once again, he had seen nothing to indicate such a thing. He was running out of ideas, and running out of time. Every moment that passed meant his chances of finding her lessened.

Even though he knew it was useless he did another complete search and once again came up with nothing – nothing to indicate what happened while he had been away. Since he had moved around and was presently in the room with the windows he stared at each one individually to see if there might be something showing up in one of them that might help. Yet once they cycled he found or saw nothing. *Sis, where are you? Are you in trouble, in danger? Why are you not here?* He received no answers from the windows, and only heard the silence that surrounded him. None of this made any sense. Elsa was safe here, and all she had to do was give it a few days . . . yes a few days and he would come back to her, which he had.

* * *

At least the female had finally entered the park, and from the way she was moving Ed suspected it had to do with nature. At least she was this far in. Now whether she remained would be another question. He could probably drop the pins on those doors and keep her in the park, but figured if he did that she might panic. Still she had brought the basket with her, and in truth she was better off in the park anyway. Everything, other than the young male, she needed was here. While he was waiting for her to exit the restroom he watched the male. *What did she call him?* He was trying to remember. During those few moments after he had arrived, it had been chaotic on his end, and he felt lucky to have gotten her name, if that was what it was. Still, it was a common enough to be her name.

On a third monitor he played back those few chaotic moments and stopped it and replayed it a couple of times. He was still having difficulty with their accent, and speech. The girl had yet to reemerge and the male was sitting down with a worried expression. Ed saw him get up and search the Welcome center once again ending up in the security office and the bank of monitors that was located there. He watched as the male studied each of them. It was obvious he was trying to locate the girl. Maybe he should contact him over the public address system, but immediately thought better of it. He'd only do that if it appeared the male was heading back out in the desert. Looking over once again at the monitor of the park he saw the female had yet to reappear. *What's taking her so long?*

He realized that once again his impatience was pushing him. He truthfully knew that all of this would have to happen on its own schedule and he couldn't influence or push it at all. The female would return to the park when she was ready, the double doors should remain open, and if the young male – again what's his name – started to return to the desert he'd have to make voice contact at that time, and other than this he'd have to wait. And after the brief period of excitement when it looked like it all would come apart, now everything was quiet and static.

* * *

Elsa was finishing up in the privy when her stomach growled complaining about being hungry. *Oh hush,* she thought. It was distracting. What was hitting her at this moment, as she stared into the reflecting glass, were those doors she ran through to find the privy or at least a place to get rid of the liquid in her bladder. If she remembered right they didn't have any handles – kind of like the doors into the privy. Although on the privy doors the inside part did have a handle so one could leave. She needed to go back and check them out because at the moment she had gone through them she had other things on her mind.

Secondly she was trying to determine if she really had heard her brother or whether it was her overactive imagination. She could have sworn it was him, but there was no way for him to be here with her. And when she had returned to the wall she could tell that however it was done nobody could be heard from the other side. She leaned on the basin; got the water running, taking a handful she splashed her face, followed by washing off the tear tracks that were there. This last moon cycle had been rough, and she knew nothing would ever be the same again for her or her brother. And what the future held, well, that was a complete unknown.

* * *

Ed took a few cleansing breaths, shifted in the chair as he continued to monitor the situation. Even though nothing was happening at the moment he could almost guarantee this wouldn't last and it would become ever more complicated and chaotic as the day moved on. In a sense he was still unhappy that the male had returned when he did, but had to admit such things were unpredictable, and just maybe he should have factored this possibility in when he had drawn the female into the lower levels. *Yeah, right! As if I could make those kinds of predictions.*

His eyes were drawn to the monitor where the camera was viewing the young male – *now if I can only remember his name, I'm sure she said it* – who stood up and began to pace the area in front of the bank of monitors. Ed could tell he was agitated. *I guess I would be if things had gone the way it appears to him. He came back from wherever he went expecting the young female to be here and as far as he can see she's gone. And there's nothing here to let him know anything. Yes, I'd be at a loss and wondering what to do.* In a way his heart went out to him. He figured he had to be thinking the worst. Ed figured he personally would have. Then when one adds into this mix the hostile environment that surrounds the Welcome center the conclusion would be bad. *None of it true, of course, but he doesn't know that. He doesn't know she's safe and actually quite close by,* Ed thought.

It was this moment he noticed Elsa leaving the public restrooms and heading back to the double doors. *Is she going to go back inside the tunnels? I hope not, she just got here in the park.* At this moment the young male headed back out of the security office and into the main area. *Now what?* With both of them on the move it made it a little more difficult to follow, and which one to concentrate more on.

* * *

With nature off her mind and her curiosity building she left the privy and with a purposeful stride headed along the pathway, but stopped a moment and looked down at what she was walking on. She realized it was rock solid, but it wasn't rock. *What is this stuff?* She crouched down and touched it. It had both a rough and a smooth surface and seemed somewhat cold. It was almost like someone had taken stone and somehow had melted it down, spread it out, let it cool, and produced these pathways. She knew from experience that the major paths and trails in and around the town had crushed rock and pebbles on them to make the surfaces better, but nothing like this.

Again she found herself in awe of the creators of this place. Not that the impossibility of all of this greenery deep underground didn't bring out the same feelings because it did. Absolutely everything she was discovering shouldn't exist here but did. Distracted for a moment she remembered what she wanted to investigate, stood up, and headed back to those doors. She noticed on the bottom section of both doors there appeared to be a large flexible metal strip, and behind this a flat piece of the same type of shiny metal. If she remembered right she pushed through the doors to come out here. Like the privies she expected handles so she could pull them open but found none. "What's this?" She asked herself. "So how is one supposed to go back?" A slight wave of panic hit her as she thought. *Maybe you're not supposed to go back through. Maybe it's only one way.*

She stood staring trying to solve the riddle that lay before her, and reached out tentatively pushing on one of the doors. She could feel resistance but at the same time it seemed to give with the pressure. She pushed harder and could feel it move but it took some effort. Now she leaned into the door and it moved inward a little farther. She let it go and it closed but at the same time moved a little past the other door. It seemed to be able to move in both directions. Still she wasn't sure and tried again and was rewarded with a little more movement inward. Again when she let it go it swung past center before settling into the center position. *Weird, really weird. Why would a door or doors swing both ways? What purpose would such doors have?*

It made no sense to her. It would mean that two people coming from opposite directions trying to go through the doors at the same time could smack each other. She stared down at the pathway by the doors and on both sides near the edges there were holes. *Now what could these be for?* Again it was something that made no sense to her. She then looked under the flexible metal sheet on the door and saw something attached there. It appeared to be a cylinder like tube with something inside of it. She crouched down and studied this new thing and found the thing that ran through the cylinder had a pin in it allowing the shaft to turn. And when she turned it the pin dropped into a slot lowering the shaft down until it touched the pathway. It suddenly dawned on her that this system would allow the door to remain open. *Wow, so simple, why didn't any of us think of this?* She reset the pin in its up position.

Standing back up she pushed harder and was rewarded with enough movement that she could enter back into the tunnels. But before going back inside she grabbed the basket of food. She'd explore this new area later. Right now she needed to eat and be somewhere she had been before.

* * *

Ed had been concentrating so much on the female and what she was doing he hadn't been following the male. When he looked back at the monitor showing the main room of the Welcome center he didn't see him there at all. Curious as to where he had gone Ed quickly brought up the other monitors in the bank and had them piggyback the cameras the security room in the Welcome center used. He picked up the male up by the natural tank. It was obvious he was heading back outside. *Darn! Paying too much attention to what the girl, ah, Elsa is doing instead of trying to follow both of them. Now he's out of voice and communication range.*

He began to follow the young male but knew that shortly he would be out of visual view. From the history and archives he knew that at one time the cameras covered all the approaches to Helms Deep. Still even this area suffered damage from the bombardment from space and approximately half the monitoring devices were destroyed. In that destruction the original entrance to the facility had been destroyed, buried, and a team had tried to provide an alternate entrance. Since most of the original inhabitants were from the construction trades it was something they were familiar with. The underground garage area avoided the damage so this provided an alternate entrance while the problem was being worked out.

Eventually a small tunnel was constructed coming in from a side direction through the sandstone that was part of the mountain that Helms Deep lay under. They used part of what had been a natural cave system to speed up the process, and had, once that hole had been discovered, marked and roped it off. They suspected it simply had gone down to a lower level of the cave complex. And it was because of this cave system this site had originally been chosen. It had reduced the time necessary for the construction, but even with these shortcuts it was too little too late.

Ed also knew, again from the archives, once the new entrance had been constructed the team working the job decided to keep the natural tank they had found and to pipe water to it so any who would be out could simply come here for water and not have to head all the way back inside. Still once all of this had been accomplished nobody used it since no one from the outside ever showed up. Any time excursions to the desert took place they were always through the hidden underground garage and supply area. In many ways he thought the effort his ancestors had put forth was a waste. But maybe it wasn't so. While no one had arrived during the original meteor strikes, now after all this time someone had. And when they had it had been through that modified entrance and changed his world forever.

* * *

She isn't here. Jay was worried, scared really. *Where did she go?* He had no answers and no ideas. From what little he could figure out she must have been sleeping when whatever happened, had happened. Otherwise the sleep sack would have been picked up, aired out, and be out of their way. While she hadn't been outside of this place since he had brought her inside he had explained what she faced if she decided or needed to leave. So with nothing here he decided to at least do a quick search out in the desert to see if there was anything out there he could attribute to her.

Filling his water bottles with fresh water he immediately headed out the doors through the tunnel, past the small tank of water, and headed towards the entrance into this place. Once close he stopped. Right here and to his right was that large hole. He wondered, and hoped he was wrong, if she could have fallen into there. He had stayed away from it, because he knew exactly where it was, but she didn't. Yes he had described it to her, but descriptions verses reality is definitely two different things. Carefully he approached the edge and tried to peer down into the pit, but could see nothing. He got down on his hands and knees and tried again with the same results. He really had no idea how deep this was.

Sliding back from the edge he found some small pebbles to toss in. He had first thought of finding a good sized rock, but changed his mind. If she had fallen in then he could inadvertently hit her, and possibly injure her more, if she had survived the fall – all conjecture of course. The surface in this area of the tunnel was solid rock so there would be no tracks, nothing to state someone had passed this way. He approached once again with great caution and on his knees tossed one of the pebbles into the darkness and listened. After what seemed too long he thought he heard it hit. *Oh my, I hope not.* He immediately sent a second followed by a third into the hole and listened. All three sounded as if they had landed in water.

If she had fallen into this and had been injured or knocked unconscious she would probably have drowned. Meaning she was dead. This thought floored him. He sat down and pulled himself away from the hole leaned back on his arms and stared out at nothing. *Sis, after all you've been through, with all the pain, fear, and agony, if you fell to your death here . . .* He could not bear to consider the futility of it all if indeed this was her fate. *No, I won't accept this. You would be more careful than this, and you were warned.* With those thoughts he stood back up and headed on out into the desert. He would do a careful and thorough search outside before returning. Who knows, maybe she simply went outside into the desert to be back in the sunlight and he would find her shortly.

* * *

Ed realized he had been working the security office since early in the day. He needed to take a break. And from what he could see the two he was watching were either beyond his view or taking a break themselves. Pushing himself back from the desk that ran the full length of the monitor bank he sighed, got up and first visited the restroom before heading to one of the kitchens. Maybe the walk away from all of this would do him good and give him a chance to think it through. When he had first seen the two of them he obviously was in shock, but as a little more time passed he felt the need to bring them all the way inside and thusly what he was attempting now.

The present problem, among many, was this was becoming much more complicated than he first thought. After all, turning off the lights, opening the entrance with its soft lighting, drawing the young lass down through the tunnels should have been simple. And with the young male out and about he wouldn't be a factor, initially making this first contact easy. Well, it hadn't been and even though she was down in the lower levels nothing had led to him meeting her. He found he had reached the kitchen and hadn't even realized he had traveled between that brief stop at the restroom to here.

He grabbed some juice and made a sandwich, went out to the seating area and sat down still deep in thought. He reached for the glass only to realize it was now empty. He hadn't even realized he had been drinking it let alone emptying the glass. It was then he realized his sandwich was gone also. *Boy, I must really be thinking hard. I just ate my lunch and don't even remember putting the food in my mouth at all.* He looked up at the clock on the wall and realized that 45 minutes had passed by also. *Guess I'd better head back. Somehow this meeting needs to happen today. With the young male, I still didn't catch his name, here and searching I've got to get her confidence and between the two of us bring him down.*

* * *

With the basket of food she wasn't sure if what was here before her was safe or not. She began to wonder where it came from. Things like this didn't just magically appear. That meant there had to be someone here – another person. She wondered why this hadn't occurred to her before. It was the only explanation that made any real sense. *So, why haven't I seen anybody?* What she was learning was this place her brother had found was much larger than either of them thought. They had been spending their time in that other place and had explored it completely. And while overall it was larger than the largest building they had it still was just a bunch of rooms. *Yeah, a bunch of rooms with magical stuff – and who'd have thought a wall that moves.*

She began to wonder if someone was manipulating her. From what little evidence that she had at her disposal it was beginning to seem like it was the case.

But how? She wondered. The only real proof she had was this basket of food. Food she hadn't touched, but eventually her hunger overcame her reluctance and she looked closer seeing what appeared to be fruit of some kind. What it looked like was a fruit she had only heard about and never seen or tasted personally. This fruit was known as grapes, and even though how she imagined them was different, now that she saw them for the first time she could tell the description had been accurate. It had been her interpretation that was wrong. Tentatively she plucked one and put in her mouth almost afraid to bite down. Carefully she did and was rewarded was a crunchy, juicy sweetness that surprised her. *Wow, they taste wonderful.* They sure beat those emergency food packs they had been eating.

She put the grapes aside and pulled out what appeared to be a sandwich, but the bread seemed so much finer and definitely softer than any she had ever dealt with in her life. Carefully she unwrapped the sandwich. Whatever the material was that it was wrapped in seemed to self-seal and it made it a little difficult to remove. She put the sandwich down and tried to open this clear stuff up and ended up, after much difficulty, with a square of whatever it was. She found that it wanted to cling to her. Eventually and frustrated by the stuff sticking to her she put it down with much difficulty and took a small bite of the sandwich. It seemed to have some type of spread, different from butter, and much thicker, plus some type of preserves. Again this was something she never had, but found she immediately loved it. And the bread, how did it become so soft and flavorful?

While holding the sandwich in one hand and nibbling on it, and with her curiosity fully aroused, she began digging into the basket with her free hand to find out what else was here, and was rewarded by a round and slightly tall container that had some type of liquid inside. And somehow it felt cool to the touch. How could that be? The container seemed to be made of glass and had a different shape as it narrowed at the top forming a small circle or mouth that had some type of lid or cap. Now if she could figure out how to remove the lid. It didn't look like a cork the type that was simply pushed in for a seal. And she couldn't see any threads so it didn't appear to twist off. She tried pulling it and that didn't work, so she moved on and tried twisting. At first it resisted then it gave away and did twist off. She was rewarded with a sound like pressure being released and she saw the dark liquid bubble and fizz. *What is this stuff?* She had never seen anything like it. She looked closely at the container, and it had words imprinted in the glass. Reading the letters it spelled C O L A, whatever cola was. She had to admit, one more time, she didn't know.

Here she was eating a simple mid-day meal and so far everything was new and unknown, and a whole new world was being opened to her. She wondered what would be next, and who was the one providing these wonders?

* * *

Jay stood up and headed back out into the desert pushing through the crack. He stood for a moment as his eyes adjusted to the bright sunshine, and the breezes that were blowing. The wind was warm and was blowing quite hard picking up sand and small pebbles when the gusts hit him. Fortunately it wasn't hard enough to create a sandstorm but this didn't bode well either. It meant that any tracks Elsa would have left would already be gone and as such there would be nothing to let him know which way she may have gone or how long in the past it had happened. From what little evidence he had found in those rooms it could have been right up to just before he had arrived.

Part of the problem he faced simply was the fact that Elsa hadn't any idea as to where this was. She had been injured, and delirious, semiconscious when he had found her. And it was days before she was herself once more. Other than what had happened to her at the hands of the raiders she remembered none of it. *Yeah leaving their camp in the dark and disappearing into the desert but that was about all.* He remembered her saying that she remembered heading out from the raider camp in full darkness and then waking up inside of the building with he watching and caring for her. Still, like all of them, she could use landmarks and such to locate and to travel, but when you had none to start with such was almost useless.

So where to look? Where should he go to search? *Maybe I can do a few full widening circles around this area. It'd give me a chance to learn a little more about the lay of the land, and if she did leave I might trip across something to give me a direction.* With his mind made up he headed on down the wash and deeper into the desert. He would spend most of the daylight working the area and then return as the sun set. He had enough water and rations to do this. Besides, once he completed his first circuit he could always return to the tank and refill his water container.

The sun was beginning to set and he was still a little way from completing his first circuit of this area. The badlands encompassed a greater area than he thought. There were literally hundreds of places for one to get lost or to hide in. He felt it would take a search party greater than the size of all the able bodied males in the village to do a complete search of this area. So how was he going to do it on his own? That brought up another question. How did he ever find this place when he had been close to death himself? He had no answers and with a heavy heart pushed on until he came to one of his markers and returned to the underground building.

He sat heavily in one of those seats that were in a row with his head resting on his hands and with his eyes closed breathed a silent prayer that Elsa was all right. At this moment this place felt empty and it emphasized his position as being the only one here. With his sister here it had given him a reason to keep going. It gave him the impetus to make plans and to take the dangerous trip back to the ruins, and to come back here. Now he was at a complete loss as to what to do. He heard his stomach rumble and realized he hadn't eaten anything all day, but still remained sitting. He felt his depression deepening, and he felt miserable and responsible. But, in truth, he wasn't here to know what happened. And to blame himself was stupid; he knew that, still he couldn't help it. When he had rescued her, not that she didn't rescue herself initially, she became his responsibility. She, after all, is his sister, and a younger sister at that. He remembered, too many times, being reminded, as he grew up, to watch out for her and be responsible. Well, as far as he was concerned, he failed.

* * *

Elsa, once she finished the food, putting the trash back in the basket, went back to those doors and pushed once again. While she hadn't really thought about it at the time she had gone through them, and in both directions, it seemed like they swung both ways. Since she now knew this to be true, since she had tested her theory, and it would be the first time she had ever encountered anything like this. Not that everything she had been discovering up to this point had been anything she had seen, because it all was impossible. And if she hadn't seen it with her own two eyes, hadn't walked the tunnels, and been in the building with Jay, she would have chalked it up as a tall tale with no truth in it at all. And the strangest part of all of this so far was what lay on the other side of this double doorway.

How could all that greenery exist? She knew from personal experience that the sunlight kept green things alive – that plus the soil and water. And then there was all this light. She didn't understand the light at all – Jay hadn't either. Yet the brief time she was out in all of that greenery she could smell it, feel the movement of the air, see the leaves in the trees move with the slight breeze – all stating these were real plants and trees. If she didn't know she was this deep underground she would have sworn she had found a hidden oasis in the desert – a strange one that's for sure, but none the less real.

This brought her full circle when once again she realized that somewhere along the line she had come to the conclusion that there had to be someone else here. Someone who had manipulated her in coming through that wall, someone who had also provided this food, and had to be hiding here somewhere, wherever somewhere was. *Maybe there's more than one.* This thought brought back a bit of fear. Still, she hadn't seen anybody, and found nothing that signified anyone living here. It was at this moment she jumped because a disembodied voice said, "Elsa".

* * *

"This is getting crazy!" Ed whispered. He was still working on bringing Elsa in so they could at least meet, and yet at the same time keep track of the young male. He had sworn he heard the girl mention his name, but with everything going on he had missed it, and for some reason he was quite busy right now and unable continue the replays or listen to them. He could see the Welcome center was still empty. He hoped that wherever the young male had gone he would return. If he didn't he wasn't sure if he could blame himself for it or not. Ed could tell from the reaction he saw in the cameras that the young male cared deeply for Elsa. Still what their relationship was he didn't have any idea. It had been something he hoped to have answered before he came back.

Ed could see the reaction of Elsa when he spoke her name. He cringed when he saw her jump. *Haven't they, or she seen or heard anything like this?* This stopped him for a moment. Could it be what he took for granted did not exist in this world now? It was something he hadn't considered, and when he began to think on it, it could be that way. So, if it was, what would they think of this place, or the security office where he had seen them watching the monitors, or all of it for that matter? All of it, including the buildings would seem to be magic, to be something created by mythological gods maybe. Well, however they viewed it he needed to coax Elsa out into the park where he could make contact with her on neutral ground, and soon.

He continued to watch her giving it a few more seconds before calling her name again. He knew that to her his voice must be hard to understand, as much as theirs were for him. Still if he spoke slowly she should understand him, and if he could get the same from her it should be reciprocal – at least one hoped. He could see her looking around trying to locate where the voice was coming from and expecting to find someone standing there. Well, even though she didn't know that it was possible, he was in a different place than she. "Elsa, look you don't know me, as much as I don't know you."

He could see her continue to look around until she finally centered on where the speaker was located. When she did he smiled and said, "Please speak to me, and when you do, do it slowly. While we speak the same language, our accents make it hard for each of us to understand the other."

Speak to him? Speak to whom? Elsa thought. She continued to look around until she centered on the area above the counter and on the wall. There seemed to be something that covered a small area there that had a lot of holes in it. She had been through the doors and knew the wall behind those desks wasn't thick enough to have a place inside of them for a person to hide. So where was the person behind the voice? And just because he had asked her to speak to him, and she was sure it was a him, why should she comply? Was he hiding from her on purpose?

Ed could almost read her thoughts from the way she was reacting. In a sense it brought another brief smile to him, but at the same time confirmed what he had been thinking. They had none of what was here. Radio, or intercom systems, would be unknown, so she would expect to see someone if a voice was heard. With this new insight he said, "Elsa, no I'm not there, and I'm not close by. Try to understand that what seems impossible to you is common for me. And no, I'm not performing magic, or am I some god or something. I'm just a person like you." Again he waited for her to say something.

Elsa held her breath for a moment trying to come to a decision, then shrugged asking, "If what you are saying is true, are you the one who opened the wall that I came through? And if so why won't you let me back through so I can go see my brother Jay?"

Brother? Ah, so they are part of the same family, Ed thought. And at the same time he gave her credit, what she asked would probably have been the same questions he would have asked. *So how to answer?* "Elsa, somehow I needed to meet with you so that you could see that I mean you no harm. To gain a little bit of trust so I, with your help, can get your brother here also. I watched him leave, and saw that this was troubling you. I don't know why, but from what I could see, you were scared, worried, had fears – I don't know, but you see from my history I had no idea that any others existed."

"What do you mean, any others existed? Have you always been isolated, away from the villages, towns, and trading centers?"

It was Ed's turn to be surprised. "You mean there are lots of people out there?"

"Out there? What do you mean out there?" She asked.

"Never mind. Look, can you come back out into the park. . ."

"Park? What's a park?"

Shaking his head before continuing Ed said, "Park huh, never heard of a park. Okay, can you go out where the green things are? You know, where the trees, and bushes and grass are."

"Oh", was all she said for a moment. "Is that what you call such a place?" She wasn't sure if she wanted to comply or not. Still she did have her knife for defense if it came down to it, but remembered when the raiders attacked that having such a weapon meant little to nothing. And from what little she had seen and understood such a weapon could be useless here as it was against the raiders. "And why would you want me to come out there?"

"Look, it's really simple. I thought it could be considered neutral ground. A place where we can see each other, and there is enough distance between us that it will give us time to decide if we do want to come closer, okay?"

One thing for sure, since he seemed to control the situation, including that moving wall, she was kind of stuck. "Was it you that provided the basket?"

"Yeah, that was me. I have no desire for you to starve. This isn't what this is all about."

"Well, thank you sir. I was always told to use manners when I'm supposed to. Still, I'm worried that you are putting me in a dangerous situation, and I'm not sure I like that. Been there already and it almost killed me."

"And that's why if we meet, like I'm suggesting, it will give you a chance to hopefully eliminate some of this lack of trust."

"Let my brother in and we can talk about it."

"Sorry, can't. Two reasons really. The first is simply he isn't in the Welcome center right now, and secondly I can only face one of you at a time. Because, you see, there is only me."

"In this place? It's so large."

"You have no idea. But think about it. In the Welcome and Processing center where you and your brother were staying, it is only the two of you yet, it could hold hundreds easily . . . So why should it be any different here? Yes, this place was designed to hold thousands, but it doesn't, and never did."

Ed needed to get this moving as he continued to monitor the situation, and as he continued to speak with Elsa he saw movement out of the corner of his eye and could see the young male, her brother had returned. He looked defeated and beat, not a good sign. In Ed's mind he could head back out at any time and he really didn't want to see that happen. Turning back to the monitor where he was watching the girl he could still see and hear the mistrust in both her body language and her voice. Well, he really couldn't blame her. If he had been in her place he'd probably feel the same way. Remembering back to the way she looked when her brother brought her into the welcome center he suspected that something really bad had happened and this would only add to the suspicion and lack of trust.

He had no answers. And time wasn't going to allow him the luxury of slowly working this out. "Look Elsa, what's it going to take for us to see each other and at least confirm that what I'm saying is accurate?"

She shrugged, not realizing she had. In truth she had no idea what she needed to feel safe or what to tell him. She realized that he knew her name but she didn't remember if he had mentioned his so she decided she'd ask. "Ah, I don't remember if I got your name. If you gave it to me, then I'm sorry to have to be asking again. But you do have mine and now my brother's. It would be a start."

"Ed, Edward Carson."

"Ed Edward Carson? That's a funny name. Is this place then called Carson?"

The way she stated it almost made him laugh. Still he had to admit he was unfamiliar with their lives and how they lived, so it wouldn't be any different for them. "No, Ed is my nickname, and Edward is my full name. And no this place isn't Carson. It's known as 'The Deeps' to any of us who lived here. Why would you think this place would be named Carson?"

She was perplexed. It was common knowledge or so she thought. "Ah, one takes their last name from the name of the village, town, or trading center where one lives, don't you know that?"

"Ah, no, I don't." When she stated this, somewhere in the back of his mind, he had seen in history, a place somewhere in this world, where this had been a common practice, but he didn't remember if he had studied it or had just found it during some research. "Look, we can continue talking this way or we can begin to talk where we can see each other. Right now I can see you, but you can't see me."

When he stated this she immediately got up and looked quickly around. *Was he here and close by?* She immediately jumped over the counter and crouched down. She didn't want anybody sneaking up on her. With a bit of fear and panic in her voice she asked, "Where are you?"

Damn! Ed wondered if he had just undone all he had accomplished. "No, no, I'm not close to you. In fact I'm completely on the opposite side of the park, and in truth a lot further away."

"So why is it I can hear you? I know I haven't seen you, but nobody can talk like this and be far away. It's not possible."

How did one explain technology to someone who had never been around it? And Ed felt he didn't have the time. Again he was afraid that Jay would leave mistakenly thinking his sister had abandoned the Welcome center and had disappeared into the desert. (He had returned once again.) Maybe he should at least contact him, but he didn't know if he could carry on this many conversations at the same time and stay ahead of them let alone even. *Again, damn. Why can't something be simple for once? I just finished, in the near past fixing that leak, and it was a bear of a project. Now I'm trying to coax someone in here that knows nothing about their true past or what we had accomplished before the bombardment.*

As he stared at the two monitors and looked back to the one with Elsa and his heart went out for her once again. Whatever had happened to her, had to be life changing. And whatever it was wasn't for the good. "Look Elsa I watched as your brother brought you out of the desert. Something bad had happened and you were unconscious. And if he hadn't found you I suspect you would have died – another victim of the unforgiving desert. I don't know how your brother found this place, but if he hadn't then this conversation wouldn't be taking place. Again, I know you have no reason to trust me, but at least come into the park and I will do the same. There will be enough distance between us so that you will be able to determine if you want to continue and meet with me."

He glanced over to the other monitor and saw Jay preparing to get up and from what Ed could determine Jay appeared to be getting ready to head out again. Ed hadn't looked to see what time of day it was on the surface, but he needed Jay to remain. So with a decision made he opened up a mic to the center and simply said, "Jay, stay put!"

Jay knew it was night out, but thought maybe he'd simply go outside and let the cool desert night air caress him giving him a chance to do some deep thinking, to possibly come up with a solution to his dilemma. Elsa had to be somewhere and he needed to know where. Overall there had been too few clues. And, in truth, the only real one had been the fact that she had been sleeping, and had left before taking care of their normal housekeeping. Other than that he had to admit there was nothing. So with his decision made he got up and headed towards the door that led out to the tank only to stop midstride when a voice out of nowhere stated in no uncertain terms, "Jay, stay put!"

He quickly looked around trying to find the source of the voice only to see nothing. He immediately began to do a quick search. Somebody had to be here it was the only explanation he could come up. Voices didn't just appear out of the thin air. It was something that was impossible. But after a quick and thorough search the results netted him nothing other than puzzlement. There was nobody here other than himself – nobody.

Ed watched in amazement as Jay stopped and began an immediate search for the one who spoke. *Haven't any of these people heard about any of this stuff I take for granted?* The obvious answer again was no. At least there was now a great possibility Jay would stay, now he needed to concentrate on Elsa. He looked back at the monitor that was watching her and he saw she was still behind the counter and still crouched down. With the action of Jay grabbing his attention he had no idea if she had responded or not. He sighed, and shook his head. He needed to be twins, then he might be able to stay on top of this situation. Right now it was anything but.

He was running out of ideas and was almost disgusted with himself for causing whatever distress Elsa was feeling. He was sure it had to do with whatever happened in her past, but in reality had no idea what it had been. Still he had an idea since people don't normally hike the desert naked – at least he didn't think they did. As he stared at the images he remained silent. *There has to be a way.* "Okay, Elsa, I'm sorry if what I said caused you a problem. Look, I'm taking this on faith. I'm heading for the park. Please come out and I think you'll see you have nothing to fear from me."

Without waiting for an answer he left the security office and headed for the park. It was going to take some time to reach it since he was close to the center of the facility. Like her, and not sure of her reaction he strapped on a knife. It was a precaution he hoped wouldn't be necessary but he really didn't know how the world on the surface worked.

Elsa was about to reply when she realized it would do no good. It was obvious whoever this Ed was he was heading to, as he called it, the park. What to do, that was the question, and she wasn't sure if she wanted to leave the perceived safety of the tunnels or not. Still, if she wanted to be honest, there was nowhere for her to go. She either stayed in the tunnels where it was just that, or she went into the park where the privies were located, and there was all that greenery that shouldn't be here but was. So her safety here was an illusion anyway. Besides, if she wanted to be honest, she getting tired of crouching down like she was. It was hard on her knees and leg muscles.

She stood back up and then sat in one of those chairs and stared out through the narrow slit of a window to see if she could see anything. Unfortunately these windows were more for breaking up the monotony than allowing a true view of what happened out there in the park. Still she felt she would remain until she saw movement or something signifying he was there. Once that happened then she would decide whether to go through those doors.

She found she was leaning forward on the desk straining to see any change, or anything, but so far she couldn't detect anything. The time seemed to be dragging and she wondered how far away this Edward could be. He did say this place was large, but how large could such a place be? *Honestly it truly couldn't be that big could it?* She was about to give up when she saw what she thought might be movement, and waited to have it confirmed. After all her imagination could be playing tricks on her.

* * *

Jay was becoming impatient. Since that one contact by the voice nothing else had happened. He began to wonder if maybe he had imagined it, but it had been sharp, and in almost a command voice had told him to stay. He wished he could locate the one who spoke. Maybe he knew where his sister was, and maybe he, whoever this was, is close by. Yet, all of it was unknown, and simply a guess on his part. He began to pace the area. *How'd whoever this is know I was about to head out those doors?* It was a good question and at this moment he had no answer. It was then he thought about those windows that saw in the distance. Maybe there were more of them somewhere else. Then he realized the voice had named him also. How is that possible?

Then he remembered there was at least one door they hadn't been able to go through. Maybe whoever this is was in that other room and there were more of these windows there. It was a possibility but once again it was only a guess. There was no way in there, and the door was solid and with what he had there was no way to go through. Still, at this moment it was the only thing that made any sense. With those thoughts he went over to that door and banged on it trying to get the attention of whoever this had to be. He even raised his voice trying to get some reaction – anything, but he heard nothing, and if there was someone there they hadn't moved at all.

Frustrated he began pacing once again and finally went to one of the lines of chairs and sat down with his arms crossed. If he heard nothing for a while maybe he would go out anyway, be away from this place, and think this through. Suddenly there appeared to be too many strange things happening, and maybe this place was actually a trap, a danger to both he and his sister. And there was a great possibility she had already fallen into it. And even though he didn't know it, his conclusion was accurate. Although not in the way he thought.

* * *

Out of the corner of her eye she caught the movement a second time and this confirmed for her that someone had to be out there. She still wasn't sure if she was ready for this or not, so she remained sitting trying to come to some kind of decision. Finally she sighed, pushed herself up from the desk and left from behind the counter through the opening for that purpose. She came around and returned to the set of doors she had gone through earlier, turned around and leaned on them still not sure if she was ready to leave this area or not. At least here she had some type of protection. Out there, there wasn't any place to hide or anything to use for protection.

Might as well get this over with, she thought. Things weren't going to change until this meeting happened. She honestly had no idea how long this Edward would wait before taking things into his own hands, and with what she had witnessed so far – wonders well beyond anything she had ever imagined – she hadn't a clue what he could do. Turning around she carefully pushed through those swinging double doors and entered the park.

She was still in awe since this area seemed to be bathed in sunlight, but this was quite impossible. She was underground and knew it. So how is it accomplished? With a tentativeness that was obvious she began to walk one of those solid paths towards the center area with her hand resting comfortably on her knife hilt. At least it gave her a bit of false confidence. As she neared the center of the park there appeared to be benches on either side of the path and sitting one of them was an old man. *An old man? Really?* Was this who she feared? He seemed harmless. But she knew such appearances could fool one. Again, with tentativeness in her speech she asked, "Are you Edward?"

He smiled back at her pointing to a bench on the other side of the walkway and said, "Yes, that's me."

Carefully, keeping him in sight at all times she moved over to the bench he had pointed to and slowly sat down keeping her weight on her legs so she could move quickly if it was required. She saw he was leaning back with his one of his arms lying across the top of the bench and he appeared to be relaxed. And thusly began the conversation between the two of them with the distance between remaining.

At the end she found herself being drawn to this oldster – one who had lived alone for too much time. It was then he asked, "Elsa, are you ready to face something different, and do you think you can convince your brother Jay that you are okay, and if the answer is yes, I will open the wall and either let you go back to him, or have him come to us – your call."

A TIME OF LEARNING, DEATH, AND THOUGHTS OF REVENGE

Elsa began to relax as their conversation continued. Ed really wasn't the threat she imagined. In fact all that fear and worry had been a waste – a waste of her time and energy. She could see that this old man was lonely, and it was completely understandable. It was then that he made an offer she hadn't expected. He said it was her decision whether to leave or to bring her brother Jay down here and meet him. She sat for a few moments in shocked silence. She really didn't expect to be allowed such a thing – and he left it totally in her hands. "I think I'd better go see Jay. I'm sure he's got to be worried about where I am."

"Yes", Ed replied. "He recently returned after searching for you, and I had to order him to stay, otherwise he would have gone back out into the desert. Look, it's going to take me a little bit of walking to get to the panel where I can open the wall, so give me time. You'll be at the wall long before it will open. There was supposed to be a panel installed at the counter where you ate, but it never happened. It was part of what was left to be done, and wasn't – just that simple. Now go, and I'll do the same. Remember I can see you and I will know you are at the wall. And I'm sure you guessed, but I can also hear and speak to you. So once you're back with your brother we'll do some talking."

She was about to get up when she became alarmed. She asked, "If you can see us anywhere while we have been here does that include the privy?" She surely hoped not. Places like that were considered private.

With a questioning look Ed asked, "Privy? What's a privy?"

"You don't know what a privy is?" She could tell from his blank stare that he didn't. "Alright, it's the place where one takes care of nature. You know empty the liquid and such."

"Oh, you mean restrooms or bathrooms."

"No, I mean privy."

Here Ed laughed, and while he smiled, he stated, "I suspect the word you use is an old word. Now I know this sounds funny, but a public restroom or a private bathroom is exactly the same thing. I think I'll have to look up the word you use when I get back inside . . . And to answer your question, no. Such areas are off limits. Yes we do monitor the entrances, more for safety than anything else, but what one does inside is their business."

Elsa smiled, "Well, that's a relief." She stood up and holding a smile turned and headed back to the tunnels. She stopped briefly, turned and watched Ed retreat back in the direction he had originally come from.

* * *

Jay was becoming more and more impatient. Since that one demand the room had remained silent. He had to admit he really didn't know what to do. So once again he began pacing this larger room. He was facing towards the employee doors when he heard a sound behind him wondering if that voice was going to speak again. He was next to the door that led into the room marked SECURITY and the place where the windows saw into the distance. So the area around the counter and the wall at the end were not in his sight. Curious, he faced that way only to see his sister magically appear where there was no doorway. He stood frozen with an incredulous look on his face. In a tentative voice he asked, "Elsa, is this really you?"

She laughed, and had a big smile on her face. "Yes, brother it's really me, and while you have been away on your adventure, well, I've been having one of my own."

He wasn't sure how to respond. At first he wanted to admonish her for leaving him in this situation. Adding to the worry that something serious had happened to her, but at the same time he was so happy to see her and that she seemed fine. Finally he said, "I'm happy you're okay. I thought the worst, and you had finally snapped and ran off into the desert. I know from what you told me before I left it could have happened. And if it had I could only blame myself because I left you alone."

"I can understand that, Jay. But, as you explained to me, there was no choice. We were running out of food, and while I don't mind wearing your clothes, I'd really prefer something for a girl. And you were trying to get those things we needed." She looked around and saw on the chairs the filled sacks, the extra sleep sack, and another bag which she suspected had clothing in it. Again she smiled, "And I can see you were successful."

At this moment another voice, the same one Jay had heard earlier adding its own comments saying, "And welcome Jay, I'm Ed. Your sister Elsa can and will explain things and once she does I hope to see you in person shortly."

Jay looked up questioningly at where the sound was coming from, and like Elsa earlier when she faced the same disembodied voice, was at a loss as to where the one who was speaking seemed to be. He simply shrugged since it was well beyond him. He looked to Elsa who continued to smile.

"Yeah Jay, my adventure. Leave the stuff you brought. We'll come back for it later. I'm sure Ed will want to see it, but first I want to show you something, a really big surprise, and something that was completely unknown to us." She reached out and took his hand and gently pulled him towards the counter. Not sure where this was leading he simply let her lead him. When they came close to the counter the wall that had been out of sight was gone.

He stopped and pointed saying, "What? Where did the wall go?"

She laughed and looked up, first saying to her brother, "My adventure." She then asked Ed, "Are you going to leave it open this time?"

Ed answered saying, "Can't. It's kind of a safety thing. So it's your decision. Once you're through I'll shut it again. Then when we meet up I'll show the two of you how to operate it so you don't feel like you're trapped or something. So what I said still stands. You can leave, or you can come on down. One way or the other I will not leave the portal open."

Again Jay was at a loss. Where did the voice originate? And it was obvious whoever Ed was he could see them, so why couldn't he see Ed? He looked at his sister pointing through the opening, with some trepidation asking, "There?"

Here she laughed, remembering the fear, the tears, and the foreboding that she had once the wall had closed leaving her on the other side. She could fully understand Jay's reluctance at wanting to go. "Jay, I thought I had lost you forever. I was on the other side of this wall, and you were on this side and I couldn't get to you, couldn't contact you, and had no idea what was happening. I was scared to death.

"You really don't know what is ahead. The only thing I can say is what's down there – and it is deeper down by the way – is another world, so different from the one we know. And the only way you'll find it is by going. But if you don't want to go, believe me, I understand completely. If I hadn't been drawn in I wouldn't have gone on my own. So are you ready to experience something new?"

Jay wasn't sure, but from the actions of Elsa maybe it would be worth it to find out. Finally he shrugged, saying, "I guess so. Lead on." He heard this Ed say, "Good boy."

Elsa laughed. "Yeah I can understand him saying that. After all he isn't young. In fact he is old, and as far as I know he is the only one here, other than you and me."

Jay remained anchored to his spot as he tried to come to terms with this revelation. "Are you saying that this place where we have been living is only part of what's here?" He knew the question sounded stupid since it was obvious there seemed to be a lot more, but this revelation was something he was having difficulty in accepting. It had been difficult enough when he had found this place. Now to learn it wasn't all there was, was enough to make him reluctant to continue. He saw Elsa stop and turn around when she noticed he had stopped. He could see her encouraging smile.

"Look", Elsa said, "I know, I really know that finding out there is more to this place after all the time we've been here is a surprise, and as far as you know maybe whoever this Ed is, is controlling me, but he's not. Look when we finally met, and believe it or not it was among trees. Can you imagine trees underground? Not only that but the light makes it seem like it could simply be one of those desert oasis's, a weird one for sure, but one anyway. Anyway, we sat across from each other on benches – far enough away where I felt safe. It was then I learned he wasn't young."

She turned around and grabbed both of his hands and gently pulled him towards the opening. He allowed her to guide him along. He still could feel a foreboding, like everything was beyond his control, and if he went through that opening any he may have thought he had would be lost forever. It was an eerie feeling, one that sent chills though his body, causing his hairs to stand up. Still from the way his sister was acting, well she seemed happy about it. Softly he asked, "Elsa, you do seem happy about this, why?"

It stopped her for a moment considering his question. "I don't know. Maybe because I had built up such a fear of what I'd find, only to learn none of it was true – that to learn what I have is a relief. All I can say is you need to see this for yourself. And so far everything Ed has said and promised he has done. Like he said, if you want to leave and head back out into the desert, you or we can do it. But I suspect if we do we probably won't be offered another chance."

* * *

Ed watched as Jay, once he had come close to the entrance to "The Deeps" entrance, stop. He listened as Elsa implored him to continue. Still Ed could understand his reluctance. Jay was about to enter a world he had never dreamed existed. And if someone had told him about what he was about to discover, Jay would have probably considered the one who spoke these things to be insane. So he remained silent and let Elsa do the talking. Even though he could still monitor the situation, and as far as he knew, these two were the only ones close, he hated to leave the wall open. Still he could feel his impatience growing with every second that passed.

Ed almost began to speak, and bit his tongue and held back. *No, he doesn't know me, not that she does. Still we've had a chance to talk, to see each other. And I suspect she realizes that if it came down to it, they could control me, which is a worry I have to admit. Still, like them, I have to chance it. I suspect this is my last chance to find anybody, and to pass on what we've lost. Well, apparently lost, looking at what they are wearing and the fact from what I could see watching Elsa that none of this is something she understands or has seen.*

He saw her turn and grab both of Jay's hands and gently pull him towards the entrance. At first he resisted slightly before allowing her to lead him into the tunnel. He would give them enough time to be safely through, and then before actually closing the wall, verbally tell them. He watched as they slowly advanced. He, at that moment remembered the stuff Jay had brought with him and wondered if it was a good idea to leave it there. Because if it was left there and someone else found this place they'd immediately wonder where the owner or owners of this stuff was, leaving them curious enough to want to explore further. And this was the last thing Ed wanted or needed. He knew he would have his hands full with just these two, and he wanted no other problems or interruptions.

Jay could see the shadows in this new tunnel, and unlike the first one he had gone through this one seemed to have some kind of lighting that allowed one to see. It wasn't very bright, but it was enough so there really were no deep shadows. Still, as long as he remained within the original building he felt safe. As they got closer he could feel the nervousness building, and he suddenly found himself in the tunnels. They went a little further and they heard Ed say, "Okay, I'm closing the wall now." Jay stopped and looked over his shoulder and watched as the opening sealed itself, and now there was no turning back. Like Elsa, he was committed.

Jay pulled his hands gently away from Elsa and looked around. He asked, "When I was on the other side how did you know I was back and looking for you?"

"I was further down in this tunnel. At the base . . . oh come on I'll just show you." At this point she led off and Jay shrugged. There really wasn't much else he could do. Standing here with the wall closed there was only going deeper in this unknown world. When he came around that last corner with Elsa still ahead of him the lights came on in the segmented way Elsa was now familiar with, but caused Jay to freeze for a moment. She turned when she felt him stop. She smiled and said, "Yeah I know, and it gets stranger. I don't know how they work either but suddenly we have all this light." She pointed further down saying, "And you can see the counter down there. Not all of it, but enough to know that's what it is." Once again she headed on down, since she was on semi-familiar ground.

In a sense he didn't want to continue, but again what else could he do? Finally he came to terms with it and followed her down until he was next to her as she had awaited his arrival. She leaned on the counter and pointed to the desks and the narrow windows that were in the wall behind the desks as she explained. Then she led him over to the double doors, stopped so he could examine them, and pushed through. When the door was open briefly he caught a flash of green, and it floored him. Like her he knew they were deeper underground now and what he caught a glimpse of was impossible. Nothing should be alive down here. And if he wanted to be honest there really shouldn't be any light. He knew this for a fact. He'd been in the mines, and it was only the torches and candles that provided any light at all. Yet, it seemed that he could be outside, how was any of this possible?

Since he had remained by the double doors for what was a longer period of time than Elsa expected she pushed back through the double doors, and again he was surprised. The doors swung both ways. "Come on bro, there's more to see, and I suspect Edward is probably waiting for us by those benches by now." She held the doors open by leaning on them and with a sweep of her arms invited him to go through.

He shrugged again. This place, yeah, this place unsettled him. There was no other way to describe it. "Okay sis. I know you've been here before. But for me this is my first time. Give me a little slack here as I get used to this. So, what I'm saying, I guess, is this time you are leading instead of me when I found the place above here." He tentatively stepped by the door, and once again stopped. "How is this done? I mean just having this much light down here is impossible, but to have trees and bushes and grasses, really?"

It was Elsa's turn to shrug. "I don't know. It's all beyond me. Like I said, or I think I did, you'd swear you were in an oasis out in the middle of the desert. And look at these paths. Have you ever seen anything like them?"

Jay looked down and had to agree with her. He shook his head and simply said, "No." He paused a moment as he looked around this place before adding, "Lead on, since you know where we are going."

She smiled, nodded, and took off in the direction that would lead to the center of this impossible place. "This way", she said, as she pointed. Soon they were what he considered close to the center of all this greenery. He noticed the pathway they were on widened somewhat and on both side sat benches. On the one to the right sat an old man who stood as they approached. He smiled although it was a nervous one. Well, Jay could understand that. All of them had to be out of their element here. He was a stranger to this old one, as much as the reciprocal. The old man put out his hand in a friendly fashion grabbing Jay's right hand. It was somewhat awkward as he had never been greeted this way.

"I guess things and times change. It is a way of greeting between friends, business partners, and such. As your sister knows, my name is Edward, or Ed for short, and welcome to 'The Deeps'. I know you are

Jay", at this point he looked over at Jay's sister saying, and you of course are Elsa, the younger sister." Turning back to Jay he said, "I heard the question you asked Elsa about how she knew you were back. Let's just say it was by accident. It turned out one of the cameras had been connected to the speaker above the counter you just came by and she heard you asking for her." He saw the look that told him that Jay hadn't a clue as to what he was talking about.

Here he smiled and said, "Look, almost everything here must seem impossible. Heck, I was surprised myself when I saw the two of you. And yes, once I knew you were here I have been watching you. Although I have to admit when I first listened I couldn't understand a word either of you said. I had to listen for the longest time before I could discern any of your words. Such a heavy accent, and the natural shift in language over time, can do that. Yeah, I know, to you I must seem to have one also. Still as we become more familiar with each other, and continue to talk this will disappear and become common.

"Look, where we are going from here is most likely going to make you feel really uncomfortable." Seeing some fear in their eyes and an unconscious reaching for their weapons Ed smiled, "No, not that way. But you see, from what I've observed, nothing about this place is familiar. Nothing here makes any sense, and as far as you are concerned this is a place of impossibilities, and could only be created by the gods from myths and such. What you've seen so far is nothing to what you are about to experience.

"Look let's sit for a little while. I need to bring you up to date a little bit so what you see here, what you are about to experience, makes more sense. It will be a much shortened version, but should help you wrap your arms around it, so to speak. So please be seated, because even the shortened version will take some time." He then sat down and motioned them to sit where Elsa had when she and Ed first met. "You've got to understand that this place, 'The Deeps', has been here a very long time. And I don't know how you found it or why, and I'm sure as we get to know each other, your past will be given to me as well as mine to you. Okay, enough of this. Now for the down and dirty version . . ." He then went on to explain the how and why of the place commonly known as "The Deeps", but officially known as Helms Deep.

The two of them sat in awe as the words of their true past flowed from Ed to them. Nothing had prepared them for what he revealed. It seemed impossible for any of what he spoke to be true. Yet, where they were presently fit the bill for the same impossibility. "You mean that what we've seen so far doesn't come close to what you are about to show us?" Jay asked, even though Ed had stated this earlier.

Ed smiled, even though it was a sad one. *If only I'd known there were others years ago, I wouldn't . . . we wouldn't have had to spend our years alone. But I guess I'm lucky enough to see that we as a species will continue on. And it's quite obvious we would have even if I died in ignorance – what a tragedy.* "Yeah, that just about sums it up."

Through these additional revelations Elsa remained silent. It was almost too much to take in all at once. And so far it had only been words. Still where and how they had lived the past days had been proof of knowledge greater than theirs. And now to learn there was so much more than what they had already seen, already used personally. *I guess for me those privies, or what was it he called them – oh yes, public restrooms – such a strange word – and to direct water like that is worth the price.* This gave her pause as the implications of this struck her. There was no way that she knew of, to do any of what appeared to be common in this place.

She saw the sad smile on Ed's face and the slight shaking of his head and wondered what he could be thinking about. It was obvious from the faraway look in his eyes that it had nothing to do with what was happening at this very moment. Then again, maybe it did in a weird way. Anyway it was private thoughts and she felt she had no right to intrude. "You know, I just realized that even the few things we've seen and experienced appear to be common and ordinary for you and I guess I can say our ancestors. Yet we can't do it today, which means we've lost so much.

"It makes me wonder if this has happened before. No I don't mean some rocks falling from the sky, and who'd have thought such could happen? We had myths saying so, but as a child, I believe is the term you'd use, I considered them tall tales. Still you've confirmed that it actually happened. So I wonder what other myths we've grown up with have some truth behind them."

Jay looked at Elsa, who was sitting next to him, and marveled at what she had revealed about herself. While he had his own thoughts about what had just been revealed his hadn't gone nearly in the direction as hers. "Elsa, I really didn't think about it, but you're right. I was thinking more practical. What I mean has to do with how much better we could live, and it would be so much easier to be aware when the raiders were close and to be better prepared. And we are basically miners, I bet there are some methods in, ah, what was it you called them Ed; oh yes archives which could improve our output. Not that it's important now since almost everyone died in the attack."

He looked with brotherly love at his sister and smiled. Like Ed's it was a sad one. It had only been a short time ago when he in his innocence wanted to climb the peaks, to take on that challenge, and to build his personal confidence. And on that fateful day their world changed forever. He saw Ed stand up and Jay asked, "What now?"

"There's a saying from my time that states, 'A picture is worth a thousand words', so I guess it's time to show you. This day has been moving on, and my stomach is telling me it's time to eat. Besides, I need to get the two of you set up in your own rooms, and somewhere along the line get those packs you left in the Welcome and Processing center. There's much that has to be done, and unfortunately with my age I don't know how many years are still available to me. I have centuries of knowledge that must be passed on. And the two of you have to unlearn everything you know. Well not everything since you both has survived out there – a place I know I can't.

"But somehow I have to teach you the technology, how the systems work, and the knowledge of keeping this place running. It's more than a full time job for me, and with the two of you as assistants it should get easier. But I know when we start it won't be, simply because you know nothing about anything here, let alone how it works. For example I heard you call those things I know as monitors, 'windows that see into the distance'. I have to admit I've never thought about it, but I guess that's exactly what they do.

"And as your sister called them, and I suspect you did too, the restrooms. I know Elsa and I had a discussion about them." Here he laughed as he recalled her shock that they could be seen almost everywhere, and her relief when she learned it wasn't allowed inside the restrooms, or privies as the two of them called them. "Anyway we need to get moving inside. All I can say is be prepared. I know you both consider where you've been to be large. But the actual facilities could fit your town or village inside at least a hundred times over."

This brought light laughter from the brother and sister with Jay stating, "You're joking right? We are underground, and from what I can guess quite deep really. I'd guess that what we've seen so far would be as large as one would dare build. The ground above is heavy and there's nothing today that could support something as large as you are saying this place is."

Ed smiled a knowing smile. "Ah yes, by today's standards you are probably correct. But you must remember this place was built many centuries in the past, and the ability to do this was common then. Not easy for sure, but it is only the size of this place that makes it different from any of the other projects that had been done in those times. Okay, enough of this. Let's go see whose lying and whose telling the truth." He bowed and swept his arm out asking, "Shall we?"

In a sense Jay and Elsa were both shocked and surprised by what had just been revealed to them. It had to be an elaborate joke. Nothing like this could exist – could it? So were both of them unconscious and somehow having the same dream? Or was it something where both were asleep in the underground building, and each having separate dreams only to have each other in them? Yet, looking around, feeling the movement of the air, smelling the blossoming plants all spoke of reality, not the dream world.

Looking at each other they weren't sure if they wanted to continue or not. What had been found and seen so far had been enough in their minds. Still a sense of adventure was there and both of them stood up with Jay saying, "I don't know how much of what you've just told us to believe, but what is around us kind of supports it. And what's happened to the two of us speaks of things we know nothing about." He looked back at Elsa and could see the sentiment reflected in her eyes. "So I guess we'll go ahead and follow you for now. No, I'm, or we, aren't threatening you. I know you said we could leave at any time, but at this moment our only way out of here had been closed to us, so we cannot even be sure if what you said is the truth."

Ed smiled, because he understood their feelings. How else could it be? He wondered if he had heard the story he had just told them if he would believe it, especially if he had just come from a primitive society like theirs. In fact he felt it would almost be impossible. Only by seeing could there be any proof. "Yeah, that's true. But I do have to protect myself. And if you really think about it, what can I do to keep you from doing anything you want? I'm not young, for heaven sake. And the two of you are. So in all ways, other than experience, I'm the one outclassed here. While I know you must trust me, think about my situation. I've allowed the two of you in here where it would be easy for me to be on the losing end. So who's risking more here, you two, or me?

"I had to do something simply because of my age. I'm the one with no choice here. What if the two of you had been part of those raiders who destroyed your town? Can you imagine what they could do with what's here? There would be no one in your world that could fight and defeat them? And what would really suck for me is that I would be the one who led them to this unfair advantage. And believe me it is. What is here would give them unbelievable power over everyone. So for me the decision to let anybody in here was close to impossible to make. It would have been just as easy to keep this place closed up, forgotten and unknown, to die, and to let this secret die with me.

"The dilemma I face is overwhelming. From the little that I observed of the two of you I felt there was a chance, a chance to bring you down here, and let you see your true past and where we were at one time. But I've only been able to see you, and believe it or not, understand you for a very short time. And in that short time I've had to come to some kind of decision based on very little real information. I could have guessed wrong. I know when I first observed the two of you, you were arguing about something. I have to admit that at the time I didn't understand a word of it. It took time before I could get past your accent."

Here he laughed. "No don't say anything since I know to the two of you I have one. Plus over time languages have a tendency to shift. Words go out of favor, and others replace them as popular. Then there are always new words entering the language. After all, that's why it's called a living language. So I had to study the recordings for a long time before I began to understand."

He paused a moment and looked at Elsa with a serious look on his face. "And on that subject Elsa, what happened to you? I know something very bad did just by the condition you were in when Jay brought you into the Welcome and Processing center – and if you don't want to tell me now, maybe later when you're ready. I haven't had a chance to go over all of what was saved when you, Jay found this place, yet."

Elsa could feel her face reddening and felt the flush of heat. *How does he know something happened? Am I that obvious to him? This is scary, and no I'm not ready to talk about it. Heck I really didn't say much to Jay other than the basic facts.* "No . . . no I'm not ready to talk about what happened, and what do you mean saved or recording?"

Ed was silent for a moment, "Okay by me. I know that whatever it was it wasn't nice or pleasant, and you paid a heavy price. And I guess the only way to explain what I mean by a recording or saved is to show you. Now come on I'm ready to go back inside. Even though this is what we call a park, a place that represents areas outside, it's still almost too much for me to spend a lot of time here. So once again shall we?"

Ed headed back in the direction Elsa saw him go when she went to meet her brother. Both lagged a little behind being nervous about what the immediate future held. They were about to enter a realm they never imagined existed. Filled with many, what they would call *magical* items. And even though Ed had called the stuff the result of technology, they really didn't know the word, let alone what it meant, or how it would affect them in the end.

* * *

How long had they been here? It seemed the years had flown, and the lives they knew, their true past seemed more of a dream than reality. The wonders this place held had left them fearful and in awe of what their distant ancestors had created and accomplished. Even in their wildest dreams or nightmares neither had imagined such existed. Ed had been a harsh task master. They knew the reason. He was an old man and his time was limited. And he was left with the question of how do you take someone who knew nothing, to one who could actually understand and become proficient enough to keep up the maintenance of this place? Overall it was a daunting task, and one both Elsa and Jay felt Ed had done admirably. He had even taken them through the tunnel where the pipes fed the water to the facility and had shown them the repairs he had made, answering the question about what had changed when Jay had been by the natural tank.

But now for both of them it was a sad time for the dreaded day had arrived and Ed was dying. It brought both of them back to their past when their family had been killed by the raiders, and while this wasn't quite as hard, it was close. The previous incident was unexpected while this one both knew was coming. Ed had been in his bed for days trying to hang on, but while the spirit was willing the body had reached the end. So both sat next to him watching him breathe his last. And in his sleep he passed quietly away to wherever one went after death. For the longest time neither moved nor spoke being lost in their personal grief and memories of the one who was no more. Finally after the longest of times Jay said, "I guess we had better move him into the crematorium. It was his final wish to join the rest who had lived out their lives here."

Even with those words, which seemed much too loud, both remained sitting. They had to admit it would be difficult to go on without seeing him around. Finally Jay stood and gently lifted Ed's body onto the gurney and together they went to this final place. Once inside the small chapel they performed the simple ceremony, read from "the good book" as it was known, and sent Ed on his final journey. Later, at his request, his ashes would be scattered in one of the many parks to remain part of this place forever.

They retreated to one of the many kitchens grabbed a small meal and headed out to one of the many eating areas and over the meal reminisced about their time in the Welcome and Processing center, the time of fear when both had been separated, and the time of first meeting Ed in person, and realizing all their fears and worries in the end were unwarranted . . . Then came that first true walk inside The Deeps. It had been difficult for them to understand the sheer immensity of this place. It was well beyond anything either had ever seen or experienced. How was it such a place could be built?

This was followed by too many wonders to even remember. And as promised the first thing Ed did was show them how to open the outer door, or the moving wall as it appeared to them. Then came the libraries. Wow, once again who'd have thought there could be such a concentration of knowledge in one place? Yet here before them lay the totality of man's knowledge, education, entertainment, and everything in-between. It was then they learned how Ed first discovered them and what they had called "windows that saw into the distance", became known as monitors and the cameras that did the actual viewing. As far as they were concerned it had to be magic. How could something look out far away from this monitor and then put that same image here for them to see?

Ed had tried to explain it. But when you didn't know the words or understand the meaning it hadn't worked. Then both of them were ushered to their own rooms. And now that the population of "The Deeps" had increased to 3 once again, they were given rooms with plenty of space and with connecting bathrooms. This had been a shock to both of them since the rooms were larger than the house they had grown up in. Of course these bathrooms, privies as they would have called them then, were something neither had seen before. The privy was outside in its own small building, and one washed down in one of the small rooms in the house using a large portable tub that one stood in using water from a pitcher and bowl. Then it was a simple wash down with cold water and homemade soap. Repeating this happened, basically every couple of weeks at the earliest, and it could stretch out to a full moon cycle now and then.

Part of the reason for this was the number of people living in the household. And because of their location, close to the desert, water wasn't as plentiful as other places. Water was more important for the animals, the mining, and keeping the fields and food growing. So bathing, if it could be called that, was last on the list. To find such a thing where all the elements were combined had been a shock. But the surprise was the showers. Ed had explained what a shower was, but the only thing they could equate it to was when it rained. Ed had to demonstrate how it worked, and showed them where something called towels were located. Again something they knew nothing about. In town they simply used old clean rags which left them somewhat damp. By going outside afterwards the air would finish the job. Of course they were fully dressed. No one would dare to go outside without their clothes.

Both protested such places. They felt they didn't deserve such fine rooms and all that came with them. Yet, Ed insisted. Elsa remembered her first encounter with the shower and remembered feeling quite nervous. Even though Ed had stated a number of times the private areas were never, as he called it, monitored, it still bothered her. She remembered going into the bathroom, turning on the light – being able to actually do something like this without lighting a candle or lantern, who'd have thought – closing the door, turning on the water – again to have actual running water – waiting until it felt comfortable – hot water what a concept – undressing and stepping gingerly and nervously into that flowing water, and realizing at that very moment how wonderful it all was. Then finding soap that smelled nice and something Ed called shampoo for her hair, followed by something else called conditioner?

She remembered she had remained under the flowing water what seemed like forever. And her skin had become wrinkled from being in too long. Then she got out and used one of those towels for the first time and felt the fluffy softness and really thought she might be dreaming. *Is this something everybody from their past shared and took for granted?* One thing she knew for sure, she would be returning to these things more often than they did when living in their own home. The bed, what could she say about this? Sheets, she had never experienced sheets, let alone blankets so soft and warm. And the bed didn't require tightening of the ropes. She remembered her first time of carefully sitting on the edge and felt it give. She smiled and with a mischievous thought jumped on it and was rewarded with a big rebound which brought laughter to her. It all seemed to be unreal, and yet Ed seemed to take it all for granted, as if it was common and nothing special. *I guess if one has lived with this all their lives it would make sense. But I haven't and I have to admit I love it!*

Then came their introduction to their education and schooling – They literally had to start over from scratch. Back in the town they had careers ahead of them, Jay would have worked in the mines, and Elsa, with other women, would have worked the fields and such. All of it hard work, but satisfying in the end. Here their education became the means to an end. And now with Ed gone it would come down to them. No longer could they go and ask the expert for he had passed on, and now they would have to be those experts. At least they had the libraries to do research if necessary.

After they got over their initial shock – back at the beginning, and after becoming a little more comfortable, both were sitting in one of the eating areas, thinking about all of this. Again to have food so easily available was a real surprise. Let alone the variety they found here. Nowhere in their previous lives were there so many choices. It was meat from the herd animals, grains from the fields, and fruits and vegetables when they could. Even though this sounded like there were many choices in truth it really wasn't so. But here the choices seemed almost infinite.

Ed came in smiling and signaled for them to follow him. He seemed to almost be secretive, and kept urging them on, finally saying, "I've something to show you. I think you've gotten over your nervousness, and there was a time where I ended up being pretty lonely. (They hadn't discovered TV's yet.) So I set up a room to see how it felt to be surrounded by the crowds from the past."

Jay stopped a moment and asked, "How is that possible? I mean if it is the past how can one be a part of it?"

Smiling Ed stated, "Ah yes, one would think it would be that way, wouldn't one. You'll just have to trust me one more time. Let me warn you though, you haven't experienced anything like this in your life. It might scare you and make you want to run away. I can understand if it does. After all, I had problems myself once I got it working."

"Working? What do you mean working?" Elsa asked.

"It's better if I show you." They continued down one of the too many hallways and he stopped in front of one of the closed doors. Next to it was a shelving unit that had some items on it. None of them were familiar at all. "Okay, let me explain what we need to do. It's not really complicated, and I'm only going to run the simulation for a short time since I only have the one chair in here. Yes there are some hard benches you could sit on but they become uncomfortable really fast." He explained they needed to put on the ball caps that had some weird device attached, and to carry something he called glasses they would need to put on once they were inside.

After donning the equipment and carrying those "glasses" inside with them Ed said, "Now be prepared for this. What I'm going to do is surround you with people, but they won't really be here. Put on those glasses. Now are you ready for this?"

Although nervous, both nodded yes. Ed had a big smile as he sat down reached for something and suddenly they were in one of the large stadiums surrounded by thousands of fans. It made both of them jump, and almost scream. Even with the warning there was nothing that could have prepared them for what they were witnessing. Breathless, Jay whispered, "How are you doing this?" He tried reaching out and touching the people around him but all he touched was the air. Turning towards Elsa he could see an incredulous look on her face as she tried to both talk and touch the ones around her only to fail.

After a short period of time suddenly they were back in the same empty room. Breathless Elsa asked, "How? This is crazy! They seemed so real."

"Yes", Ed replied, "Didn't they? You've got to understand they are real, or were real at one time, but have been dead for a very long time. What I showed you is something that was popular before the bombardment, and what was happening back then was the beginnings of what was called the 3D revolution where, with the help of this equipment, one can create the illusion of being surrounded by images like in real life. Later they made it portable, but for me this was the best way." It was one of the many revelations that lay before them.

This brought her back to the present. And yet she remembered one other thing that had been a surprise. *The clothing . . . oh my, so many fine things.* Again, from her time of growing up and living in their small town the life style determined what one wore. While the town was supported by the semi-precious stones they mined, theirs was never a rich town. So all the clothing, even the ones who seemed to have more, were made in the town. And because she, as well as most of the other women, worked the fields, things like dresses were only worn for special occasions or get-togethers where one's finery could be shown. Normal day-to-day stuff was pants, heavy shirts, and when one could afford the materials, course undergarments.

Here, in "The Deeps", what was revealed to her seemed beyond comprehension. Such finery, so many choices, and undergarments were beyond anything she had ever dreamed of, or imagined. *Is this how it was for the women of old?* She wondered. Then she learned about how women handled their fertile cycle, and after all the mess and such she and all of the other women were used to dealing with, it was a shock to learn that these ancients had come up with a better – so much better – way to deal with the bleeding. And for once back in the Welcome and Processing center she had been happy to see that old thing arrive. It meant she wasn't carrying one of the raider's children, and she could get on with her life. Well, maybe, since she still bore the scars, mostly inside, from that encounter.

Jay continued to watch Elsa knowing that the pain and suffering she had endured during her time under the control of the raiders had left a mark. She tried to hide it but he knew her too well. And with Ed now gone and not harassing them over doing something wrong, or pushing them to do their lessons, he now had more time to concentrate on her. Although he had to admit there was plenty of work to keep the two of them busy.

When they had first been introduced to this place he thought how wonderful it all was, so many strange and wonderful things – so many conveniences to take over something that they used to do themselves. So many changes and ideas, and stuff well beyond his imagination. Yes, their ancestors had created much. Yet, now, as both of them had learned about all of this stuff, studying hard, trying to grasp concepts they had never heard of until now, it was becoming obvious this stuff wasn't perfect. He wondered how Ed had ever stayed on top of this place. It seemed the maintenance was never ending, and things broke all the time.

Ed had explained the reason for this had to do with both the limited time the ones who had built this place truly had, and the fact this place was old. This meant simply age could cause things to wear out, to break, and to fail without any warning simply because it was well beyond its expected useful life. That didn't mean he or he was sure Elsa liked to be wakened by some type of alarm letting them know something needed to be fixed. He really did wonder how Ed stayed on top of all of it.

It was during this time of one of the many repairs he began to realize how far Elsa still had to go to be her old self, if that was even possible. It got him to thinking about the raiders, and how they were the scourge of the earth. And if only they weren't around then such tragedies as what happened to their town, and to Elsa, could be eliminated. Well, if not eliminated, because there were always those individuals who did bad things, at least reduced. It was then, in the back of his mind, as he again watched his sister, and the lines of stress he saw, that maybe with what they had learned, what they had available, they could do something about it. Maybe it was the reason they had been led here in the first place, so very long ago. It was the only thing that made any sense.

They had personal experience of the danger of these people. Maybe because of this they could be the ones to eliminate them and allow the world to grow again. And because they were here in the desert it would be the last place the raiders would search, if for some reason the two of them screwed up, and botched an attack. Here in the badlands within this vast desert would be the last place someone would expect to find any living thing. And if they were followed back, once in the badlands it would be easy to lose them. And most of the ground was sand, leaving no tracks to follow, making it more likely they would never be found.

One day as they were replacing a pipe in one of the hydroponic greenhouses he decided to broach the subject. "Elsa . . ."

"Yeah Jay", she answered absent mindedly.

"You know we are in a unique situation here."

Here she smiled, "Yeah, you're telling me." She stood up and stated, "We, from a world where none of this exists, and now living here, the home of the gods." She then returned to what she had been doing, trying to keep the smile off her face.

"Ah, right. Look I know, and don't you deny it because I can see it. Anyway I know that what happened to you still weighs heavily. I'm your brother and I can see it in your face, see it in the way your eyes appear to be haunted when you let your guard down. It's bothered me that I haven't been able to help you."

She stopped what she was doing, stood up once again, turned and faced him, with her hands on her hips. "Yeah, I know, and I really had hoped by now I'd be mostly over it. I'm not, and I still have nightmares. I still wake up screaming, finding I'm soaked in sweat. Having the need to get up and take a shower. To wash it all away, like the soap suds do when you rinse off, but it hasn't gone away. Lessened somewhat I think, but not gone – why do you ask? It is my problem and someday one way or the other I have to come to terms with it."

"That's probably true, but that doesn't change the fact that I'd like to help you, but can't." Here he paused before continuing and stood up himself with his hands on his hips, like she was doing. "I've been thinking, and no don't you try and lighten this up by saying something smart. What do you think about payback?"

She had a questionable look on her face, "Payback? Payback for what?"

Taking a slow breath before replying Jay said, "Look, there has to be a reason we found this place, and then was allowed inside. I think with what we have available to us we can seek a little revenge on the raiders. Think about it. We don't even have to get close. We can strike from a distance and let a lot of fear and uncertainty into their lives, like they did to you, like they do to all the towns and villages. And maybe in time we can track down the ones who did this to you, and indirectly to me, and give you the satisfaction of taking them out and in the process maybe help you heal and have some final closure to all of this. I don't want an answer now, only for you to think on it. Besides, we will have to study, and then practice. All of it will take time."

He could see that she was thinking about it. He turned back to their repair work and let it lie for now. The seed was planted, so to speak, now it would be a waiting game. And because of where they were, and the time they still had available to them, the answer didn't have to come tomorrow, or many tomorrows in the future. But he suspected in the end she would agree. And with those thoughts began to prepare for what was ahead.

Elsa wasn't sure if what Jay had proposed was a really good idea. Still she had to admit that after all this time since her abuse by the raiders she still had nightmares and woke up in cold sweats. She still would get the feeling she was being watched and at times feel the fear and the desire to run push into her conscious mind, which she had to fight down so she didn't panic. And she had to admit getting a little revenge for the ones who had suffered at the raiders' hands and subsequently died wouldn't bring them back, but maybe, just maybe it would even the score somewhat.

She could feel herself almost smiling at the thought of seeing the ones who had done this to her and the others of the village dying with her either witnessing it or being directly involved in their death. Still she hesitated. Was she really ready and willing to take this step? To become a killer? She was a woman; a person by her very nature is nurturing, and willing to save lives, not take them. Still what Jay had said, and at least she would give this to him, he hadn't pushed once he had presented his idea, had a certain appeal, one she couldn't deny. To actually give them what they did to others would, would what? Here she smiled as she imagined them dying in droves never to bother anybody again. It was this more than anything else that appealed to her. No more worries, no more problems from those lawless ones who cared less for others.

Jay felt, as both of them continued working the many areas that required the constant maintenance, she was slowly processing what he had suggested, but knew better than to push. He knew personally he could be stubborn, but knew from experience Elsa had as much if not more of a stubborn streak in her. It seemed to be one of the family traits for which all of them were constantly reminded over time. So he remained silent and simply carried on the small talk that family and friends always did. Talk that five minutes after the words were spoken would be forgotten.

He found on those days where they had time off from their schedules he would return to the Welcome and Processing center, followed by going out into the desert through the original entrance he had discovered so many years ago. He knew it was probably wrong to leave the wall entrance open during these times, but there had been no one but them. While during the time of the original inhabitants they had finally given up on finding anyone alive on the surface, Jay and Elsa knew better and had periodically reviewed the recordings. And other than seeing themselves there had been nothing. Not even a desert animal. It was as if they were the only ones in the whole world. No wonder Ed and the others had believed what they did.

* * *

He was just returning from his last foray into the desert and was most of the way through the park when over the speaker system he heard Elsa, "Jay, you need to get down here to the security office. I've confirmed the wall is closed . . . just in case."

He felt a chill run through him as he asked, "Just in case what?" He knew she could hear him, and when he, or she for that matter, made a trip to the surface the other would monitor the situation from the security office where Ed had discovered them, so if something happened they would be aware.

"Just get in here, okay?" Was all she said.

He immediately began to run and in short order joined her. What's up sis?"

She pointed to one of the monitors that showed some distant images making their way across the desert. In their time with Ed they had learned a lot and had found that many of the security cameras had been destroyed both during the bombardment, which they finally had seen for themselves, and just the normal wear and tear. So they had replaced most of them and had added others that would monitor the open desert. This was one of them.

He stared at the distant images. Whoever this was wasn't a small group of travelers. Using the zoom-in function he felt chills run down his spine followed by goose bumps. Once zoomed in it became obvious these travelers were raiders. There was no doubt. He turned to Elsa asking, "Did you know?"

With a grim look she said, "Yeah, I zoomed in, and before you ask, no, I didn't recognize any of them, but it's obvious they are heading somewhere. And both of us know when they are on the move like this someone is going to pay heavily for it – just like we did." She was silent for the longest of time as she continued to watch as the raiders steadily moved on until they were no longer in sight of the cameras. She turned and faced Jay stating in no uncertain terms, "Others are about to suffer the same fate as we did, and while I really don't know how much of an impact we can have, any we can save from that fate is a good thing. I'm in. When do we start?"

And just like that they began their planning, and training. With only the two of them they would have to be very good at what they planned and carried out. Sure they had what "The Deeps" could provide them, giving them an advantage over their enemies, but history had shown them time and time again that having superior technology never gave one a guarantee when it came to fighting, battles, or wars. Unfortunately they were not prepared at this very time, so whatever these raiders had planned would happen, and the ones who would be the target would suffer. It was something that pushed both of them hard as they prepared.

* * *

There were other more modern weapons they could have chosen but they settled on an old tried and true rifle. It was one both of them could shoot, so either could be the gunner or spotter. They had learned their lessons well. It had taken a lot longer for the two of them to become proficient with the rifles. Since neither had grown up around them, let alone had ever known such existed. They learned about positioning themselves, giving themselves escape routes out of the area if something unplanned happened. And one of the things that was continually stressed was the fact that the unplanned usually happened, so be prepared.

The weapon of choice, oh yes, was the military and modified for sniper duty M14, 30 caliber, with the 7.62 NATO round. Highly accurate it had been around forever. And with the specifications on file they had been able to fabricate a number of them and the rounds needed for the weapons. Then they practiced in a range they set up in the garage slash storage area, being sure to keep the bullets from going anywhere where they could damage anything. This was followed by forays into the desert where they could sight in the weapons for distance. Being sure to practice on days when the winds were strongly blowing, and days where it was variable. Plus learning to deal with the heat waves that always radiated off the desert sands which could distort images and distances until all of what they learned became second nature.

And, of course, during all of this training, they still had to maintain the facility. And at the end of those days out in the desert it was always nice to return to the coolness of the facility and take a long shower. Soon they would be ready. And it would then be time to see if all their efforts, all their training, would be enough.

* * *

The raiders had returned to their hidden canyon semi-permanent encampment. It was one of the many canyons that emptied into the desert. The leader felt they were safe here, and because they did most of their traveling through the edge of the desert before they moved in and attacked their targets, they were well away and hidden. No one traveled the desert. He had to admit it was even true for them. Yes, they traveled the edge of the desert, just far enough in to be unseen, but only fools went deep into it. It was a place of only death, not that they didn't bring death themselves. This brought a smile and a slight chuckle. His mate who was lying in his lap looked up and asked, "So what is so funny"

Shaking his head he said idly, "Oh nothing, nothing really. Just thinking about the desert and how it's a harsh mistress that nobody survives and only death comes out of it. And of course we are death." They were in a large communal tent, and he heard chuckles from the others who were inside. Looking around he saw all the under-leaders of this clan and felt good. The last raid had been very good, and they had come away with much to sustain them in the style they liked for quite a while. And the females they had before they killed them and threw them away were fun. Not for those females, but so what, that's what females were for, other than bringing brats into this world.

These thoughts brought warm thoughts to him again. Yes those young ones, those who had never experienced a male were very enjoyable. Their fear would tighten things up nicely increasing the pleasure. And to share them with all of them, what could be better? Then when done with them leave their bodies to the scavengers and birds so there would be no witnesses, no one to point one of them out. Although he suspected with the fear they showed, they probably wouldn't remember any of them if they had survived the ordeal. After that it was simply taking the time to take what they wanted before burning the place to the ground.

It reminded him of the other outlaw clans he'd keep in contract with. About two-thirds of the leaders stated they worked the same way as his clan. Go in take what they wanted, killing all, and leaving no witnesses to their atrocities. But there were a few that would laugh stating they were doing it all wrong. There was profit in the slave trade. Shaking his head at these thoughts inwardly he laughed. *Slave trade, right. More trouble than it's worth. The ones who state they do this talk about their trek inland to the northeast somewhere towards the center of this land where there's great expanses of grass and one can see forever into the distances. And that the journey takes many days.*

He remembered laughing at these comments about the many days of travel. Then stating, "If it takes many days, that's too long. All you have is trouble with the ones you've taken, and with that kind of distance one or more could escape and then get back to someone who could make it difficult for us. Not worth the time, not worth the effort, and definitely not worth the risk, in my mind." He remembered the others who were involved in this slave trade laughing at his comments.

The one he had been talking with smiled casually and looked around to others who like him was involved in this trade. "No, as far as I know none have escaped. We know who to take and who to leave dead behind us. Besides, these we plan on selling in the markets to the east give us something to do with our time. The journey can be rough, or it can be pleasurable. And I personally prefer the pleasure we derive from our merchandise. It kind of prepares them for the life they are going into anyway." Here he turned to the others of like mind asking, "Isn't that so?" This brought about a lot of rowdy laughter."

Still unconvinced, he smiled back stating, "Too much trouble for me. Besides my people prefer to go in, have a great party, take what we need, and leave with just the stuff we can carry to either continue on or to sell. Other than that we see such journeys as a waste of time and a chance to be discovered by others who don't care for what we do. I really don't think we'll be changing each other's mind. Yeah, I can see the pleasures that would be derived from such a trip, but it's not something that holds any interest." That finished the conversation, and the night was beginning to fall. It was time to return. Night was the time of movement and preparation, and they needed to move out and be back to their hidden encampment anyway.

Yeah, that last time we had gone to one of the clan meetings this slave trade had been pushed hard. But in the end the ones who did this type of trade weren't able to convince any of us who weren't interested. Suddenly he found his thoughts and concentration being broken by his woman. She began to tease him in such a way that his mind and body began to think of those physical pleasures. He looked down where she had been laying in his lap and could see a wicked grin on her face. She was very good at this kind of thing, and knew what to do to get him interested. He smiled down at her and she kept at it. Finally he whispered, "Okay you wench, let's go and take care of this need." She laughed but didn't say anything as both stood and headed out the flap and proceeded to their own tent.

Soon they would have to leave the area; head north to one of their other camps, and let this area cool down. But such a move and the planning of that move was for later. Right now there was a greater need that needed to be filled. As he thought about what he had just said in his mind he laughed. It was an appropriate description – *A need that had to be filled.*

* * *

How long had it taken for the two of them to track down these raiders? Too long, but all of this was becoming harder than either Jay or Elsa thought it would be. Both should have realized it would be that way since they had found, as they were growing up, what projects they were tasked to do always took longer than they thought. It was never as simple as it appeared when the work was first looked at. So why should this be any different?

The clues were difficult to find, and then to trace out. And every time they believed they were close the lead would disappear like the dust in the wind, or the smoke of a dying fire. And they would have to start again. Since it was only the two of them they also had to be very careful. In the old days they would have been called an insertion team – one too small, but such is life. One worked with that they had. If the ones they were tracking ever learned the two of them were doing such, an ambush awaited. And if the ambush didn't kill them outright, both knew torture and a slow death would be their fate.

So many times they had almost given up figuring it was all a waste of time, and a waste of their lives, only to find something that moved them a little closer. Now here they were lying out in the desert behind a small sand dune looking towards a narrow entrance into what had to be a canyon. They had followed a couple of known raiders to this place. Still they couldn't be sure if they had it right. The distance necessary to keep from being discovered was great enough that they had lost them here in this area. Carefully, and remaining out of sight, since if any were watching from the heights, they couldn't afford to give them something to alert them, they searched beyond this narrow entrance and checked to see if maybe these raiders had double backed and were now heading in a different direction.

Any and all of these options were available. The raiders had to be good at covering their trail, remaining hidden, and being good in wild land skills. Then their leader, or whoever the leader designated, had to be good at planning attacks and retreats, otherwise they would have been destroyed a long time ago. So these ruthless individuals were the best at what they did. Jay, looking at Elsa said, "I don't know. We can't afford to make any more moves. And I suspect we won't be able to get any closer to that canyon entrance. I haven't seen any movement on top either. So, either this is the beginning of a trail that goes deeper into the hills, or it is simply an entrance into a hidden canyon. I don't know which it is and we have no way of knowing. I guess we need to pull back and watch this place for a while. Unfortunately it appears the only way into this area is from the desert side, which means we are easier to see.

"At least we have these tools that allow us to see into the distance. When Ed first showed us binoculars I was shocked. Again it felt like magic . . . yeah I know, no such thing. And now here we are with the tools from "The Deeps", which we cannot allow to fall into the hands of these raiders. Can you imagine how much worse it would be for ordinary people if they got their hands on what we have?"

"Yes", Elsa said, "I can, and I agree there's no way we can allow this to happen. So if this first attempt comes to nothing, well better that than losing, and giving them the advantage. Look, I think there's some movement on top – in fact on both sides of on top. I mean on either side of the trail heading inside those walls."

"Yeah, I see what you mean. You watch the one on the left, and I'll watch the other one. We need to spot them so we know where they are exactly. Then we will see what we can do."

"Works for me", Elsa stated.

Jay signaled for them to pull back. They needed to wait until darkness before they could move into the next phase of their plan. With their desert camo clothing they were as close to invisible as one could be. Still from their studies he knew it was movement that caught one's eye. And with the ones posted high on the ridgeline they knew these watchers could see great distances. Both hoped they were good enough to move in such a way that it wouldn't give them away. Plus they had hope the ones watching were bored and would be staring out at nothing in particular biding their time when their duty was over and they returned to the camp.

When they had pulled back and dropped into a small wash that was deep enough to prevent any from observing them until the ones searching were literally on top of them, both relaxed. Neither had realized the tension and pressure they were under while observing that entrance. "Whew, glad that's over for now." Elsa whispered. Although why she was whispering she didn't know. They were well away from where they had been, and with the winds this time of day it was doubtful any would hear them talking. Still it didn't hurt one to be cautious.

"No arguments from me", Jay replied. They leaned against one of the banks of the wash trying to find some place that wasn't hot. The sands they had been laying on had been really warm and uncomfortable, and the heat almost unbearable. They had left their backpacks here and Jay opened his with Elsa following, grabbing something to drink, and both prepared to wait out the long afternoon and once dusk settled in to begin. With only the two of them there could be no mistakes, and when they left there could be no one left alive to let anybody know about what they were using or the fact they had even been here.

From Jay and Elsa's point of view this would be the same as what the raiders did to the villages and small towns they destroyed, and this was to be a warning to the other raider clans out there that the rules had changed. Now they could become the prey instead of the regular status quo where it was they who did the preying.

* * *

Back at "The Deeps", when they were researching and training for this, Jay had found a section in the archives that talked about the many small wars that seemed to spring up all over the world. It was such a surprise that it had been this way. But then again when they had learned how many people supposedly lived on the planet it seemed to them it had to be over populated. Meaning that as the population continued to grow resources would become scarce. And with the scarcity people desperate for the resources would fight to get them. This meant that with the pressure of the fighting, devices had been created to help one side have an advantage over the other.

When they began this they had thought small. Just learn to use the sniper weapons, take out a few, maybe one or two, harass the enemy, and move on only to do it again at a later time. What they discovered here changed all of that in an instant. They were in awe of the myriad of ways the human race had found to kill each other. The arms race, as it had been called, continued to bring out better and better weapons, and here in the present, in this time in history, they had the best by far. The weapons of the day were knives, long knives, bows, and pikes. Any personal protection normally was constructed of leather. Not the best but it helped.

While the two of them had flak vests and head protection for their personal survival, what they had gave them the advantage on the ground making them almost god like. They had learned about night vision goggles, with this by itself providing an unfair advantage. Nobody in this time had such, and had to rely on their night vision which was always poor. The first time they had tried these things on it had been one of the blackest nights out in the desert. They had used flashlights – flashlights wow – to see their way out of the garage area. Once out, they turned off the lights, waited for their normal vision to adjust to the darkness, and stood there afraid to move. The only real things visible were the stars. Then Jay put the night vision goggles on and was shocked. So much so he stated in a surprised voice, "Wow!"

He turned completely around and it was as if night had become day. He took them off to be sure it was still night and found he was back in the ink blackness of night. He turned to Elsa and said, "You're not going to believe this. I don't know how it's done, but the descriptions we read did not lie. Here you try it and see if you agree."

Elsa, could hear both the surprise and the enthusiasm in Jay's voice, but still felt nothing could change night into day. Where would the light come from? Yeah, the explanations in the archives stated it gathered starlight. She looked up at those stars and while they lit up the sky, in the daytime one couldn't see them even though they were there. So it didn't make sense. Still her brother's reaction surprised her. She shrugged, took the goggles, put them on and adjusted them to her. Instantly night became day. She caught her breath, and then realized she had been holding it and let it out slowly. Jay had been right. She could see everything as if it was daytime. Like Jay, "Wow", was all she could say.

After testing out the night vision goggles they no longer had any doubt about the descriptions presented in the archives and lessons. They then searched small scouting teams and found two groups that were used and were famous for their successes. Most of the time they would go in silently, do their assignment, and withdraw successfully, leaving their target confused and damaged, with minimal casualties. These two groups were known as the Navy Seals, and the Army Rangers. And since they were only two (There were other such teams in other parts of the world, but these were the better known.), the tactics used by these specialty forces would have to become their way. It had taken them over two years of hard work to learn what they could. Still with no one alive who had been part of either team, they could only use what they had, and hope for the best.

* * *

Still both were a long way away from being ready to attack the raider clans. One of the most obvious facts lie in the fact they had no idea where any of the clans lived, camped, or gathered. It is one thing to be ready for revenge, but another to carry it off. While they both knew who they wanted to destroy, it still required a target or targets, and at this moment such didn't exist. Yes they had caught one of the clans on the move, but it would be stupid to attack a force that was ready for battle. And to be honest with only two of them such an attack would be pure stupidity, let alone suicide. "So bro, how are we really going to do this?" There was incredulity in her voice. "I mean it's all good and well that we are prepared. Well as much as we can be. Still here we are and somewhere in the great vastness of this place there are the raiders and all the ones who help them, and nowhere do I see something that says 'X' marks the spot . . . Unless I've overlooked something."

Jay shrugged what else could he do? What she had pointed out and had asked really did sum up what they faced. "I don't know. I guess we keep practicing what we've learned, but there must be some way to begin to track the movements of the ones who are responsible. Come on sis, back when we were both innocent and our village was still alive our lives were going in a completely different direction. I'm sure there was some boy back there you had a crush on just like there was a girl I was interested in. And if life had continued, at this time in our lives, we would have possibly looked back on how naïve we were when we first began looking at the opposite sex.

"I suspect we would have followed in both our parents and our older siblings' direction. You know, be with our true love, probably with children of our own, laughing about the first ones of the opposite sex that caught our attention. Instead of that future, this is the one we are living now. In a sense it's ironic. And what I mean by this is we are living our future through the past of our ancestors. Not our sires or our family, but our ancient ancestors. We are using ancient technology and methods that haven't been rediscovered yet. And other than each other we have no family. They are all dead. And we have decided – yeah I know I kind of pushed it a little – that it's only right that we should return the favor to the ones who changed our future forever." He stopped and was silent as he continued to think.

A little subdued by his response, Elsa said, "True. Everything you just said is true. To be honest I think I'd prefer the future that was to be to this one. But no one ever gets to go back. What is is, and what was shall remain. Look we still need to figure all of this out. Yeah we have the most important part of this behind us, but now what? In a sense we live in a vacuum here. We have no contact with the world outside of 'The Deeps'. So we are kind of isolated here. And maybe that's our answer."

"Answer? What do you mean answer?"

"We haven't been outside of here other than maintaining the equipment. Maybe it's time we go and see the world. Well, not all of it. Still we need to get out there."

"Hmmm, you're right we do. So how do we do this?" Jay shrugged. "I guess we could be just who we are – sister and brother. Maybe with the different traders and caravans we can tag along using them for safety."

"Sounds good, but from what I remember from our own traders and the town meetings most won't take on strangers for obvious reasons."

"True and it makes sense it should be that way. After all, you really have no idea who the strangers are and what their purpose is when joining a caravan." Both were silent. Then Jay continued. "Maybe we just go out by ourselves for the first few times. With only the two of us, the modern or ancient weapons, to be honest, that we have, we should be safe – more or less – and maybe start to become known. I know we do have some distant family members, or at least I think we do, in some of the villages further to the south. Maybe we should seek them out and maybe tag along with their traders."

"It's a thought. Maybe for the first couple let's just head out to the west and see if we can find some of the trading centers our traders went to. Maybe we can use the fact that we are the only survivors from there – our village, as a way in. I don't know. Still somehow we need to get out there."

"Okay, let's do it. Still we have to figure out ways to follow the raiders when they are on the move and not be seen or caught. Otherwise all of this will come to nothing."

"Maybe we'll have more ideas once we've done some traveling on our own."

"Might – just might. So when do you want to do this? At this time we don't even have the clothing that would match what we used to wear. And to be honest, while we still have our old stuff I doubt either of us would fit into them now."

Elsa laughed, "No doubt about it. It would be funny to try, but we are no longer teenagers and both of our frames have filled out."

It was Jay's turn to laugh, "Yeah, and you especially. Yup, you definitely have filled out and you're no longer that skinny little urchin who always bothered her older brother. If I was looking you surely would be one of the first to catch my eye."

She blushed. She had never heard Jay talk this way. In fact when he first started to comment she could feel anger rise a little. *Filled out indeed!* Yet he, in the end had actually complimented her. He was full of surprises. "Ah, I guess, thank you should be my response?"

Again he grinned, "You are most welcome, sister of mine."

* * *

How long had they been away? Overall it wasn't that important, still their time on the trails had been eye opening. Had things changed that much or had it been them who had changed? Of course both knew the answer – it had been them. In a sense it had brought them back to the time of the first conversations with Ed. They hadn't realized that their way of thinking and of speaking had moved to the old ways. This became obvious the first time one of the caravans overtook them as they headed south on one of the main trails. Both at this time were trying to be more observers than participants. They had been away much too long to jump right back into the society they had left.

As the caravan had passed they waved and smiled, and first saw suspicion from some of the ones guarding, but once it was obvious there were just two it went away. And as any came close they'd pass on words of pleasantry – words that would be forgotten almost immediately. The problem for the two of them lay in the fact that they couldn't understand them at all. Both looked at each other shocked by this revelation. So they smiled, waved and didn't say anything. After the caravan passed and was out of sight they pulled off the trail where they could remain hidden. Elsa asked, "Did you understand any of that?"

He shook his head, "No, not at all." He was silent for a short period of time. "This isn't something I expected. Okay, I guess this means we have a lot of additional work ahead of us. I think I now know how Ed must have felt when he first heard our conversations."

"Yeah, really." Elsa could feel her nervousness grow. At least their first contact had been brief and on the trails. What if they had been entering one of the trading centers or maybe one of the villages where they might have relatives?

In the end they cut this first time out short. Once back inside "The Deeps" they went to the archives and began to study the recordings Ed had made of their conversations when they had been inside the Welcome and Processing center. And it was during this time they had come across ways to become others in those same archives. It appeared that spying and spies had existed throughout written history. And when they saw the many disguises the spies used it became obvious it was the route they would need to go.

....

THE HUNT

Jason stood behind the makeshift bar that was located in the corner of the roadhouse, (An old word whose origins were unknown.) that he, his wife, and their children owned. Of course they ran it also. There never had been enough coming in to be able to hire anyone. Here at the bar they served beer and wine – made on the premises of course. His roadhouse was on one of the major trails just outside of one of the larger trading centers. And when he had chosen this site, too many years in the past to count, he figured it to be a good location. Far enough out that it would be a good stopping point, a place to refresh before entering into the trading center proper, and all its hustle and bustle, and close enough that they could go there to get anything they personally couldn't supply themselves. And there had been trees of plenty so they could use some of them to build this place. And the water from the well was sweet – some of the best in the area. So he and his wife decided it would work. Work it did, but never to the level expected.

What had happened was something they hadn't anticipated. At first, once they were open for business, things went well and they had many visitors, and many who would stay the night. And in those first few years they continued to add to their buildings. But now during the heavy trading season they couldn't fill their rooms and while they had enough income, it barely met their needs. Because of this they had expanded, growing their own food, and running a small herd of cows to provide milk, meat, cheeses and such, which they would sell here and in the market places inside the trading center. Yes, this trading center had been successful and as such began to grow in their direction, shortening the distance where eventually they were being bypassed because of the proximity of the center. Now any who would stop, would do so because they had arrived at the end of the day or because they had left late on the way back to wherever they might be going.

It was as this growth had been happening and the lessening of the customers that led to creating of the small bar area, plus a few round tables and a small sitting area. It had forced them to begin to grow the grape vines for wine and plant the grains necessary for the beer. The first few seasons had its share of failures, but now after all this time their product was consistent and that was all one could ask – thusly leading to the regular clientele he saw here today, in the late afternoon. Some were from the trading center, and a few were local farmers and such. Still, there were always a couple that remained secretive, and to themselves. He suspected they were spies for the raider clans, but they always behaved themselves, bought a few rounds – generally beer only – and would leave. They would arrive one at a time, and never sit together or even acknowledge each other's presence. Still it was obvious they knew each other.

When they first began showing up and he surmised who they possibly were, he worried that they were scouting his place. Yet, over time nothing bad had happened, and so he figured they were here to see who might be coming into or leaving the trading center. Still, in the end, he had no proof – none at all . . . Just an uneasy feeling that all was not right with the world. This brought an inward smile. *Of course all is not right with the world idiot. Word comes in often enough to let us know that the raider clans are strong and dealing death and destruction wherever and whenever they decide. I guess being this close to the trading center, and one of this size, gives me some protection. I don't think they'd attack such a large settlement. And, for whatever the reason, some of them spend time here. Maybe that in itself gives me some protection also. In the end I have no way of knowing. And the ones who stop by and loiter about never do anything to raise suspicion anyway.*

As he wiped down the bar with a damp cloth he shook his head. He and his family were stuck here, and while they have been doing okay, there had never been enough to make a move, or change their location. Well for good or bad here they'd stay. He had been looking down when he heard the door open. It surprised him in a way, since this was one of the two doors – this one opened to the bar, the other to the area where one rented the rooms. And while on that subject he had been approached a few times where some of the lower class members wanted to use their vacant rooms for the oldest profession. They said they would pay well, and he was sure it was probably true . . . But he and his wife didn't like that kind of thing – the selling of one's body, and he knew that in the end they would be drug down into the lawless underworld for which they wanted no part.

All the regulars for this time of day were here, and while the day was close to ending, any arriving now would be looking to spend the night. It would be some time before the night regulars showed up, and began their tall tales of today's business. And he suspected this was another reason for the ones he considered spies for the clans to be here. Looking up he was surprised to see a young – not a bad looker either – woman who obviously was wealthy, enter.

She stopped once she had come inside, and with what appeared to be indecision, stood there for a few moments as her eyes adjusted to the dim interior. No surprise since he only had a few candles on the tables, and a couple of oil lamps sitting on the counter, in a room with no windows. *Is she alone? No one is that stupid – especially a young woman such as this one. She has to be in her mid-twenties, and with what she's wearing she must have guards somewhere. And usually someone would precede such as this one into any unfamiliar building.*

She smiled, even though it was a nervous one, "I'm sorry, I think I've entered through the wrong door. Does the other lead to where I can rent a room for the night?" There was an innocence here, as if this was her first time away from wherever she came from. "It seems we are arriving late, and we decided to stop here instead of heading into the trading center where at this time of day it would be difficult to find lodging. You see we are looking to set up a contract and supply some needed items." Here she paused followed by a frown. "Oh, I wasn't supposed to say that."

Jason smiled and asked. "You said we, can I assume that whoever is with you is out taking care of your animals?"

Once again she smiled a dazzling smile, and nodded. "Yes! Yes, that exactly what he's doing."

"He? You mean there is only one other with you?"

"Oh, we can take care of ourselves if that's what you mean." Her response was quick and somewhat defensive.

"It's a nasty world out there. Usually someone of your class has a small army to protect them, why only one?"

"It's simple really. And it's something we've done a lot. With just the two of us it is easier to move, to camp, and it requires less supplies, animals, cost, and such to make the trip. With two we can disappear and not be seen unless we want to be."

At that moment a male stepped through the door, He had the look of a servant, but seemed to look somewhat like the female albeit older. And Jason had to admit, even if it was to himself, he appeared to be able to take care of himself and this young woman. "Ah madam I believe you have come through the wrong doorway. We need to leave here so I can get a room assigned for you for the night." He took a quick look around eyeing all who were here and shook his head. "I find nothing but trouble here. Maybe we should move on and chance it in the trading center."

She smiled at him and shook her head. "No, I'm not ready to face that crowd. We'll spend the night here." Once again she turned towards the bar and smiled that dazzling smile. "I'm sorry if I interrupted anything. We'll be going now." With that she withdrew back out the door with the servant following.

After she left he could see knowing smiles on much of the crowd and a few cat calls. *Naïve that's all I can say. How'd they ever get here alive?* Well, however it had been, luck must have been with them. One of the things he noticed as the two of them left was an increase of interest from the ones he suspected were spies from the raider clans. Not a good thing for those two, but who knows, they just might be able to disappear like they said. Still he suspected that the next time they disappeared it would be permanent and their bodies plus what they carried would never been found.

* * *

After closing the door Jay smiled. "It looks like you did a great job. Even I could have been taken in by the way you acted. I'm sure everybody in there, and I know you heard the cat calls, thinks we are fools, and I'm only here because of your demands. Did you notice any that seemed too interested?"

Here Elsa smiled. "Yeah, I noticed a couple in the shadows – not that the room was anything but shadows – that immediately perked up. And while they tried to hide it, they even glanced at each other. I think the leads we've been following so far are correct, and this is one of the places they spend time trying to locate targets. So are we going to spend the night here, or pull back and camp? In truth I'd prefer a night in a bed. Yeah I know what is in these places could hardly be called beds – especially since 'The

Deeps'. Still they are not the hard unforgiving ground, and I'd prefer not to have to spend another night that way for a few days."

"I can understand sis. Yeah, let's do it. We have enough of the bars we use as currency to do it. Besides it will help with the illusion of our wealth. After all, we are gem traders . . . well you are, and on this outing, I'm just your humble servant and protector. Besides you said we were staying the night anyway. Next time we'll have to become a couple. One thing for sure we couldn't pull off a parent – child relationship. We're too close in age."

This brought laughter from Elsa. "Now that's funny, besides being impossible."

"Yup. Still being a married couple will be almost as difficult to pull off. And this is why I like it this way. I mean, and don't take this wrong sis, I don't think I'd want to be in your bed to maintain the illusion we are married. I think you're beautiful, but that's just a brother's pride." Here he stopped for a moment and had a mischievous smile, that she recognized immediately. "I know that it would be easy to misinterpret that statement, but let's be honest family does look at things differently." He paused for a moment with a more serious look. "Still, from the reaction you got from the ones drinking in there they thought so also. Still . . . it could be the beer talking."

Trying to change the subject, since there continued to be a bit of teasing in his comment, and still answer, she said. "Yeah, that's true. Still with what I'm wearing, and I have to admit it's rather tasteful, after all, these clothes show off the best of me." She knew this part of the conversation would have to play itself out.

"Now I thought your mind was the best of you. Are you trying to say your nice curves are the best part of you?"

She shook her head as she pushed him, "Males!" Was all she said. Still inwardly she smiled. He had always been good at teasing her, but she could sense a brother's pride there also.

Both had pulled far enough away that what they had been saying couldn't be overheard. The two of them headed, with their mounts, to the stables and found one of the owner's children there, paid the fee, and had the two horses taken care of. Jay then stated, "We'll be here early in the morning for them. Will they be ready for us?"

The boy, who refused to give his name, replied, "Of course, most that stay leave early so we are used to having the animals ready."

Jay nodded in reply knowing that most preferred to remain anonymous – it made it simpler that way. The two of them turned and headed for the door that would lead to the rooms. And with a quick glance over his shoulder Jay took the large pack and hefted it to his shoulder, While Elsa carried a small bag. As they headed for the door the two glanced quickly at the entrance to the bar and could see the door was cracked with someone looking out. The two continued on unconcerned – or so it appeared, and entered through the second door. Once inside they looked at each other knowingly but said nothing. Looking ahead of them and their surroundings they saw a well-lit desk ahead, and to the left a small eating area, with stairs to the right and a second floor where all the rooms were located. The two had guessed, from the size that there were probably a dozen rooms. Still it was also obvious that the owners were surviving – barely.

As they approached the desk an older woman came out and greeted them. She must have been the wife of the one who stood behind the bar. They made the conclusion from the similarity of family. The boy who had stabled their horses looked a lot like the two. She smiled and asked, "And what can I do for the two of you?"

"I need a nice room for madam, and it must have two beds. I cannot leave her unprotected. I do not require much but she does. Do you have such a room?"

She smiled before answering. She like her husband could sense the wealth this young woman had, "Of course. We've faced those kinds of arrangements before. Although with an unattached woman, and one of wealth, she usually has other women with her, with servants staying in the next room. While this is unusual, it is not that it hasn't happened before. Such a room has dividers inside so that privacy can be maintained as required. Still such an arrangement does cost more. You can afford such can you?"

The young lady looked at the woman in distaste. "Of course I can afford such a room, and it's an insult that one has to be asked!"

The servant turned to her shaking his head, "Madam please, she doesn't know us or *you*, so it is a valid question."

Sniffing loudly she answered by saying, "I suppose so. Still it gets old to being asked *that* question all the time." She then nodded in agreement, although it was obvious she really hadn't wanted to, "Okay we will take such a room . . . and I suppose you want payment in advance?"

The owner's wife smiled, "Yes, since this is the first time here. If you return to where we know you then other arrangements will be made."

With a grimace she looked at her servant saying, "Pay her what she asks."

From around his neck he pulled out a rather large bag that was attached to a leather band and looked expectantly at her, "How much ma'am?"

* * *

Once in their room and sure they were alone Elsa laughed as she whispered. "Did you see how big her eyes got when she saw that bag? I think our reputation will be everywhere by the time we leave tomorrow."

"No doubt about it. Look let's take the time one would take to inspect a room, and then go get some food. Maybe this one will be better than the last one. I swore they were trying to poison us there. Yet, the rest seemed to be enjoying it."

Elsa shook her head. "It wasn't that bad. And I suspect with the passel of kids I saw here putting on a good meal is normal."

"Yeah, probably true, but one never knows . . ."

"Quit it Jay. We aren't in 'The Deeps' where we can get anything we want. It's back to what we grew up with."

Again, he laughed. "Yeah, I know sis, still one can always hope."

* * *

Leaving the Trading center and heading back out. Both felt they had done a good job of establishing their reputation or her reputation as a gem trader. Of course back in the time when "The Deeps" had been constructed what they were trading would have been close to worthless. All the gems they were trading were synthetic – fakes, but in this world such things didn't exist. When they were trying to come up with some way of tracking down the raiders and their networks they had thought and discarded lots of ideas. And in the end it came down to what they knew. Their village had dealt with semi-precious stones for generations and even though they hadn't realized it, because of their age when the village was destroyed, they had absorbed a lot of knowledge on the subject. Plus it was only the two of them, and they had no plans on adding any others to the mix. The stones they created would be easy to carry.

Once they had established what they were going to do, now came the problem of getting the gems. One thing for sure they were not equipped to go mine them themselves. So off to the archives they went. It was here they learned about artificial or synthetic gems. It seemed their ancestors had been growing them for all sorts of uses. Many of the uses, even after all the time they had spent at "The Deeps", were still well beyond comprehension. As an example of this was the use of these gems in the building of lasers. The only thing they could get out of what lasers were was concentrated light. And why any would want to concentrate light was beyond them. Still, if they survived, there might be a time where much of it made sense.

So, they spent time on learning the processes of creating synthetic gems, and once they had they created a good supply and began to build who they would be. One of the earlier times out they had joined one of the caravans and after a short time realized they would have to fine tune their aliases. On this one trip they remained who they truly were – brother and sister. Still they had changed their names, their location, and how they came to own such a supply. It had been a nervous trip, since, and by the time they had reached one of the trading centers, the majority in the caravan believed they had stolen the gems and were trying to find a place to sell them. So once they had arrived they quickly separated themselves from the caravan and disappeared back into the wilderness. They really had no need to sell the stones other than to begin to establish their worth as traders, making them interesting to the raiders. And once back inside "The Deeps", they breathed a sigh of relief and began to work harder on who they were to be.

* * *

This was their second foray out as sellers of semi-precious stones, as mistress and servant slash protector. They knew from the knowledge of their town that they had better stay with these semi-precious stones. Yes, there were stones of much higher value, but they didn't really exist in this part of the world. Both knew that when their town traders would return they would discuss the more valuable stones that came from foreign lands. And even though there seemed to be rare finds that was the problem, they were rare. So if they had arrived in one of the trading centers with a large amount of these stones they would immediately fall under suspicion. Besides the ones they were selling were the ones they knew best – which meant, in the end, they knew what the market value would be.

One of the things they studied at "The Deeps" was bartering, and the ability to buy and sell, getting the best price. There they practiced buying and selling whatever came to their minds, at times bordering on the ridiculous. And after their first failure they also studied and practiced the art of disguise, acting, and the ability to carry out the roles they had chosen. Now in the rented room both sighed a sigh of relief. With the walls between rooms being thin they really couldn't really fall out of character. Still it wasn't an issue. Another lesson they had acquired while they had been searching the archives turned out to be important in this endeavor, and that was sign language. So while they continued to carry out their roles they signed to each other.

Elsa: "So what do you think? I know with the brief time I was inside the bar there appeared to be two who might be part of the clans."

"So servant, unpack my bag. I need to get out of these travel clothes and into something comfortable!"

Jay: "I was in there less than you were, but I agree. It wouldn't have been the two at separate tables sitting against the back wall where they could watch the door would it?"

"Yes, my lady. I'll get right to it. And what outfit would you like to change into, if I may ask?"

Elsa: "Yes, the very two. They perked up the minute I entered the room and while they tried to hide it they both seemed very interested."

"I don't know . . . just pick something out. Not my finery of course, that's for when we are in the trading center . . . After all one must keep up appearances."

Jay: "Yeah, I noticed the same thing. I suspect they have left, or if not, will soon. But before they disappear to wherever they will be going, and I bet they will leave separately, and I suspect our gear that's with the horses will have been searched."

"Will the blue one work?"

Elsa: "I'm sure you're right." She looked down at what passed for a bed and shook her head. One thing for sure it didn't take long to get spoiled. Their ancestors surely had it better.

"Look at this bed. Is this supposed to be something someone of my class is to sleep on? And yes, I think the blue one will be fine. After that you can retire to your side of the room behind the barrier."

Jay: "So I guess we might want to be on guard tonight just in case one of them wants to search the room. From what I could see the owners seem to be honest. At least they are trying hard to make it a go. And the rooms are clean and neat."

"Will there be anything else?"

Elsa: "That's always a possibility, still we really haven't revealed anything to anyone as of yet. It's only been the way we are dressed and the way we act. I'm sure it will change once we have completed our first trip to this trading center. In fact I suspect that the only information our informants can make is we may be potential targets."

"No, that will be fine."

Jay: "And by keeping it small, not that we could be more than two, it means if we are attacked, it should be by a small group, and not the full attacking clan, which is a good thing. A small group we can handle, but anything larger than four or five might become a real issue. Still by booby trapping our camps we're probably as safe as we can be."

"Yes, madam. And if you need anything further . . ."

"Yes, yes, I'll let you know. Now please withdraw." She could hardly keep from laughing. Yes, she, the younger sister, bossing her older brother around, like she was their parents, or maybe the leaders of their town. Still, what they were doing was serious business, and both hoped the results would be worth the effort.

Jay, smiling because he could see the way Elsa was thinking by the smirk on her face, just shook his head, turned around and headed back behind the screen. She'd pick her own change of clothes, and he was sure it wouldn't be the blue ones they had discussed. Still, for both of them, since they were middle children, to be the one in charge like this was so very different.

"I hope everything was to your satisfaction . . . ah . . . madam?" Jason wasn't sure about this one. She and her servant were so different. And what really bothered him was the fact that neither he nor his wife had been able to figure out the difference. Yet both of them had left them nervous, and from the way both had acted around them there seemed to be no reason for this nervousness. Yeah they balked at paying up front but only for a moment. And after overhearing the conversation between them last night (With the thin walls in was impossible not to.) they had been quiet causing no trouble or problems. Still he would be glad when they were gone. Funny thing, when she had made that brief appearance in the bar she seemed out of place and genuinely apologetic. Still he couldn't help but notice the interest two of his regulars paid to her and her servant.

Breathing out loudly she said, "Yes, yes it was all good. I've slept on worst beds and the roadhouse was as quiet as one could expect." Here she paused for effect, "And I guess if it came down to it I would spend the night here again. Still only time will tell if I happen to be by this way again. It's all according to how well I do in the trading center and what price I can get for the stones I carry. After all there is more than one of these – ah, trading centers and roadhouses – around." She turned to her servant and asked, "Is all prepared, and are we ready to be on the trail? I want to be where we need to be early so we can be heading back."

"Yes, madam, the horses are prepared and awaiting us outside at this very moment. All I need to do is to place your pack on yours and we can be off."

She turned back to the owner with that dazzling smile. "Are we finished here?"

He bowed and responded by saying, "Yeah, yes ma'am we are done here. May your journey be successful." He watched as they headed out the door and once the door closed he went to one of the closest windows (real glass and expensive) and watched as they mounted and headed out towards the trading center. *Trading in stones,* he thought. *I wonder what kind?* He was about to turn around and leave when he noticed a movement outside and waited, curious as to who might still be around. The two had been the only ones staying the night and the children were at breakfast so this had to be someone else. Eventually he saw the two who he suspected were part of the clans and in a leisurely fashion began following the woman and her servant. *Now what? Am I finally going to have some proof that my thoughts about them are correct? Or is this just a coincidence?* He shook his head, coincidence or not, seeing them head out left him with an uncomfortable feeling. He wondered if the two would make their destination, but in reality they were too close to the trading center and doubted these two suspected clan members would have time to waylay them.

He felt someone come up beside him and knew it was his wife. She asked, "What has your interest this time of the morning? Oh, and by the way your breakfast is getting cold."

He turned and smiled saying, "Nothing, oh nothing really. Just caught some movement, was curious that's all." He reached out and hugged her and together they headed back to the kitchen where the family ate their meals. They had a full day ahead of them even if no guests arrived.

* * *

After Elsa and Jay left the roadhouse they went as far as necessary to give the appearance of heading off towards the trading center. The day before they had scouted the area for a place they could pull off and be completely hidden and still watch the trail. First they rode past and then carefully backtracked covering their returning tracks, dismounted and tied their mounts back and away from the main trail. Elsa turning to Jay asked, "So how long before you think those two will show?"

He shrugged. They were carrying what would have been considered a tablet back in the past. They had left a small camera with a transmitter back at the roadhouse. And while the range wasn't great it wasn't necessary. As they left he had activated the camera and pulled out the small device, watching as they trotted away. Sure enough, in a short period of time both saw the two from the bar begin to follow. They were no more than ten minutes or so behind them. Still once they had left, all four of them, Jay and Elsa suspected the two would have slowed down so as not to overtake them anywhere where it might be inconvenient, and require an explanation. "I suspect any time now." And almost before he got the words out both of them heard approaching mounts.

Both pulled back deeper behind the brush and watched. After all, what they were hearing might not be the two that were supposedly following them. This was the main route into the trading center and as a result it could be others who were heading there. Still it was early, and if both wanted to be honest they really felt it had to be the two. In a short time, and as expected, it was the two, and the suspected clan members continued on, unaware that they were the ones being watched. After the dust settled Jay and Elsa looked at each other and smiled. Jay made sure the tablet had recorded the images of the two for future reference as they continued to develop their list of known clan members and collaborators. They headed back to their mounts and began to follow the two. Their plan had been simple, and so far it had worked. They had identified two additional members of the raider clans. It wouldn't be long before they would be out of the range of the one small camera and its transmitter, but from what could be monitored there had been no others that had left the roadhouse. So they felt safe that there were no others behind them who could box them in between two groups. And that camera, it had a solar power source, would continue to record until the memory was full or they came to retrieve it.

They kept their horses at an easy gait with Elsa commenting, "It's becoming a beautiful day. I admit it was a bit chilly for me at first but invigorating to say the least. And that damn semi-auto pistol I'm carrying was really cold when I strapped it on under my outfit."

Laughing Jay said, "Yeah, I know. I could hear you yelp. Not to change the subject, but to change the subject. I wonder if those two ahead of us have figured it out yet. Or have they taken off figuring somehow we were running our mounts and they are trying desperately to catch up."

She smiled a wicked smile, "Don't know, don't care."

Just ahead in a rather large flattened area forming a large bowl sat the trading center. Like all cities, villages, and towns of the time it had a defensive wall around it. As they approached the wall grew in size – at least it seemed to – and once they were even with it they had to crane their necks to see the top. Shaking his head Jay said, "Must had taken a long time to build something like this. Hey, maybe it's one of the reasons this area is so flat."

With other thoughts running through her mind Elsa just nodded absently. She – they had never been in a trading center of this size – could feel the excitement building within her. Still, she suspected that in comparison to "The Deeps" it, over all, would be a disappointment. No one here could be aware of their true past, and all the differences between then and now. And since they had been away trying to track down the clans, and their underground, the differences had become more apparent. Still, this would be more people together in one place than either she or Jay had ever been around (other than virtually). It meant that they would be facing clan spies, let alone the normal thieves, pickpockets, flimflammers, and other scum of their world along with legitimate businesses and people trying to earn a living. To be honest, she wasn't sure if she was ready for this, let alone to be able to carry out her role.

Jay could see that Elsa was far away and deep in thought. He reached across and touched her on her arm and saw her jump slightly. He smiled when she looked across to him with irritation. "Come on sis, we have to be alert. Once inside of these walls we have to be even more so. And I suspect the two who were following us are here and will be looking for us besides all the rest of the bad that is here. We've got to concentrate."

She smiled, and once again nodded. *He's right.* It definitely wasn't the time to daydream or not concentrate on the tasks at hand. They approached the gate, and here it narrowed forcing the ones coming and going more into crowded areas making it easier for pickpockets to work their trade, and for the ones guarding easier to control the masses. Jay could see the guards were being careful, studying the crowds, and there were crowds, and any who were riding such as they were. Eventually it came their turn to pass through the gates and with a stern look from the guards they were inside. The area immediately opened into a plaza with tiles laid in a mosaic – forming patterns that one's eyes tried to make into something familiar. In the center was what would be called a fountain from the literature studied back in "The Deeps". The only issue was the fact that it simply was more of a tank, made of brickwork of course, without a flowing or spraying fountain. He wondered how it was kept filled since there didn't seem to be any obvious source.

Behind this and towards the far end of the plaza were a number of pathways leading to the different sections and just before them appeared to be a large sign like structure. It lay in the shadows making whatever was on it illegible. So they walked their horses over to it and found a map of the trading center complete with images directing any to their destinations. Elsa smiled, "Smart." Jay had to agree. It made it much easier than fumbling around. Still at the moment he couldn't respond as an equal since here he was simply a servant. As they studied the map he saw the area they wanted was to the right and down a pathway named Simmons Way. Then both of them got a whiff of cooking foods and noticed that all along the edge of the plaza were eateries, and carts. And it had been a few hours since they had eaten breakfast and both heard their insides rumble and their mouths were watering. Again Elsa quietly said, "Smart. It's obvious this place has been here awhile and they have figured out many ways to separate one's earnings from them. Should we be tourists and imbibe?"

Quietly, since they were surrounded by the crowds Jay replied, "Probably. I really don't know how long we will be here, and once we begin to negotiate with the buyers I don't know how long that will take." Then with a louder voice he asked, "Madam, would you care for some of this food that is being offered?"

Both were avoiding signing at this moment since they didn't know if there were others who might know this language of the deaf. Elsa responded, "Yes. There seems to be a lot of choices. You know what my tastes are; go find me something to tide me over." She handed Jay a small bag that carried the currency of the day (He still had the larger sack underneath his shirt). He dismounted, handing the reigns to her. She followed on her horse with Jay's following along. He looked over the delicacies before deciding, bartered with the cook, and then brought the meal back to Elsa. As he stood there with her on her horse he looked around in a casual fashion and after searching the crowds located the two who had attempted to follow them. He looked up at Elsa giving the appearance that he was asking if the food was okay, and alerted her to his discovery. She gave a slight nod acknowledging she understood and located the two herself. She realized that there seemed to be at least one other with them. *So the spies grow. Oh well, what did you expect? For the raider clans to do what they do they have to have a rather large network.*

* * *

Again, when they got back to "The Deeps", they reviewed the Intel they had added to their files. Both of them laughed when they looked at the footage of their introduction to one of the buyers of gems, (They carried personal cameras that recorded all their actions.). Even though, at the time, Jay hadn't been too happy. When Elsa had approached one of the shops that appeared to be doing quite well, and the proprietor saw her approaching there seemed to be a look of distaste on his face. It appeared he had just eaten something quite disagreeable. Elsa remembered that kind of look from the past and then glanced at Jay with devilment in her eyes. He had shaken his head but she just couldn't help herself. She walked right up to him with an innocent look and asked, as if she was new to this, "Do you purchase semi-precious stones?"

In the corner of her eye she could see Jay wasn't happy with her, but she was tired of the attitude she was seeing around her. In truth she probably knew more about gems because of their study back in "The Deeps", and, of course, growing up around them, than this merchant or any of the others would in two lifetimes.

With a haughty expression he asked, "Why would I want to deal with the likes of you?"

She smiled a wicked smile saying, "Oh maybe because I have what you want, and I'm not talking about intimate relationships between the two of us." She could see the shocked expression from her blunt response. Such a thing from a woman was unheard of after all.

"And what is it that you could have that would interest me . . . and I'm not talking about what you suggested."

With an innocent expression she asked, "Is it not true you deal in these stones?" Here she pulled a couple out of the small pouch she had been wearing around her neck on a leather cord. When she had dumped a couple out she made sure that others within the pouch were visible. She saw a change come over the buyer and inwardly smiled. *Greed seems to always win out in the end doesn't it? Well, his attitude just cost him, because I'm only going to show him, but not offer to sell any to him.* "And I thought you were the type who was interested in such items as these, but I can see that you won't deal with a woman so it's your loss. There are plenty of others here who will be interested in what I have to offer . . . and don't go where that statement can take you or how you may want to go with that." She turned and put the stones back into the pouch and said to her servant, "Come we will not deal with this one." And with that the two of the left the shop.

She could see that Jay was angered by the way she had handled the situation. Because of the roles they had set up he couldn't say anything. Still she knew once they had left she would hear it. "Okay, I know, maybe I came on a little strong", she whispered, "but he was such an ass and deserved it. Still I think I accomplished what we set out to do. I'm sure you saw that there were a couple of others who were in the shop whose eyes grew large when they saw what we or I had. I think if we head back out to the plaza area that we will be approached by some of his competitors, and the word will be going out making us 'persons of interest' to certain people we are trying to locate."

"Maybe so, still we don't need a reputation where everybody in this world will shy away because of you and your attitude. Yeah, I know there are many in this world who think the only thing a woman is good for is producing the next generation, or to take care of one's needs, but most aren't that way and you know it. Again, I know we find more that are like this in the more established markets and higher end items. I suspect, as the archives have shown us, that some women are drawn to wealth and what it offers. In a sense they are exactly what these men think women are. So it is no surprise that they have such an attitude. Look we – you have to be approachable."

Anger flashed in her eyes, "And what is that supposed to mean? Am I to grovel at their feet because they feel so superior? Never happen. When our world came apart and somehow we both survived I vowed never again would I submit unless it is on my own terms. Yeah, I know, if I was to fall into the same situation as I did earlier I'd have no choice. I'd be raped and beat up until they were through with me and to be able to escape a second time would probably never happen. Look, I'm sorry, but he just set me off. I promise I'll be good."

He had trailed behind like he was supposed to in this role and their conversation had been kept low and private. Suddenly they were back at the plaza and to his surprise it had to be close to midday. While the sun felt warm and comfortable at the moment, especially since they had been in the shadows created by the buildings, with a cool breeze that had whistled down the narrow pathways, soon it would become hot. "We need to find a place to sit and see if you are right about this." He looked around and found an area that had been roped off. Inside were a number of tables and chairs. They were sitting under a small copse of trees. When he looked closer they appeared to be cottonwood trees. He had always loved the sound of the wind blowing through them. The sounds were soothing causing him to relax. He could see that Elsa had seen them also and with a nod of her head they went over to the entrance which had a gate across it. Both saw someone standing next to the gate with a table in front and inwardly both shook their heads. The trading centers were obviously a place to make money and everything had a price. Even entering this area would cost them.

Looking expectantly at them the man stated four copper bars to spend the afternoon. She looked over at Jay and said, "Pay the man. I'm looking to get out of the sun." Jay pulled out the necessary fee and both entered, found a table that was both isolated, and still visible. So if any of the other buyers came looking they'd be easy to find.

And that was exactly how it had gone down. In the end, she had been right and others came looking. In the end they had sold their supply of stones furthering their reputation. In the end they had performed the same routine at four other trading centers. And in each case they were able to identify more who were either part of the raider clans or had to be working for or with them. Ahead of them was a lot of work necessary to begin to unravel the underground network where the raiders sold their stolen items.

While it was possible the clans only traded among themselves, they both doubted it. And some of the rumors they were now hearing were disturbing. Both hoped that these rumors would prove false in the end but knew within their own hearts that they were probably true. Making the nightmare that Elsa had lived through mild in comparison.

The rumors spoke of slavery and the slave markets to the east in an area of flat lands and rolling hills. A place where the grasslands went on forever, and men, women, and children were the commodities. Yes, as property to be bought and sold – to be used up, and once used up, to be thrown away as worthless, as a broken tool, or trash. The only way they would ever learn if these rumors were true would be to follow the routes inland, to see for themselves. But for now they had other plans. Maybe if they were successful in their plans of revenge, then, and only then would they find their way to where these markets were rumored to exist.

It had bothered both to realize that there were some out there who appeared to be honest merchants but were actually – and they had discovered the term while studying – "fences" for the clans and made the stolen merchandise legitimate items to be resold to unsuspecting people. Again, through their studies, they had found that this was something that appeared to be common no matter what part of history they searched or studied. What was it about society that led to ones who lived this lifestyle? Did they not realize the suffering that the ones who had originally owned this stuff had gone through, or did they not care? Both wondered how one could not care. Yet, what had happened to the two of them, and more so to Elsa said that there were many who didn't care at all for others. And so they pressed harder in finding the small clues, and began to map out the routes, the trails, and they began to track the ones they either suspected, or knew to be part of the underground network. And to the surprise of both of them it had turned out to be huge. Much more than just the two of them would ever be able to cover or handle. Still in the end they wouldn't give up.

* * *

Jay, shaking his head as they looked over a photo map of the desert said, "I never realized, first off how big this desert is, and secondly how many routes actually exist on the edge here close to us. I suspect none of the villages and towns, like ours, are really aware of this. After all, the desert has always been considered a place of death, and it really is. But it means that we know so little about it or the fact that it is an easy and generally a safe way to move without being seen."

Elsa had been leaning over the table resting on her hands and arms remaining quiet. There was no doubt this area was huge, but what intrigued her was the fact that not too much further in – to the east – there seemed to be something that could pass, or could have passed as a town or village, or maybe even a city. And if that was so, how did the ones who lived there live? What did they do, and how did they ever get any water? At least by being here at "The Deeps", it was obvious that there was water under the desert. Still it wasn't easy to reach. And it had been the old technology that had found and reached it, not what existed today. Yeah, their old village or town – since it bordered on being a town – had a couple of wells. But in comparison to the depth of the wells that kept the tanks filled here, they were shallow – hand dug – no deeper than sixty feet. (Feet – a measurement that they had learned, again, from the library, and one of the two prominent measuring systems of old.) The maps they were using were actually photos, images taken after the bombardment, overlaying a topo map so they could both see the actual terrain and see the elevations by the lines added. When the photos were taken neither had any real idea since a lot of time had passed after the bombardment, but it helped visualize the land. Still it made it easier to understand what the actual lands were that the maps represented.

She looked up and could see Jay concentrating on the trails they had added to the map over time. Yet as far as she could see there were none heading out deep into the desert, and none heading towards this hidden city. More to herself she asked, "I wonder? Hmmm . . ."

Jay looked up with a questioning look on his face and asked, "Wonder what?"

"Huh? Oh, I'm sorry . . . Was speaking more to myself. But look Jay, doesn't this area out here look like it could be a town or city? And while it's obvious that there's no one or nothing there now, it appears at one time there was."

He was irritated for a moment since they were trying to come to some conclusion as to whether there was some type of schedule that the ones who plied these trails were on. But from what little they had there wasn't any proof. They'd need to place hidden cameras on them and then go collect the data, then once collected try to compile all of it. And all of this would take time – something they'd been spending a lot of. He glanced over and immediately saw what she had seen and wondered why he hadn't noticed it himself. At that moment he knew it was because the rest seemed unimportant. He studied it for a few moments and then leaned over to get a better look. "I think you may be right. Why would anybody want to live out in the middle of the desert?"

She smiled, "You're asking me? I know I wouldn't."

He shook his head and smiled back. "Yeah, I was asking generally, not that you didn't know that, still this is intriguing. Look we have a few days before we should go out again. And we need to make some decisions on how we want to try to track our targets.

So, if I get the gist of this, maybe you'd like to go and check it out?"

"No, no, not really . . . although . . . hmmm . . . it is intriguing, as you said. Maybe it would be worth a visit." She thought about possibly heading out to that village to the south and getting the horses they used during their time out as gem traders but thought better about it. Neither knew anything about this part of the desert, and while it might save them some time, in the end it just might kill the animals. They'd be better to do this on foot.

* * *

Distances on a map, and on the ground always seemed to be very different. What seemed somewhat close, and where their destination turned out to be was far different. Looking at the map they had planned their route and again it had seemed to be well thought out. In the end what they had thought might be trails weren't and some had changed over time from when the maps were first made to now. If they had thought about it, it probably would have been one of those "DUH" moments. Even though things changed slowly over time, they still changed. And to not factor that possibility in had been stupid. Still they had brought plenty with them, especially water. Jay had learned his lesson back when he had almost died because he didn't have enough. Yet, as they got closer it became more and more apparent that there had been something out here in the middle of the desert.

To the shock of both the first signs that there had to be something here were large fields that had to have been worked deep in the past. And considering the size they probably could have put eight or nine of their own worked fields inside of just one of them. Standing there in awe Jay looked around. "Look at the size of this thing. And there must be at least forty or fifty of these things. How'd they do it?"

She was just as surprised as Jay. And while she knew the question he asked was something she had no answer to, she understood. After all she had worked those fields back in their home and she had felt theirs had been large. But now here before her was proof that they weren't. "I really don't know. I know what it takes to work fields and to work these fields like we did would require, oh I don't know, maybe hundreds for each one." All she could do was shake her head.

The breezes were hot; no surprise considering it was late in the day. "I guess," Jay replied, "we'd better find a place for the night, and spend tomorrow looking this over, and then head back. Knowing this is here, and we probably, now that we've been here once, can make better time next time, might be important. And I guess if we want to be honest, here is further proof of the old technology that we've been learning so much about. Still I never thought about it from this end."

She had to agree. "Look somewhere close to here, if I'm reading this map correctly, should be where the people lived. Maybe we can find something that will get us out of the elements. It surprises me but it looks like there still might be some trees alive – how I don't know." Both looked further to the east and even Jay had to admit that what they were seeing did look like trees. As they worked their way across the abandoned fields they came across small canals showing how the fields were possibly irrigated. Still it was only one possibility. To them it seemed to be a waste of water. With the heat of the desert much of what was here would evaporate and not provide what was needed. Still they knew so little about how it was done and their conclusions could be completely wrong.

Shortly they found themselves on what they would consider a main trail, but knew that in the past such large trails would have been called roads. It seemed to border many of the fields, and once they reached the edge of the fields it curved away and disappeared into the distance. In places they found it to be covered in sand blown in over the ages, and in others it disappeared completely being destroyed by what had happened to this world in their past. In fact just before entering what they considered the town they had to skirt around a large crater. They could immediately see the damage it had caused, destroying much of what was here. "I guess this is probably what finished this place", Jay said. She couldn't disagree. Even after all of this time the scorch marks on much of what still stood were visible to the naked eye. Then Jay continued, "I for one am glad I wasn't here when all this took place."

When he had stated this she felt a shudder go through her as she imagined how it must have been. Yeah, they had seen the destruction through the cameras that had recorded the event. But actually being at one of the places where a strike happened made it more real even if time had dulled the impact. "How'd any of us survive? I know 'The Deeps' had been created to give us a chance, and it failed. Still some of us remained – enough that we are here now. How? I mean how? Look at this – I mean really look at this. I suspect that this is probably a minor strike in comparison to others; still it destroyed most of what is here. And maybe, and this is just a guess since I have no way of proving it – maybe the survivors of this place moved to the mountains on the edge of this desert and eventually became us."

Jay thought a moment as they continued to stand there, "That's a possibility. Still how would one know where the ones came from that inhabited the areas outside of this desert. I mean it sounds logical that our ancestors could have come from here. Still we have no way of knowing if any survived this and we could be building fairytales because it seems like a strong possibility." He shook his head with the total impossibility of it all. "I wouldn't even know where to begin to figure that one out.

She had to agree, how could they? There was too much unwritten history. And she was sure that chaos reigned supreme as the survivors tried desperately, well, to survive. "I don't know if we'll find anything fully standing or not but maybe there are a few sheltered areas that were missed." Looking around again with new eyes she thought she could see where there were foundations of some of the destroyed buildings. It was hard to tell, but she suspected that the further they got away from this impact area the less the damage would be. As they stood on top of the crater rim she noticed that even after all of this time that there still were patterns spreading in all directions with the crater being the center. The scars ran deep and even time couldn't erase them.

Jay looked to the south and noticed that the lands seemed to drop away somewhat. So maybe there was some of the original buildings still standing since there was a chance they would have been protected from the blast. Still knowing nothing about how the energy waves, the heat and fire, the winds created would have acted there was really no way of knowing. Turning back to Elsa he said as he pointed, "Look there might be a possibility that something might have survived over there."

She looked in the direction where he was pointing and could see how the area seemed a bit lower. It could be, but she doubted it. Even after all of this time the power and destruction caused by this impact was highly visible. *What truly could survive such a thing?* She shook her head saying, "I don't know about that, but let's go look anyway." They headed in the direction indicated by Jay and passed by outlines of foundations where homes had one stood. In many ways, even after all of this time it was a depressing sight. For Jay it reminded him personally of their home even though after the fires had died and left a few ruins there was still more back there than here. The difference lay in the fact that their village or town had been destroyed by man, while this place had been destroyed from the skies. Destroyed by an uncaring universe where life and death was determined by the living and dying of suns. So what happened here meant nothing in the overall scheme of things.

They reached the distant area that he had seen back at the crater and found that there was a small cliff like area, and yes it did provide partial protection to some that were furthest down. Still everything showed signs of damage and none escaped the fires. It said volumes about the amount of heat generated with the impact. At least, in his own mind, death had to have come quickly to the residents, unlike the members of their village. They found a trail that ran down into the small valley and towards the far end found a partially standing home. Here they set up camp for the night. Tomorrow they would head back after some exploring. He suspected that what they had found here would leave marks on both of them as the past became real to them. Not some images on a screen, or words written down describing what transpired during that horrible time. Still what they found here said that it was possible to live in the desert and be successful. The size of this place had been a surprise and the fact they were growing things meant the lands were fertile – something to remember.

* * *

They had been back at "The Deeps" for at least a week. In a way they had fallen back to the way of tracking time in the ways of their ancestors and were no longer using the lunar calendar. In a sense they had no choice once Ed had become their teacher and mentor. He and all who had lived here in this place had maintained the old system of years, months, weeks, and days. Both were studying the images they had taken of known agents of the raider clans when the alarms went off again. Shaking his head Jay asked, "I wonder what's broken this time."

She laughed remembering how much in awe of this place they were when they had first entered it. And now with all the breakdowns, and equipment needing maintenance, reality had set in leaving them understanding the weaknesses in the systems, and the facility itself. Yeah, originally it might have seemed to be something from the mythological gods, but now it was obvious this place was manmade. "I guess we'd better go find out, don't you think?" As they listened to the alarm both realized that what they were hearing wasn't one announcing a breakage or failure but one originating from the security system. This caused chills to run up and down their spines. Their light hearted approach turned dead serious when they realized the difference, and both sprinted to the closest security office.

Out of breath once they arrived they changed the views the monitors were showing to the cameras inside the Welcome and Processing center, and to the cameras outside the facility. The ones monitoring the inside showed a vacant center. Turning back to the other set they watched as the images rotated through the different cameras showing empty desert until one showed what looked like two individuals working their way south. They zoomed in and immediately recognized the two as members of the clans – ones who scouted out potential targets. In fact they were the two they had seen in that bar inside the roadhouse just outside of one of the larger trading centers. Both looked at each other with Jay asking, "I wonder where they are going?"

She smiled, "You're asking me?" She looked back at the monitor as did her brother who had switched the images to another monitor.

He shook his head as he remembered what he had called these things back in the beginning – *windows that see into the distance.* He had to admit for someone ignorant of the technology it was an apt description. He leaned back and stood back up. He had been using the shelve that ran the length of the monitors to lean on. "We need to follow them. Let's grab our packs and see where they might lead us. We might finally get some leads on where the clans travel and camp. That surely would help, especially in our future planning. You know from our training we've been doing we really need to know more."

"Can't deny that. Okay, let's do this, and maybe this is the break we need. We knew we would get one sooner or later."

* * *

By the time they had vacated "The Deeps", the ones they wanted to follow were out of sight. Somehow the two had approached closer to their location than the ones who normally passed this way, thusly setting off the alarms. And normal here meant once or twice a year. After all, their location was at least a full day's travel inside the desert. And that would be if you made a direct shot here. Normally, following the trails that led one through the area it was closer to three. Still "The Deeps" wasn't close to any of the known trails, and thusly why it had never been discovered. Any who had to travel the desert knew they must stay on the proven trails or die. It was just that simple. This desert, and Jay with Elsa suspected it was the same with any desert, was unforgiving. You lived by its rules or you died. There were no second chances here. Although, if Jay wanted to admit it, he, in a sense, had been given one by finding that water source so many years in the past. One that originally had been natural but later had been converted by man.

As they tried to figure out where the two had gone he knew, back at that fateful day that both of their lives had been changed forever, so much could have gone differently with neither surviving the raider attack. Elsa should have died back in the raider camp from the abuse she endured, and he should have died of thirst, yet now years later here they were. "Those two were on foot how could they have disappeared so fast? I mean this is the desert after all, and mostly open. Yeah I know, that overall it isn't true. Still it's open enough that someone shouldn't disappear this easily."

Here Elsa smiled a knowing smile. "Right. After all, you didn't get lost here, and I didn't disappear here, and something as large as 'The Deeps' shouldn't be hidden here, yet all of it is fact. And, as you so apply pointed out, there are badlands, canyons, gullies, ravines, washes, and so many other things here that is unknown unless you travel it."

He shrugged; yup all of what she said was true. "I guess if you state it that way . . . I don't know, we should only be fifteen or twenty minutes behind them and yet there's nothing. Should we give it up this time or push on?"

She stopped with her hands on her hips. "I don't know. We haven't seen any sign of them, and this sand isn't good for producing tracks. Maybe we should head back and think this through. Besides whomever they are could be stopping now and then watching their back trail. I know, especially after our training, I would."

"Good point. All we would need to do now is walk into some type of trap or ambush and then all we are looking to do, all we have planned, would be over." He looked down at the ground and shook his head. "Okay, let's head back. We really weren't ready anyway." She nodded in agreement. For a short time they remained where they were looking over the vast desert that surrounded them and then began their return. Here they spread out and kept a distance between the two so that they could watch more of the area. All they needed was to be followed themselves revealing their hidden location.

* * *

"Well, that was an exercise in futility. I think I could use a shower." Elsa headed for her room. And as she did she stopped and turned around seeing Jay was still standing where he had been. "Look we need to come up with something soon."

Once again he shrugged, she was right they did need to do a better job of this. Maybe it was time to send a message to the raiders. Maybe it was time to make them worry like they did to every other person in the area. The time they had spent putting together their list, and both felt it was accurate, maybe it was time to test their skills with those sniper rifles and remove a few of these small teams. "Okay, you're right. Go take your shower. I think it's time we give back."

"What do you mean by that?"

He waved at her in a shushing manner, "Just go clean up then meet me back in this security office."

With a questioning look and with it in her voice she said, "Okay." She turned back around and headed to her room. Even that short jaunt into the desert had left her feeling sweaty and dirty. And a quick cool rinse would do wonders.

He headed back to the closest security office and brought up the information on the numerous members of the clans and their collaborators they had identified and what they knew about them. It was time to find their patterns so they could be ambushed and he wanted enough of the information available before him so he could present it to Elsa when she returned. And even though they hadn't found any of the temporary camps, or where they clans actually lived, if they were successful on this first part of their planned operation a message would still be sent. The clans would know that they were just as vulnerable as the ones they attacked and destroyed. Who knows, maybe, in the end, it would make the raiders more cautious, less likely to attack. Here he laughed a bitter laugh. *Yeah, like that's going to happen.* He knew that a few of their own were killed in their attacks. It couldn't be any other way. So losing a few of their infiltrators would only mean they would have to get new ones inserted. And in the end it would simply mean a loss of time, nothing more.

* * *

It was their fifth foray out into the world of the hidden trails the raiders, their collaborators and spies used. So far they had been successful, as snipers, to remove from this earth nine confirmed collaborators or raider clan members. They had been sure of their guilt and had picked the loneliest most isolated areas to make their attacks. In any of these operations they had alternate sites to work from. When they took these clan members out it had to be in a place where there would be no witnesses. And once they had confirmed the kills – from a distance of course – they would inspect the area with their glasses, clean up any sign they had been here, police their brass, and silently withdraw. Both had to admit that there was some satisfaction in seeing the raiders take casualties, and maybe with their attacks they were beginning to make the raider clans doubt, maybe be a little tentative in their future plans. Of course there was no way for them to know since they had no one on the inside. Still what they were doing had to have some effect. Both knew it would be that way if it was them.

Both were in what was known in the past as "Ghillie suits", named after the inventor of this method of camouflage who had created it for hunting. It made them virtually invisible. It had taken months to set this ambush up. The two they were targeting were very good at disappearing at inopportune times, to take alternate and unexpected routes, and to simply disappear for a period of time. In fact it had taken a while before they could establish the fact the ones they were waiting for had been part of the clan network. Eventually all the pieces fell into place and it had been an ambush set up by their two targets that finally had identified them for who they were.

Elsa and Jay had been inside one of the trading centers watching the two when they suddenly withdrew and left. It had been sudden and unexpected, leaving both Jay and Elsa wondering what could be happening. The subjects had never acted this way before. They looked at each other and when they were sure no one could see them they quickly signed questions. They heard a commotion and realized that one of the smaller caravans was preparing to leave and wondered if this might be the reason for the sudden change of character. They decided to follow the caravan from a safe distance. In fact they headed out a few minutes later and climbed some of the ridges, with each of them taking opposite sides of the main trail so they could cover the whole area. With the glasses they carried they didn't need to be close, and they could see far ahead – such an advantage that didn't exist in this world of today.

They stayed with them keeping in contact with each other with small tactical radios following the caravan throughout the day. From what they could observe, it appeared it had a good sized group of armed guards. In truth they didn't know what the caravan was carrying if anything. Still from the number of guards there must have been something of value. Yet, the two persons of interest had simply disappeared, and as they watched the caravan settle down for the night they began to think that someone unknown to them simply had come up to the persons of interest and had given them a change of assignment.

As darkness approached, both remained back where they could observe the area, the camp, and any of the approaches to the camp. Both had switched to night vision goggles and continued to observe. Still nothing happened and it was getting cold. Neither had anything with them to combat the chill and as they became more chilled and uncomfortable both had come to a decision to give up and set up their own camp. It was then Elsa radioed, "I see movement!"

"Where?" He whispered back.

"Towards your side, coming down a small ravine . . . It's hidden from you but give it a couple and you should see them also."

He tried hard to pick up the moment but couldn't. He looked over towards where Elsa was located and quietly stated, "UT OH."

"Now what?" She asked.

"Another group approaching the caravan camp from your side." Zooming in he realized that two of the leaders of this group that he could see were the two persons of interest. "And guess what, the two we've been following are part of the ones I can see. I think we have our answer."

From the tone of Elsa's voice it was obvious that she wanted to warn the caravan when she quietly said, "Yeah, I really didn't need it confirmed this way . . . I wish . . . oh well."

"Yeah I know, but we can't. All we can hope is the guards are well trained and they can take care of what's about to happen." Still it was obvious that the ones that were about to attack knew what they were doing. While the area the caravan had picked to set up camp had been a good one – especially for defense – even the best could be overwhelmed or compromised. And in the end it was that way as the attackers first came in from one side drawing attention away from the main force that was hidden on the opposite side of the encampment. And with the defenders looking towards where the first attack appeared they were unprepared for the second. It was over quickly. Both withdrew once the outcome was obvious and finally came back together miles away from the site of the attack. They felt sick and had their answer, now it was the planning and finding the patterns of their targets then picking the best possible locations for the ambush.

And so here they were on this day awaiting their targets to show. If all went to plan it would be over in moments and they would disappear into the surrounding desert as the dust the winds picked up and blew around. The sun was hot on their backs and they were cross canyon from each other giving both a complete view of the portion of the trail they would be targeting. Both had a few blind spots, but overall what one couldn't see the other could. Both yearned for a drink but it had to wait. The hours drug by with only a circling buzzard and the lengthening shadows to mark the passing of time. Then their tension rose as they caught movement on the trail. Both, using their glasses, confirmed that the ones who were approaching were their targets. Then both searched the back trail and found it vacant as the blue steel sky which held no clouds. Jay said, "Clear. Take the target closest to me, and I'll take the other. We are live."

There were a couple of loud cracks like the sound of thunder, then only silence. Nothing now moved in the isolated canyon where the trail wound its way through. From the surrounding ridges there was movement then nothing, with only the buzzard to witness what had transpired here.

* * *

With these successes then came the work of finding one of the encampments the raiders used, and by trailing a couple of the collaborators – success. And with this first one finally located, they would be going in this very night, using the tactics they had learned and find out if all the time and effort they put in was worth it. One thing for sure, if, in the end, they screwed it up neither of them would be alive to regret it. So here they were, leaning back against one of the banks of a wash, waiting for the sun to set. Soon it would be time.

* * *

It was full dark when they moved cautiously towards the canyon entrance. They split up and arrived from opposite directions. Even with the lookouts being high up it was doubtful they could be seen. Still it was better to be safe than sorry. They had chosen one of the darkest nights to make this attack. With the night vision goggles they had no problems seeing and moving in silence. Once they began their approach there would be no speaking and everything would be handled by hand signals. They had thought about taking out the lookouts with silenced sniper rifles but decided against it simply because they had no idea when the ones would be relieved and replaced with new lookouts. On this foray they carried 9MM automatic pistols for protection, leaving the rifles at their rendezvous point.

Leaning against the canyon walls that rose up into the night sky, leaving a dark shadow, blocking out the stars producing an almost complete darkness, they with their night vision equipment, had no problems at all. With the prearranged signals one led down the narrow trail with the other following and watching their rear. To the surprise of both of them the trail into this canyon turned out to be short. It opened into a large area where they could hear water running, and see many campfires burning. These fires indirectly lit the area reflecting off the canyon walls and revealed the number of tents within the encampment. It shocked both of them by the sheer size. It looked like this hidden oasis could easily hold twice of what was here, and the raiders who were here had to number in the three digits. One thing for sure they couldn't afford to be seen. If they were there was zero chance of survival.

Now that they had a chance to see what they were facing, they set plastic explosives along the exit point of this camp. Then moving as close as they dare they set up a number of tripwire explosives with the plan of setting off a flash bang to startle the camp into action, and to hit the number of traps they had set. They lined the walls of the canyon with remote and tripwire claymore mines, when set off would shred the camp with its deadly loads. Both pulled back and began seeding the area with surface antipersonnel mines, followed by lining the canyon walls along the trail with more claymore mines. These would be set off remotely when they could see the majority of the raiders heading out of the canyon trail and beginning their exit into the desert, and additionally more set up by the trail exit (Some, close to the encampment would have trip wires).

Once the two of them were back in the desert they set, in a fan shape, another series of claymore mines with every other one having a tripwire. The others could be individually set off as needed. Now it was time to get this show on the road. With Elsa remaining back at their rendezvous point Jay went far enough in so he could see the camp and tossed the flash bang, turned and immediately ran. He knew he didn't have a lot of time before the camp would be stirred into action by the explosion.

The flash bang had a delay of about ten seconds giving him time to be at least half way out by the time it went off. He heard it explode followed by a flash of light that lit up the trail briefly casting heavy shadows on the narrow trail walls, turning night into day. It caused the images from the goggles to go white as the light overwhelmed the electronics. Just as quickly it returned to darkness and everything was as it was.

Only now it was as if he had stirred up a really nasty ant or hornet nest. He could hear screaming, shouting, and confusion coming from behind. After this came the next in a series of explosions as the traps were tripped setting off the explosive devices they had left in the camp. Then he was back in the desert. They had figured the guards, or lookouts would be looking back at the camp when the action started, and if not, that was exactly why Elsa was where she was. With the lookouts in her scope of the sniper rifle she could target and eliminate them if they proved to be a problem. Eventually they would be eliminated anyway. There were to be no witnesses to what was transpiring here. No one could learn of how this was done or by whom.

With his heavy breathing from running the full distance, Elsa could hear Jay approaching, and eventually she spotted him. He apparently was alone which eased the worry somewhat. There was still much that had to happen and she needed to return her concentration to those lookouts. Jay jumped into the depression where they had set up got his breathing back in control and began to watch the entrance. After what seemed like too long of a period of time, and with his impatience growing, the first of the raiders showed at the entrance.

This should mean the camp was on full alert status, and it was time to set off the charges they had placed around the camp including the claymores that lined the canyon walls along the narrow trail. Between the two traps very little to nothing should be alive afterwards. He pushed the button, heard and saw the glow from the explosions. He then counted to three and set off the claymores placed along the canyon trail. Both waited to see if any more of the raiders would be coming out through the opening. Jay picked up his sniper rifle and with Elsa took out the lookouts that had exposed themselves as they tried to figure out what was happening.

Then a small ragged element of the raiders entered the desert. They appeared to be pretty shaken and leaderless, but still began to spread out. All of them were in the range of the mines set up earlier, and most were killed when they tripped the claymores. The rest died from the ones that had been remotely set off, or by being shot, and then there was silence.

Nothing moved, the smell of gunpowder, and explosives drifted off into the night air and everything returned to the normal quiet night sounds. In the distance and in the area of the encampment they could see a glow. It appeared the camp area was burning. Both remained in the ready position not sure if they had accomplished their goal or not. Only in the daylight, towards evening, when they could venture back inside that canyon of death, would they know.

* * *

Back at The Deeps, they talked about the successes and failures of this venture (And there are always failures.). While it had been satisfying to give back what these raiders had been doing, it still didn't give them any closure. It was a bothersome and painful thing to extinguish that many lives in such a short period of time. It made both of them realize that war is hell. And while this wasn't a declared war, it was the same thing with them being the avenging ones against the destroyers. They expected to feel good about what they had accomplished but instead found it had left a bitter taste in their mouths. They had gone from innocents to the killers of men, women, and children. And no matter how they tried to rationalize it, both knew something had changed and they would never be able to go back. It seemed to have affected Elsa deeply – very deeply, but it had left its mark upon Jay also. Still, to have been this successful on their first attack on one of the raider camps had been rewarding.

RECONCILLIATION

Both of them remembered how it was after their attack. At this point neither knew how successful they had been. It had been a night attack, and while the engagement appeared to be short, in the end, more time had passed than they thought. Neither got a lot of sleep being on an adrenaline rush. So the next day they remained where they were to see if any more of the raiders would be exiting the canyon. Finally the sun was heading towards the distant hills marking the close of another day. Jay and Elsa remained in that shallow depression all that day continuing to watch the skies where the raiders had their hidden camp. The smoke that had come out of that canyon was finally beginning to disappear. And the silence that surrounded them was almost overwhelming. And while that last few hours in that silence seemed to drag, it continued to move on unconcerned by the amount of death and destruction that happened around it the night before.

It had been crazy there for a short period of time. Well, it seemed like a short period of time to them while they were involved in the fire fight. With the explosions, the mines being set off by the retreating and attacking raiders, and the attempt by both of them to keep all of this in their sight and not be flanked by someone who may have figured a way around the ambush – the night vision goggles had been the deciding factor. But eventually silence reigned supreme, the dust and smoke outside of the canyon, and here on the desert floor, settled down. The stench of death, of burned flesh, and the smell of the smoke from both the exploding mines and burning bodies drifted off as the desert breezes picked up in the morning sunrise and moved the odors away from the sight of destruction.

Both of them felt drained, tired, beat, and as the silence continued to assail them, they found their attention and alertness beginning to fade, with the need to sleep, to rest and replace their flagging energy reserves. Neither had expected this. Even with the descriptions of battles, the visual recordings they had studied back in "The Deeps", none of it had prepared them for actual battle. And even the ambushes that they had set up and accomplished didn't prepare them. Yes, the classes they had taken to make such an attack had warned them that there was no way such things could actually prepare them, but they hadn't believed it. Yet, now after living through their first major battle, they had to admit the instructors were correct. The chaos, the noise, the smells, the intensity, and yes the sounds of death, and of the ones who died slowly, ate away at their humanity. Both wondered how the raiders, the ones they had just brought down, could do this. It made no sense.

Jay, looking at Elsa said, "Look why don't you nod out for a few. I'll wake you just before sunset. If nothing has happened by then we'll recon the canyon and make sure we were completely successful. There can be no survivors."

Shaking her head, "No, that's all right. I think if I fell asleep right now I'd begin having those vivid nightmares all over again. This brought it back to me, even though we were the ones dishing it out. You really want to go in there?"

"Not really, but I really don't think we have much of a choice. Someone could still be alive in there waiting for darkness and then try to escape, and we can't allow that. If any of what we did here, and how we did it gets out then it will be close to impossible to do it again. So it has to be everybody period. And no I don't look forward to the idea of being up close and personal to finish this, but if it is necessary I . . . we must. With this attack we've officially began our war against the evil in this world – not that those ambushes we performed counted, because they did. Whether this is right or wrong doesn't matter now, since it is over and done.

"If any are to escape and we have been seen then it will make us targets for any of the raider clans out there. Especially now since we ply the trading centers. And there is no way we can know every one of them or every individual who resides within those clans. So any time we take on a target like this it has to be total – no witnesses, no one left alive. And if either of us gets squeamish then all we have to remember is what these and others like them have done to our town, our village, and our people. In a sense we're being generous by just killing them. You know personally that they have and will take it much further to include torture and rape. And however much pain and agony it causes their victims it doesn't matter. All we're doing is killing them as fast as we can.

"Whether this makes us better than they are, I don't know. But I feel there has to be some type of justice in this world, someone willing to try and set things right. For whatever the reason we were chosen. We learned of the old technology which has allowed us a great advantage over these killers, rapists, and torturers. I just hope we are up to the task, and that in the end we do not become so hardened that such sights mean nothing."

Shaking her head Elsa said, "Quite a speech, Jay. But how does one not get sick over watching people die like this? Yeah I know I was a victim of theirs and through whatever providence escaped. And I don't know how or why I ended up finding you and where you had been hiding. So maybe this is what we are supposed to do. Still, as I just said, this makes me physically ill. I don't care whether they were good or bad people, only that they were people. They had their lives and future ahead of them. And who knows, maybe some would have had a change of heart and left. But we've made sure that none of it is a possibility. We have made sure their future ended today.

"Are we right doing this? I don't know. Do I feel good about doing this? To be honest I feel numb. I thought I'd feel great getting some payback to ones like this . . . but I'm feeling nothing, nothing at all. I know we've opened the war between us and the others, and probably there's no turning back. Still, even now, I'm not sure about this. Can we go back? Of course not. But before we do this again I'm going to have to do some serious soul searching." She stopped a moment and saw the shadows lengthening. "I guess we had better go in and check our handy work. Looks like it won't be long before the sun sets behind the mountains. I suspect the canyon is already deep in shadows."

"Okay, yeah you're right. We have a lot to think about. So shall we see if this has been as complete as it needs to be?"

* * *

Two weeks had gone by since their successful attack on the raider camp. Elsa still was abnormally quiet, and had a white pallor to her. It was something that worried Jay, but he understood, not that it helped. This was something she would have to come to terms with on her own. Once they had gotten back to "The Deeps", they had discussed what had worked and what seemed to be a little weak. But it couldn't cover the shock when they entered that silent camp with the dead lying all around. Had it been only men then maybe it wouldn't have been so bad. Still for both of them, other than when the village was destroyed, neither had seen so much death concentrated in one place.

Elsa caught her breath when she saw the dead child, a young girl. He could see that seeing this brought Elsa immediately back to the attack on the village, and the killing of everyone who was there, other than the ones the raiders had taken back to their camp for their pleasure. She froze and refused to go on, and there was nothing he could do to persuade her. So he had her rig up the sensors and small cameras, find a way up to the top where they had seen the lookouts, and find a place to place a small antenna so they could monitor the canyon entrance. He continued his search through the camp and found no one breathing. Even all the animals – pets and such – were gone.

He had to admit that this scene of destruction left its mark on him also. And if he really wanted to admit it, it brought images back from what he had found when he had returned to their town after its end, finding the town burning, and all the bodies lying as they fell. And what made this one worse – and he knew no one in the raider camp – lay in the fact that he and Elsa were responsible. He knew since they had been back Elsa had only been going through the motions. It seemed more like she was sleepwalking than living.

Like back on that day when he had left to find them food and other needs, he worried she'd go over the deep end and he'd lose her forever. Again, like that time, he couldn't find the words to console her, to make her better, to help. She, like he, went into this with their eyes open. Still when someone has never done anything like this, how can one claim to know? He wondered, as he suspected she, how could the ones who were raiders do this kind of thing and not have it affect them? For who knew how many times he looked upon the haunted face of his sister and asked once again, "Elsa, are you okay, is there anything I can do?"

She would look through him as if he wasn't there, just shake her head, and then leave. And every time she would leave he felt that she was withdrawing further into herself – not a good thing. Once he had finished working that camp, he didn't pass on to her that there were other children, and not only that but many women – women who were probably the mothers of these dead children, that were scattered like fallen leaves in the fall. The one body of that young girl, probably three or four, was enough for her.

Shaking his head he had no answers, and again hoped time would be the healer. Still with all that had happened to the two of them in the last few years, it just might take a lifetime for them to come to terms with it. With these thoughts, for whatever the reason, his mind went back to what Ed had showed them about their history or the time of what was considered the last days. What the ones in "The Deeps" witnessed should have been enough to drive any sane person crazy. And while what had happened here in the present was by their "own hands", in comparison, it really meant little in the overall scheme of things. Not that taking lives by their own hands was something to take lightly. Only that by doing this they probably had saved countless other lives – lives that would have been at the mercy of these raiders.

When they had carried through their plans and in the end been successful, Elsa felt only relief. What she had expected to feel, she really didn't know. Still, she was sure it wasn't relief – elation possibly – but not relief. After the fight, and the time they waited she'd found she was exhausted. So much so that the longer she remained in the ready position the harder it was to stay awake. She knew she had dozed a few times before Jay told her to go ahead and sleep. And when they finally entered that silent camp neither of them knew what they would find.

The last thing she expected was finding that dead girl. In her mind she was fighting raiders, the worst scum of the earth – ones who could care less about others, and would kill just for fun, or to watch the fear from their victims before doing to them as they pleased. All of these images were dashed when she saw her in death. It meant that no matter how bad these people were, they had families too. And at this point she and Jay had done to them exactly what the dead raiders had done to others. *No, we didn't torture and rape, but did this make what we did right?*

At this moment she had no answers, and until she came to terms with what she and Jay did, she would forever feel remorse and guilt. Once they had returned she found the fears and nightmares which had faded over time had returned, and she would find herself waking up screaming as those images from her past, ones she thought were buried deep inside of her, would return – causing her to relive her own time of personal terror.

* * *

Jay continued to monitor the remotes they had set up at the canyon entrance, and the area around the camp. He needed to know if there would be someone coming who would be making contact with this particular raider clan. He knew from their research that the raiders had some type of network, an underground of contacts that allowed them to keep in touch with others of their kind (they had tracked a small part of this). No one lived totally alone and isolated. Well, most anyway. Even their village had contact with the caravans and members traveled to the trading centers to buy and sell. These raiders, and their ilk, had something similar – mostly unknown of course. Places hidden from the common folk, places where they did their trading, and the updating of information, and possibly to plan their attacks.

So far there had been nothing other than the carrion eaters. They would arrive tripping the alert alarm where he would come back to see who or what may have arrived only to find it to be some animal or bird taking a meal from what was there. As this continued he eventually began to ignore the alarms and come in periodically and run the recordings to see if anything had changed. It was late in one of the days where he had been eating the evening meal, and was running through that day's videos when he stopped mid-bite. Putting his fork down, he stopped the playback, backed it up, and ran it at normal speed.

From the hidden cam set at the entrance of the canyon he saw three approaching. They appeared to be hesitant, and spread out making the approach as careful as they could. It was obvious they knew this place because they came directly to the entrance and did no searching as they approached. They stopped and the one who could have been the leader said something to the other two who only nodded. One of them remained out in the desert, while the other two began the trek down the canyon trail. Shortly they were out of sight from the one feed and it would be a short time before they reached the next one.

His concentration was interrupted when Elsa came in. He looked up at her and smiled. She still looked like hell, although she seemed to be coming around, at least a little. Pointing to the monitor he stated, "Looks like someone has finally showed up to see what may have happened. I'm watching them now." He could see some curiosity from her as she got close enough that she could watch over his shoulder, but she remained silent. With the way this had affected her he wasn't sure what to do – whether to continue to track down the raiders or to leave it where it presently was. One thing for sure he knew he couldn't do it by himself. And if she remained as she was, even if she went with him, he might as well be by himself.

He turned back to the monitor with his meal forgotten for now. It could always be reheated in the microwave later. He could hear Elsa breathing as she continued to watch and then suddenly she turned and left again with no word or explanation. He had a sinking feeling that once the discovery was made of finding the dead child, that her heart was no longer into avenging their family and friends. He could understand it. To not believe the raiders could have families was stupid. And yet when one saw what they did to others it was an easy conclusion to make. Why would any woman want to be a part of something so cruel and evil?

Maybe it would be something he'd understand later in his life. But for now it was an unexpected revelation. And no he hadn't wanted to bring death and destruction down upon children. Most were innocent, unaware of what was happening in the real world. Still that didn't change the fact that the adults were not innocent at all. So was there a way to take out the raiders themselves, and not touch their families? And if it came down to it, could they maybe rescue the children, the young ones who were completely unaware and eliminate the rest? He had no answers, but at least he could think about it. Yet, right now it was important to watch the feeds. He watched as Elsa disappeared through the doorway out into the hallway and headed in the direction of her room. Sighing he wished he could see his old sister once again, but the scars ran deep and it seemed that they had come out again, once she had seen that dead child.

He found he had to stop the video once again and run it back so he could watch the two enter the camp area. When he did he watched as the two stopped in mid-stride, look around at the destroyed camp, make a quick circuit around the area and quickly leave. Soon he saw them meet up with the third, discuss something for a short time and then head straight out in the desert once again, and finally disappear from the view of the feeds. At least he had a rough idea of the direction. Not that it mattered at this time. There was a very good chance that in the end it would only be information, something that could have a future use. He truly suspected that their days of being avengers of the innocent were over.

He kept going over in his mind what Elsa had said about them being no better than the raiders, and while, during their attack, it had felt good to give back, he had to admit in some ways she had been right. Still what was one to do? How did one handle the bad element that existed in this world? If there was no one willing to take it to the raiders couldn't they eventually destroy all that is good? He had no answers, only questions. So if, in the end, they couldn't bring death and destruction down upon the raiders, what could they do to help? There had to be something, but what?

* * *

Elsa woke once again finding the pillow wet. For the third time this week she'd been crying in her sleep. The only thing she could attribute it to was finding that child dead, and knowing she and Jay had been responsible for her death. She suspected, when she had entered that silent dead camp it had triggered her own memories she had buried deep inside of her, when she had witnessed the destruction of their own town, followed by being captured by the raiders, and then all the unspeakable things they had done to her and the others that had been captured with her.

When her brother had presented the idea of giving back to the outlaws and what they were doing to others it sounded great. Yes, she had to think about it, but all along she knew she would be for it. After all, who wouldn't want to get a little revenge against the ones who had hurt you, destroyed all you knew, and when they were finished, to move on and do it again? All the training they did should have given her a hint of what could come out of it, but when one's mind is made up, the little details seem to be ignored. Little details like when one takes up arms in the end the innocent would suffer. It was part of life. There would never be any way one could guarantee that only the bad ones, the outlaws would suffer.

So when they returned to the encampment they had destroyed, those little things were pointed out to her immediately, and she realized at that very moment she no longer had a desire to continue. She no longer wanted to bring vengeance down upon the raiders. Let others do it. She was finished, done, and she hoped somewhere in the near future the tears and nightmares would end and she could get on with her life, scarred as it was.

Sitting on the edge of the bed in her nightgown she could feel the redness and burning in her eyes, and she felt as if she hadn't slept at all. *Maybe a shower will refresh me. If not . . . I don't know . . . maybe I'll just stay in here today. No, I really can't do that either. There's a lot that needs to be done and I can't just stay here acting like a spoiled brat because things didn't go the way I thought they should.* Still she couldn't move. That took energy and right at this moment she didn't have any.

Finally she pushed up off the bed, got her clothes together for the day, moved into the bathroom, turned on the shower, disrobed and walked under the refreshing hot stream of water. As the hot water washed away the wariness that seemed to penetrate deep into her soul, her mind drifted in many directions never staying on any particular subject for very long. Eventually her train of thought moved in the direction of the fact that she and Jay were orphans, thanks to the raiders. She began to wonder what happened to others like them, and she had to admit she didn't know.

In fact, if she wanted to be honest with herself, this was something she had never thought about. Since she, and her brother of course, had come from a large loving family, and the town had been almost family, so such thoughts of others without would have been something foreign. *I guess it takes living it to understand it. I miss mother every day. I miss the spat my sisters and I had, or the fights between us – my brothers and sisters. And the many times we came together as an extended family celebrating some important family event. All making me who I am, and in a short time having all of this stuff taken away forever. Sad, so sad. Wish there was a way to go back, back to those wonderful times. Yeah, if only . . .*

She exited the shower, toweled off, got dressed, but all of it had been just going through the motions. Her mind was far away on those days in the past before the world had changed forever. As she walked down one of the hallways towards one of the kitchens to grab breakfast she found the beginning of an idea forming in her mind. She grabbed a bowl of cereal and went out to the tables, sat down, and began to automatically eat not really paying attention. She was deep in thought staring out at nothing when she realized Jay had joined her, and she had no idea how long he had been sitting there.

* * *

Jay had come out of his room a few minutes behind his sister and could see she was already in the kitchen. It would take a few for him to catch up with her, but wasn't sure if he wanted to or not. She was like a dark cloud on a sunny day. He worried once again that all the bad that had happened to her was back and fresh in her mind. Again, like when he had saved her life, he still felt inadequate. He couldn't fix it then, and he knew he couldn't fix it now. Even with all the knowledge that was available and at their fingertips it really hadn't changed anything at all. She still was that lost little girl with those deep scars and fears. And even after all this time she refused to say any more, yet he felt it might help if she could just talk it out.

But he understood why, or at least he thought he did. He was a male, and it had been males that had hurt her, so it was something that would be almost impossible to do, to talk to him even though he was her brother. She needed another woman, and he suspected the best for the job wasn't available. She was dead, and had been for many years. He suspected the best for the job would have been their mother. And with them being the only ones here there would be no other who could fill the bill, or help.

He finally reached the kitchen and saw Elsa was already sitting at one of the tables with a bowl of cereal, although it appeared to be mostly untouched. Looking closer he could see her staring out in the distance at nothing.

He thought a moment, grabbed a bowl of cereal himself, not that such a thing would hold him for long, and joined her, sitting opposite. He could tell she was completely unaware that he had joined her. *Wonder what she's thinking about?* He smiled and asked, "Penny for your thoughts?" He knew it was an old saying, but to be honest he really didn't know what a penny was. She looked at him and appeared to be surprised he was there.

"Jay? When did you get here? And what did you just ask me?"

"Nothing really. I could see you were deep in thought and wondered if there was anything I could do to help. And while we are talking I'll ask, how was your night?" He could see the redness in her eyes and knew it had been another rough night, but again he was helpless.

She could see that lying about it wasn't going to work. She really hadn't looked too close in the mirror when she left her room and suspected her eyes were probably bright red. They sure were raw from her side. She shrugged and said, "Another bad night."

He looked down at her bowl of cereal and found it had turned to mush from being ignored, stood up grabbed it and said, "Here, let me get another. This would taste horrible." As he headed back to the kitchen he asked once again, "Is there anything I can do?"

She knew he meant well, but there wasn't anything he could do to help, other than to be here for her, and he was. Shaking her head, she simply said, "No."

He already knew the answer, since it had been the same one from all the way back. Still some day it might change. He doubted it, but at least, and as far as he was concerned, he would keep trying.

Later in the day Jay approached Elsa once again. She was in one of the security offices monitoring the feeds from the desert, something both of them did at least once a day, and it was her turn. It seemed since their first successful attack on the raiders that a barrier had been building between the two of them and it was something that needed to be fixed. Soon, if the wall didn't come down he knew he would lose her forever. He could tell she was aware of his presence so he asked, "Anything happening or going on?"

In a distant voice that trailed off she responded by saying, "No, just sand, rocks, the wind, and dust." She never looked up or at him.

"Look Elsa", he pleaded, "we started something and we really do need to finish it."

She rotated around in one of those swivel chairs with anger, "Finish it? How can we finish it? I believe we could do this kind of thing for the rest of our lives and there will still be bandits, thieves, and raiders. There have always been bad people out there, and I really believe there will always be. After we did what we did I realized that if we continue down this trail we've started that in the end we would be nothing more than killers. I suspect that anything of what we are would be lost along the way.

"Yeah, in the beginning I was all for it, all in for revenge. I watched unspeakable things happen, was a victim of those same things, and the idea of giving back a little of my own to that scum really did appeal to me. It really did until I saw that little girl. You have to understand that she had no choice being there. She knew nothing of what her parents did, or what the people around her did. She was innocent. Innocent, don't you get it? And we came in to avenge what happened to us and our town, all the people we knew and loved, but what did it prove? Did it bring any of them back? Did it remove what happened to me personally? No. Nothing can change the past, nothing at all." She turned back to the monitors with the anger still showing in her posture.

Jay stood quietly as he absorbed all her anger and her words. He took time to think before saying anything. Somehow this impasse had to end. "So, I guess we are to become like Ed. You know, stay here until we die and let the secret of this place die with us. Is that what you are trying to say?"

He could hear her breathe out heavily and saw her shoulders slump, but she remained forward with her back to him looking at the monitors. Although he suspected she was probably looking at nothing. In a soft voice she said, "No . . . no that's not what I'm saying. What is here should become available to everybody, but there's a real problem thinking that way also."

"Yeah, I know", Jay replied. "With what this place holds it would be easy for someone to decide they needed to play god and everybody would have to answer to them. And they could find enough like-minded to literally control the world, with no one being able to stop them."

"Yeah, exactly right. So do we destroy this place? Do we abandon it? Do we allow it to become a place where only the ghosts from the past roam?" Her voice was still soft and distant as if she was somewhere else.

"I guess it would be the easiest way, but can we leave it? Can we in good conscience do such a thing? I mean, think about what's here. Yeah, we know and used the system to train for the fighting we did, but we also got an education that puts us centuries ahead of any out in the real world. It means we really couldn't blend back into what we were before. It wouldn't be possible. And I think I really wouldn't want to give up what we have here anyway. Yet, there are those other dangers you've so aptly pointed out, or have been pointed out.

"So, if we aren't going to seek revenge, or abandon this place . . . And one thing for sure, we can't take the chance and bring others in here like Ed did with us – he really did take a great chance bringing us in – as he stated so many times, he really only had that brief time to make a decision about us. Yes, it worked out in the end because we really are just ordinary folk, but could we be that lucky again? I really don't know, and I for one do not want to take a chance. Yet, we are sitting on the most important thing in this whole world, and I don't know what to do?"

She slowly rotated around and looked up in her brother's eyes, and shook her head. "No, I really don't know what to do either. I know that once we went inside of the canyon and I witnessed what we had done that in the end it brought back all those nightmares, bad dreams, night sweats, the fear and foreboding that I had back when you found me in the desert. And what made it worse this time was the fact it had been my hands that had created what we saw.

"And like you, there's no way I want to leave this place. And I agree, we can't just bring others in here. And no I don't want to stay here and die leaving the place to become a home for ghosts and only the past. And you're right we can't really become part of this world with the knowledge we've gained. Maybe we could head out find places that needs help, and work on giving them solutions, then disappear and return here. But I suspect this is something that wouldn't work either."

"It's something I hadn't thought about. Why wouldn't it work, Elsa?"

"For the very same reasons we can't bring others in here. Somewhere someone would want what we know and we would become their prisoners using leverage against us by using fear of one or the other of us becoming victims unless we cooperated."

"That's true. There's always that minority that only sees personal profit in anything, and they could care less who it hurts. So, if none of what we've been discussing is an option, what is it you want to do?"

Shaking her head once again she said, "I don't know. I really don't have any ideas at all."

Jay thought, *success! At least a little anyway. She's at least talking. Maybe we can keep doing so.* He nodded his head inwardly. *A small step, such a small one, but better than nothing.*

For Jay to abandon the attacking of the raiders was frustrating. But at the same time he wasn't sure if he could have continued either. He had to admit, even if it was only to himself, seeing women and children killed in their attack had been a shock. In his mind he had only considered the ones who carried out the attack. And as far as he knew generally it appeared to be men. He hadn't considered the fact that these men would have had families – although, after the fact, it should have. And in some ways even after learning this he felt it important to carry on.

At least he was honest enough to know that he probably couldn't do this himself, he could possibly carry on in a limited capacity. Yet, here they were in a forgotten and unknown structure buried deep in the earth whose purpose had never been fulfilled. And while it held promise for the future of them, and the rest of the world, it was also a curse. As both of them pointed out, if this place fell into the wrong hands it would mean the end of all that is good. So this couldn't happen. So how did they avoid such a thing? And he knew from the conversation he just had with his sister they wanted to do something, but what?

For the next few weeks they continued in the normal routines of "The Deeps". Both would eat their meals together and talk. Once they were finished and back to the work neither probably could say what they had said or discussed. What it did do was to bring them back together so the wall that had been building between the two of them was now gone, and while it could never be like it had been before the destruction of the village, they at least felt they were brother and sister once again. Still somewhere somehow soon they needed to come up with something that they could do. It would be easy to follow in Ed's footsteps, and all the others who had lived here, remain isolated, live out their lives, and die, having the secret of this place remain with their deaths. But neither wanted that kind of future.

Still while the bad out there in the real world was in the minority, they still wielded a lot of power. So how did one keep this knowledge away from them, and make it a benefit for all that is good? He didn't know, and when he had asked Elsa she hadn't any answers either. So both continued in the day-to-day routines and let the questions they had work through their subconscious mind. Maybe some idea or inkling would come to them, and they could begin to work towards those ideas and plans.

* * *

Both were outside inspecting the hidden cameras that kept the area under surveillance, allowing them to know if any were passing through the area. The location of "Helms Deep" was such that it would be the last place any would look, so they felt relatively safe. Still it was important to keep the area monitored. After all, however it happened, Jay had stumbled upon and found this place, and if he did others could. It was pushing midday when Elsa stood up and stretched. This particular camera was located inside a split in the rocks and required one to be bent over to insure everything was still functioning. Shaking her arms to release the tension she said, "That really sucks. I know we have to put these things in places where they can't be found, but really? We know where they are since we set them up, but to go out here and maintain them is a bitch, a real bitch. Still, I guess it's better than the alternative."

Yeah, that's true", Jay replied. "I'd rather be aware of others around than be surprised." He'd been acting as a spotter, a lookout while she worked on this particular security camera. The next time she'd be doing the lookout duty while he inspected the camera. He unconsciously looked out towards their late home with his mind drifting back to when it had been full of life, and they were no more than ordinary people looking forward to their place in life, with dreams all young ones seemed to have. Now all of that seemed more like dreams of fiction instead of being their true past.

Elsa, watching Jay could see that faraway look in his eyes and asked, "Penny for your thoughts?" She smiled inwardly as she realized that she had picked up phrases from the deep past that would have meant nothing to them a few years ago.

"I don't know, just thinking back before the world went to hell for us – I know that you are still fighting those demons. And I have to admit there are times when I wake up from a nightmare of what I found when I returned to the village finding all the death and destruction there. Sometimes I really wish none of it happened and both of us were back there dealing with the normal stuff being ignorant of everything we now know." He saw she was about to say something and he signaled her to wait. "Yes I know it's something that's impossible to do. Yet, I seem to remember our sires doing the same thing. You know something they wished they could change. I guess it's just part of who we are." He could see that somehow he had triggered something with Elsa as she suddenly appeared to be in deep thought. "What are you thinking sis?"

"I've never been back to our village, can we go?" Elsa asked.

"I guess. It's been years since I was there. In fact the last time was when I resupplied, although, in the end, none of it was needed."

She smiled, "True, but neither of us knew that at the time. We didn't know "The Deeps" existed, and both of us, even though I was in worse shape then, knew we'd have to move on at some point. So when?"

"I guess we can do it tomorrow. There's nothing on the schedule requiring immediate inspection and repair for a few days. Still it's almost a five day round trip, and I'm sure there would be nothing left, which means we'll have to carry everything we need. I guess sometime in the near future we need to see if we can get or build a desert buggy or something. It'd make traveling through the area quicker, although they do have their own problems. Still it would make a trip like we are planning much shorter. Something to think about I guess."

* * *

The hot desert winds were blowing, with dust devils dancing among the ruins that had been their home. Simply, a village known as Sandy, and thusly their last name. There was a silence that spoke of honoring the ones who died here. Everywhere they looked there were piles of dust building against any wall still standing – speaking volumes of the abandonment, leaving only ghosts roaming this place. For Elsa this was the first time she had seen it since the destruction. It had still been burning when she had been abducted and hauled off somewhere into the desert where she and others faced the fate that awaited them.

In some ways it was shocking, what she was seeing now, how fully the destruction had been. She hadn't even recognized the pathways through the town and the many gravel surfaces and paths that marked the division of the homes and businesses. And while some of it almost seemed familiar, it had taken her a moment to recognize where their home had stood. Now after all this time there was little to outline the actual structure. A little charcoal, a few odds and ends, and a broken cast iron stove that had been used for cooking of the meals, and very little else. It surprised her how small the area seemed to be. She swore the house had been so much larger than what this showed her.

She could feel a heaviness in her soul, and depression beginning to lie upon her, not that she hadn't been fighting her personal demons. Now after seeing this, she yearned for those uncomplicated times when the outside world meant nothing to a young child growing up in a loving home. After who knew how much time both of them moved on and found a place to break and eat something. Their conversation at this point was subdued for obvious reasons as both of them were deep inside themselves. After all, this had been the only home they knew until that fateful day. A day that ended all the innocence either had possessed.

So much had happened since then. And while those innocent and ignorant ones still existed inside of them, they now knew more than anyone in this world. Had even taken advantage of that new, to them, knowledge and had brought some payback to the raider clans. After the meal both of them continued to walk among the broken buildings remembering and talking about what they had done when this place still existed and was full of family, friends and townsfolk. It was then as if on cue both of them stopped and began to speak excitedly. Here Jay laughed and said, "After you, ma'am."

"Well, thank you sir." Again she laughed. "I guess we came up with the same idea, or at least I think we did. Look, we are only a few days out of "The Deeps", which means we probably could use this place as a starting point." She could see her brother smiling and nodding his head, encouraging her to continue. "Okay, we know that not only from the attacks made by the raiders, but other things happen to create orphans like us. So why not use this place as a gathering place to bring them all together. Make it a home where all orphans are welcome – even those young ones who may come from the raider clans. Only if they are young enough to not know the way of life that the raiders seem to prefer.

"Even though this place isn't rich, one can still be comfortable here. And with "The Deeps" so close we can augment the protection to prevent a repeat of what happened here in the past. Not directly, of course, but here we could begin the reintroducing of the old technology. And after a time establish a hidden town by using ones from this one to establish it. Maybe that one we found in the middle of the desert would work. From that one we could begin to send out teams to begin the spread of what we have. You know how to improve agriculture, shelters, roads, schools, and so much more. What do you think?"

Nodding his head as Jay smiled, he said, "I'm all for it. But it won't be easy – in fact it's probably going to be quite hard. And I'm sure we'll have many problems and issues to face. But, in the end I think it will be worth it. And by keeping 'The Deeps' isolated and unknown, it will remain protected."

EPILOGUE

What were they? Both stretched their aching backs. They were in their fifties and both wondered where the years had gone. In so many ways when they looked back to that time when they had visited their destroyed village they had been naïve, and somewhat idealistic. The idea of rebuilding and bringing in orphans like themselves turned out to be so much more difficult than either ever imagined. Yet now Sandy was up and operating once again. Obviously not on the scale back before it had been destroyed, but enough that if both disappeared it would continue a slow growth. And yes while the core of the village had been orphans, now there were children from ones who had married.

Yes orphans were still brought in, given a place to start over, and begin their lives once again. And it was this that became common knowledge. But there had been an underlying secret goal that became known only to certain of the residents. And only a few knew the real truth. And yes, that town lost in the middle of the desert was coming to life once again as it became the place of learning of the old ways. To be able to join the ones there, one had to prove their worth in Sandy. Once that worth was proven only then would the truth be revealed and they would make the move. In the end, once Jay and Elsa passed on, a teacher, a "Keeper of Knowledge", would be chosen from those who worked the hidden town – a place where teams went out into the known world to teach. And whoever this individual was would then move into "The Deeps" to continue the reeducation of the world so that the old technology would be available to all. Yes, both realized there would always be problems, but that's what kept it interesting, kept one on their toes.

Smiling at his sister as they stood there, he said, "I think it's time we leave this to the young ones. I'm getting too old for this."

She laughed, "You? Old? Never happen. Although I must admit my joints and body keeps trying to tell me something. And we are starting to see a little gray, although you won't get me to admit to that."

He shook his head and smiled. Elsa was still beautiful to him, and in truth together they had accomplished so much. Yeah, they wouldn't live to see the changes they had begun, but it wouldn't be that hard to see that it would happen.

Together they walked towards the gate. It was time to head back to "The Deeps", at the finish of another day. He with his arm across her shoulders and her arm across his waist leisurely headed out through the gate past the guards. They smiled as they carried on a brief conversation with them before heading out towards the desert.

One of the guards looked as they disappeared. He shook his head. "I wonder where they go."

The other laughed, "Now that's their secret. And I think with all they've done for us they should be allowed that, don't you?"

The other shrugged. He couldn't disagree with what had been said – no, not at all.

ABOUT THE AUTHOR

F.D. Brant always wanted to write, but life got in the way. Finally after retiring he got his chance.

Storytelling and writing has always been F.D. Brant's passion, but responsibilities took preference. And because of those responsibilities it took retiring to allow those passions to come to fruition. Since retiring he has written 9 books, and maintains a weekly eclectic blog, Words in the Wind.

Growing up in the backcountry he learned the appreciation of "doing things for yourself". Because it was impossible to call in someone to repair anything one either did it themselves or went without. This led to the appreciation of the natural world, and the daily struggles that one faced as nature threw problems at the family that had to be overcome, leading to confidence and self-sufficiency. This led to the strong characters that populate his stories and books. And his female protagonists are strong willed and confident – something that he saw in both in his mother and sister.

www.ingramcontent.com/pod-product-compliance
Lightning Source LLC
Chambersburg PA
CBHW050611170726
48283CB00001B/200